THE JUSTICE LOVERS CASE

To Annie —

by

Bob Bertolet

Bob Bertolet

Hope you enjoy this first novel!

Library of Congress Control Number: 2008905912

ISBN: 978-1-934035-48-1

Cover Art: Simone Bryan

Cover Layout: Ashley Spears
AES Graphics & Design

Book Format: Jonni Anderson

Trent's Prints & Publishing
Chumuckla, Florida
www.trentsprints.com
866.275.7124

Trent's Prints & Publishing
Chumuckla Florida
www.trentsprints.com

AES Graphics & Design
Chumuckla, Florida
www.aesgraphics.com

To my children, Barry, Toni and Todd,
better known as B T & T.

AUTHOR'S NOTES

The author has taken liberties in the discussion of law, medicine, and psychology. To better enjoy the story, it is requested that the reader overlook those flaws that enhance the flow of the story.

Although the author is fond of his characters, Mike and Tess Miller, he does not agree with their behavior, nor does he advocate anyone becoming their disciples. His views are identical to those of Attorney Mack Franklin, as expressed in Chapter 47.

To order books or contact author
www.bobbertolet.com

PREFACE

Do horses run upon rock?
Does one plow the sea with oxen?
But you have turned justice into poison
And the fruit of righteousness unto wormwood—

Amos 6:12 RSV

PROLOGUE

Every human being, whether humble or proud, influences societal evolution. Their contribution may be negative or positive, insignificant or awesome, evil or benevolent. History, the "Great Overseer," measures and assigns the contribution to the trash barrel or to the treasure chest.

A momentous event typically disguises itself to the casual observer. A generation may elapse before history recognizes that event as the catalyst for alteration of the human equation.

In October 1996, two courageous people made an extraordinary decision. History currently judges their actions. Assuredly, some will call the two people heroes; others will label them misfits. Significance, like beauty, is always in the eye of the beholder.

CHAPTER 1
October 15, 1996 (Tuesday)
Jackson, Mississippi

The large screen plasma TV with the Bose® surround system created a virtual reality to eye and ear. Like a hawk searching for a tasty ground hog, Tess Miller scrutinized the 6:00 p.m. newscast for some kind of uplifting news. Because her Type-A personality demanded that time not be wasted, she scanned the October issue of *Time* magazine during the commercial breaks.

Exuding all the charm of a plastic Ken® doll, Farley Winston, the white male newscaster for CMTV channel 14 in Jackson, Mississippi, spit out news items with the rapid-fire delivery of a used car salesman.

Tess glanced at her husband, drowsy-eyed from working a crossword puzzle, and then let her eyes return to the TV image. *Get a load of Farley tonight,* she thought. *He must have used a whole can of hair spray to look that neat. Maybe he has a date with Rolanda after the show.* Tess looked with disdain toward the talking head. *I cannot trust someone who never smiles and is too pompous to be a newscaster.*

Reading skillfully from the Teleprompter, Farley continued in dulcet tones: "The polls show that Bill Clinton is going to trounce Bob Dole to win a second term."

Feigning humor, Farley added: "Some more bad news. There are now 15 million worldwide cases of AIDS. The first confirmed case of HIV-1 occurred in Africa in 1959. In 1981, the CDC termed this ruthless killer with the innocuous name of Acquired Immuno-Deficiency Syndrome. AIDS probably will not reach the 100 million deaths caused by the influenza outbreak of 1918. The tragedy is that both epidemics could have been avoided with isolation of the initial victims."

Mike Miller, lying back in a black leather ergonomic recliner, shouted over the stentorian Winston, "Hon, what is a six letter word for an atrioventricular valve?" Juggling his paper, he readjusted his body to hear his wife and to write the answer.

"Mitral," Tess answered without hesitation. Since she was a nurse, medical vocabulary was second nature to her. She also knew that the *New York Times* crossword puzzles got progressively harder from Monday to Saturday. Surprised Mike asked for help on a Tuesday, she thought, *My husband must be getting senile in his old age.*

The TV camera zoomed in on the black female co-anchor, Rolanda James. The throaty baritone voice hinted at a two-pack-a-day smoker. Tess thought, *Get ready for chemo.* The stern countenance predicted the seriousness of the message to follow: "And now for the lead story: It's the thirtieth anniversary of the alleged brutal murder of three black teenage boys from Tipton, a small town in the northwest part of the state."

The video camera panned slowly over a group of mourners marching in the background, holding candles and singing "We Shall Overcome".

"Hey, Mike, listen to this news story. These murders happened near my hometown when I was 13 years old," Tess exclaimed.

Rolanda continued: "A teenage girl claimed that she was a witness to the murders and told a gruesome story to the local sheriff three months after the crime."

Tess and Mike studied the four pictures appearing on the TV screen, one each of the three dead victims and the witness. The pictures looked like high school yearbook photos.

Rolanda added: "The location of the bodies remains a mystery. Residents believe that the burial ground is somewhere in the dense woods that cover Longstreet County. The Cantrell brothers, Bobby Dan and Carter Lee, were indicted for the murders. A jury found them not guilty in spite of the eyewitness testimony of the teenage girl and a mountain of circumstantial evidence."

Rolanda arched her brows meaningfully and leaned toward the camera. "No Mississippian, black or white, was surprised at the verdict. In 1966, it was best that a black kept his mouth shut and stayed out of sight."

Two grainy black and white pictures, resembling post office wanted posters, filled the screen.

Mike and Tess noticed the aura of evil in the two unsmiling faces with pointed chins, narrow noses, furrowed high brows and eyes of obsidian.

Tess offered an opinion, "The Grinch had a bigger heart than those two apes."

Mike answered, "Two Neanderthals with clubs looking for trouble."

Rolanda continued: "Carter Lee, on the left, died of emphysema in early 1985. Bobby Dan is now working at a gas station in Tipton." Rolling her eyes, she nodded toward Farley.

The camera panned back to Winston. A brief contrived grimace for the camera: "Um! Such an American Tragedy! And now turning to the weather. . . Parts of the Southwest are getting widespread showers, but drought-stricken Arizona, Oklahoma and Texas are becoming a modern dust bowl."

Tess hit the remote power button with force. The normally demure southern belle was mad. "Damn it, Mike, the national news is going to pick up this story. CBS and that egotistical Dan Rather already think that everybody in Mississippi walks around with rocks in their shoes and straw between their teeth. I will admit that there were some barbaric lynchings in Mississippi. It sickens my stomach to read about Mack Charles Parker and Emmett Till. I resent having to continually take the hit for a few murderous hotheads that today hardly know they're in this world."

Mike recognized the pursed lips and the squinting eyes as the prelude to Tess's preaching a sermon. Hunching his shoulders and burying his head in a newspaper would not be a cool move. *I'd better pay attention if I don't want to skip supper tonight.*

Tess paced up and down the room. "Mike, you remember the sixties were, indeed, Mississippi's Dark Age. Both blacks and whites were terrified of the Ku Klux Klan and the Citizen's Council. Law enforcement sucked. Mississippi should have retried Cantrell, found him guilty and fried his ass at Caseyville State Prison. That simple action would have sent a clear message: *We don't care who you are! Don't break the law in this state or you're going down!*"

On a roll, her face flushed bright red as her blood pressure spiraled upward, Tess enjoyed a captive audience, even if only one.

Mike, less easily provoked by news stories, warned in a controlled voice, "Calm down or you're going to have the 'big one' à la Fred Sanford." He spread his right hand over his heart and cried, "Ah! Tess, you know that the state cannot try a man twice for the same crime! It does surprise me though, that some irate family member hasn't popped Cantrell in all these years. There are still a lot of people in this world, including *moi,* who believe in an eye for an eye."

Mike's innocent statement triggered bitter memories for his wife.

Tess fought to stem the rising gall in her constricted throat. Suppressed events crashed to the surface from an abyss, flooding into her conscious. How the so-called legal system failed to render justice for her brother, James Arnold Taylor. How she sat that horrible day in the courtroom behind the prosecutor, her heart pounding, her head splitting with tension, her stomach tied in knots, waiting to hear justice carried out for her brother. How her eyes riveted on the judge's lips as he declared he had reached a verdict. She saw the hand, speckled with lima bean-shaped brown spots, running through the thin gray hair as the old purveyor of justice waited for the murmuring to cease. The interminable wait for everyone to hold his or her tongue, the overwhelming smell of sour sweat permeating the poorly ventilated courtroom, and then the sweet words: "I find the defendant guilty." How exhilarated and giddy she became. How someone shrieked, "Hallelujah, praise be the Lord." How she realized it was she who shouted out those words, and the judge pounded his gavel demanding silence. Then, a phrase out of hell created a landslide of emotions: "I am suspending the sentence." Those words split her head open. Reeling with shock and inexpressible grief, Tess felt a sinking sensation of helplessness and confusion overwhelm her.

Tess heard other words bubbling out of the cauldron of her mind. "This sure wasn't what we wanted, Tess," the prosecutor sadly mumbled to her, patting her on the shoulder, "but you are gonna have to find a way to live with this. You're young and intelligent. Please don't let this injustice ruin your life. We did the best we could for your brother. He would not want you to waste your potential."

"What did you say?" Tess whispered to an imaginary audience. Tears of white, hot anger streamed down her face. *I know he was trying to comfort me, but could he possibly believe that I could live with this stupid decision? Did he say we did the best we could?* Stumbling into the aisle, she nearly ran headlong into the defendant, Buddy MacFoster. She said, "If I only had a gun, you drunk bastard!"

And then the murderer smiled at her. Perhaps unintended, the cold smile transmitted by the damaged brain of a chronic alcoholic said more eloquently than words: *I was lucky to get away with it one more time.*

Clenching her teeth, she was suddenly filled with an icy resolve. *Oh no. I won't be living with this. You didn't get away with anything, Mr. MacFoster*, she answered the unheard statement.

She watched with hatred, as the one she once held in respect sauntered out of the courtroom. Even an unversed sixteen-year-old like Tess thought, *Justice was on trial in this courthouse and today it was found guilty. MacFoster was a pawn, a beneficiary of a system so sick it needs hospitalization.*

Tess struggled to push away the nightmarish memories and clear her head. With a quick vengeance, she resumed her preaching. "Mike, I believe in the Eleventh Commandment: The law shall punish the guilty!"

Mike did not interrupt. He figured Moses would not be angry with his wife for this minor addition to the Ten Commandments.

She continued, "When injustice occurs in a runaway society, the law must use a legal big stick to make the wayward behave. Well, the big stick has been put in a wood chipper. People are doing what they damn well please because there is no punishment. The law now gives people a pat on the back and a handshake for absurd behavior."

Mike nodded but made no comment, wryly musing that his wife was surely coming to the end of this not-so-yellow brick road. He knew Tess would continue her argument to the logical conclusion. *Look interested and be patient. Throw in a nod or two for good measure.*

"Tell me what's wrong in these pictures, Mike. A clumsy woman in Louisiana gets a five million dollar award for spilling boiling hot coffee in her lap that she purchased at a drive through window. If the coffee had been brewed in her kitchen, we wouldn't be hearing about it. She and her attorney made a raid on the deep pockets of the franchise. The bogus jury, the arm of the law, awards big bucks. When you read that story, does it instill confidence in our justice system?" Tess lifted a long forefinger upward signifying example number one.

Tess continued, "A Texas parole board, under a stupid overcrowding issue, and a court order by a do-gooder judge, released a prisoner who committed a murder during a robbery; the convict now certified as rehabilitated by the prison psychologist. The bastard wasted no time in killing a young bank guard in the commission of another bank robbery. If that judge really wants to see overcrowding, he ought to hang out on a troop ship. Society should be allowed to handcuff a murderer to a fence post and let the victim's family render punishment. Just kidding, Mike." The middle finger joined the index finger in forming the famous Winston Churchill V, in this case signifying example number two, not victory.

"Here's a case that is too nutty even for the wacky California Court System. The California judge ordered a stalker to keep at least 300 yards away from a young starlet. Big deal! Ichi-ban protection! One week later she is dead at the hands of the defiant psycho." The ring finger popped up, joining its brethren, signifying example number three.

She continued, "Is there any sense to these decisions, Mike? I believe anger and anxiety, caused by disgust and frustration, are at a dangerous level. People are beginning to understand the enormity of what is happening to American society."

Mike, able to do two things at one time, completed the first and second parts of the crossword puzzle quip while listening to his loquacious wife.

Part 1 read: *Two antennas met on a rooftop and decided to get married.*

Part 2 commented: *The wedding was a big disaster, but. . .*

Mike recognized a change in Tess's tone of voice. For his continued good health, he decided to defer solution of the quip to make a logical comment. "Tess, griping won't help. My Dad always said: 'Do not leave it up to the other guy because he'll leave it up to the other guy.' Tess, you can either do something or just keep your mouth shut." Mike hoped keeping her mouth shut would be Tess's choice.

Tess said, "Mike, we have financial security. In fact, I guess some people would call us filthy rich. Your employees can take care of the business and I'm not working anymore. We have cash, plenty of leisure, no children or parents. We aren't fenced in or tied down."

"I agree. So what's your point?"

Tess, with eyes closed, sat in deep thought for several minutes.

The impatient husband quipped, "I smell rubber burning and hear gears grinding. Give it to me straight."

"Mike, do you think you and I could do something about the Bobby Dan Cantrell ilk of this world? The U.S. of A. needs a mouthful of no-nonsense Wild West Justice."

Clowning around, Mike stayed with the frontier metaphor and said, "I'll buy that idea. I want to be Pat Garrett. You can be Belle Starr."

"Belle Starr was a whore, and to have such a pretty name she was hard-core ugly. Pat Garrett got shot in the back while taking a piss, you idiot. Now be serious. We aren't working crosswords. Did you think I wouldn't notice your lack of Wild West knowledge?" Tess admonished.

"Sherlock Holmes detects a bit of sarcasm from Dr. Watson," Mike teased. One could almost smell the aroma from the great detective's

Meerschaum pipe. "What kind of measure shall we mete out?" Mike asked, incorrectly quoting Saint Matthew.

Tess answered in a calm, firm voice, "There's only one punishment that we can effectively dispense to those slobs who have evaded judgment. I believe the idiom is termination with extreme prejudice."

Mike, submissive to his wife in most matters, held up both hands and managed a weak, "Whoa. Boy, Bobby Dan Cantrell got into your head tonight. You're all riled up and sounding a little crazy. You're talking serious stuff, lady."

"Sometimes a patient is desperately ill and will die if nothing is done. As a last resort, you use an unapproved medical technique or drug to save the patient." Tess paused for effect and then said, "Are you listening? Mike, believe me, we have two vitally sick patients in this country, our society and our justice system. Quit working that damn crossword puzzle! What do you suggest we do if you don't like my idea?"

Mike finished the last part of the crossword puzzle quip.

Part 3 was the punch line . . . *reception was exceptional.*

He did not laugh, but got up and gave his surprised wife a big bear hug. "Let's hit the sack," he whispered in her ear. "We can talk about some of this stuff in the morning when our heads are clearer. Right now, I don't have a good answer to your question."

* * *

October 16, 1996 (Wednesday)

Tess and Mike sat in the alcove that served as a breakfast room. The morning sun, blazing through the bay window, cast the room in a restorative golden glow. Tess drank freshly brewed coffee. Mike sipped herbal tea.

"Okay. You've slept on my idea for eight hours and twenty minutes. So give me your opinion, worldly geologist." Tess looked at Mike intently, expecting approval of her idea.

"You're actually serious, aren't you, Tess? I agree that the judge erred in your brother's case and all the problems you mentioned. I'm just not so sure we could or should carry out this radical idea of yours."

"Come on, Mike. You said just last night, 'Don't leave it up to the other guy because he'll leave it up to the other guy.' There's been way too much of that in our society. A blind man could see what's happening. Somebody must do something. I need you with me on this one, but I'll go it alone if I must."

Gazing into the fervent eyes of his impassioned wife, Mike relented. "Look Tess, I'm not exactly thrilled at being an executioner, but if you're bound and determined to do this, you'll need help. I don't want you going off half-cocked on your own." Although it was never recorded that Belle ever met Pat, Mike said, "Miss Starr and Mr. Garrett will ride out together, even if we ain't got no horse."

Tess, victory secured, was glad that Mike changed the mood. "Sounds like a rejected title for a country song, but glad to have you joining me, Mr. Garrett," Tess quipped. "Let's hope I don't get ambushed like the 'Queen Bandit' and you don't get assassinated like the 'Man who shot Billy the Kid.' By the way, Pat, people around here are saying there is one bad desperado in Tipton that escaped the law. What do you think, Sheriff? Do we go after him?"

Not to be outdone, Mike asked, "Is there any reward posted? I don't hire out cheap."

"A Yankee dime," Tess puckered her lips and provocatively stuck out her tongue.

Mike grinned like a possum at his sexy wife but remained silent for a few minutes, reflecting on their decision. He shocked Tess when he said, "Enough of this cowboy-cowgirl humor. This project requires we both chip in with some serious discussion, especially considering the risks involved."

Tess grabbed a yellow legal pad and ballpoint pen, compliments of Sammy's Quick Print Shop. "We need some guidelines on choosing someone as a target. Okay. Give me a list of reasons for selection."

Mike had recently read about a guy who threatened a 24-year-old jogger at knifepoint, forcing her into the surrounding woods and raping her. Quickly identified, the rapist was taken into custody. The creep just finished a five-year sentence for rape and was out on supervised probation. Mike thought, *Now, that guy would have been a prime selection.*

Tess tapped her pencil, signifying impatience with Mike's thought process.

"Just getting myself in the mood," Mike said. "The reasons for being a target are rather simple. Anybody who commits a vicious crime, an act of atrocious stupidity that causes harm to another, inflicts malice, or practices unfettered greed makes the list. We don't really need a list, you know. We'll recognize the bad people when we see them."

Tess added, "I've a short list of whom we should not choose. We do not select anyone under the age of 21. That may be arbitrary, but anyone younger is still a kid in my book. Naturally, we don't select anyone who is *non compos mentis*. That should be a relief to you, Mike. It'll leave out all of your relatives and friends."

"Thank you very much," Mike said, impersonating Elvis. "I've learned from reading crime novels that there are a few dos and don'ts we should take into consideration: No boasting to the papers, no tokens left at the scene and no taking souvenirs. Them's the don'ts. We do advance planning. We do handle each case differently to avoid being tracked by an easily recognized *modus operandi* (MO), and them's the dos."

"I like the way you're getting into this project. Anything else?" Tess asked.

"We don't attempt the impossible, like bumping off Bill Clinton," Mike cautioned.

"Hey, I think Bill is cute. No problem there," Tess cooed.

"My final suggestion is that we do not go after more than one target per year. Too many ventures and we'll get careless. We get careless and we get caught," Mike added.

"That might not be such a bad outcome," she said. "Our getting caught and put on trial could lead directly to publicizing our motive and method. We'll be on trial, but so will the legal system and moral decay. We had the guts to declare that if the law can't or won't punish the misfits, then the citizens must respond."

Mike warned, "The media might accuse us of being the incarnation of Sacco and Vanzetti."

"Mike, we are not misguided anarchists. We are not against government and laws. We are against the failure of government and laws to protect our society and to encourage morality. We have to encourage society to change the way things are in our justice system. Publicity will be the catalyst."

The sound of the toast popping up diverted Mike's train of thought. "Right now, I'm convinced that I'm hungry." He removed the low cholesterol spread from the refrigerator and spread it on two pieces of lightly toasted wholewheat bread. He gave one slice to Tess and asked, "Cherry or blackberry jam?"

"Cherry. I've selected our first target. Guess who?"

"That old slime ball, Bobby Dan Cantrell," Mike said. "Gimme a hard question."

"He's perfect for our first target, *n'est-ce pas*?" Tess said. "Cantrell lives only a few miles from where I was born and raised. Knowing all the roads and places should make the job easy."

Mike spoke the last words on a life-changing decision. "People will probably applaud when they learn Bobby Dan Cantrell has finally gotten whacked. And many of those will be Mississippians of both races."

CHAPTER 2
November 18, 2002 (Monday)
Quantico, Virginia

The man sat in his office chair at the FBI Academy Behavioral Science Unit in Quantico, Virginia, peering out at the ashen cumulus clouds. He got up and touched the window pane to get a ballpark estimate of the outside temperature. *Cold as dipping your hand in an ice chest for a cool one,* he thought.

The weatherman predicted an Arctic front booming down from Canada. So the meteorologist was right for a change.

Agent Gable worked in the Behavioral Science Unit (BSU) using his knowledge and training in social behavior, psychology, and sociology, and to record and analyze depravity in connection with criminal activity. He networked with two sister units, the National Center for Analysis of Violent Crime (NCAVC) and the Critical Incident Response Group (CIRG).

Though it was almost quitting time, Supervisory Special Agent (SSA) Clarke Gable—first name spelled with an "e"—never cheated the government by leaving work early. In fact, he often joked, "Overtime is my middle name."

* * *

Clarke F. D. Gable rarely used his middle initials and never revealed they stood for Frederick Douglass. Like his movie star namesake, Clarke sported rugged good looks, the same square jaw, the high forehead with pronounced brow, the squinting eyes, chestnut brown wavy hair and a neatly trimmed mustache. More striking than the added "e" in the first name, he differed from the movie star in a skin deep way—this Clarke Gable was black.

* * *

Clarke's parents had the lustrous skin tone of anthracite coal. In a genetic quirk, Clarke ended up a light brown color. A Caucasian with a summertime tan might have been an apt description. There was no kinkiness in the thick chestnut-brown hair. His lips thin, having none of the Negroid fullness, the narrow nose delicately concaved with no noticeable flaring of the nostrils, only the eyes truly reflected his ancestry, being luminous light brown with a ring of amber flecks.

Early in his life, he learned to accept the things he could not change. A black with a white movie star's name attracted taunts from even his good friends. Clarke skillfully parried a bad situation with humor, often converting tension to amusement. When one of his classmates scornfully asked, "Why are you so light, boy?" he said, "I guess there was a white guy in the wood pile."

On another occasion, Bessie Mae Jacks, furious at him for flirting with a pretty cheerleader, yelled, "Listen, Mr. Clarke Gable, if you keep messing around with that cheer girl, I'm gonna be *Gone with the Wind.*"

Clarke instantly replied, "Frankly, Bessie Mae, I don't give a damn."

They both laughed, and she treated Clarke extra nice that night.

An event occurred in his senior year that indelibly stamped his memory. At a high school dance, he asked Cindy Lind, a white girl in the band's trumpet section, if she would like to dance. On the way home that night, three football players, including Cindy's brother, accosted him. The brother snarled, "No nigger is gonna dance with *my* sister." Clarke knew his sense of humor was not going to keep him from getting his ass kicked. His only consolation was that he got to throw some damaging punches.

Although six-foot three and 195 pounds, Clarke disliked sports and concentrated on academics, music and theater. Students called him the tallest, biggest, meanest-looking trumpet player in Maryland.

Clarke, born and reared in Towson, Maryland, graduated salutatorian of his class and then crossed the country to attend San Jose State University in the budding Silicon Valley, California. SJSU, which prided itself on racial diversity, offered the talented, personable top-flight senior a full scholarship.

Clarke's earliest desire was to be a writer. His idol, F. Scott Fitzgerald, once lived in Towson. Fitzgerald had his wife, Zelda, committed to Pratt Hospital for treatment of depression and alcoholism. Clarke heard some of the old-timers talking about the wild Fitzgeralds. After reading *The Great Gatsby*, Clarke could not imagine anyone not admiring F. Scott.

The fistfight with Cindy Lind's brother caused a dramatic change in his aspirations. It sidetracked and finally derailed Clarke's high school ambition to be an author. He thought: *Cindy and I are band members and friends. One dance was no big deal. What made a human being bypass their good judgment and do an insane and hurtful thing? Well, I'm going to find out how the mind functions.* One-word answers to his question like "prejudice" or "redneck" did not satisfy his curiosity. Clarke abandoned his goal to master the written word. He became a psychologist.

At SJSU, Clarke managed a double major in Behavioral Science and Psychology. He found time to play in the Spartan Band and still graduate Magna Cum Laude. Clarke then traveled back across the country to Tampa, Florida, where he obtained a Doctorate in Criminology from the University of South Florida. In his thesis, he attempted to decipher why serial killers were almost exclusively white males. The analytic part of him wondered if the choice of this topic was his subconscious slap at white society.

* * *

Clarke was awed when he first came to Quantico, forty miles south of Washington, D.C. on the west bank of the Potomac amid 58,000 acres of woods. He learned that here the United States Marine Corps trained its officers, developed assault techniques and tested weapons. He felt uneasy in the shadow of the military, until he came upon the large complex that resembled any metropolitan beltway commercial development—the FBI Academy, his new home.

* * *

The phone buzzed and Clarke answered, "Agent Gable."

"Hello, Mr. Gee, it's Jezzy." The 58-year-old live-in maid never referred to herself by her formal name, Jezebel. She treated Clarke like her own son. His mother still lived, but Clarke liked to tell his friends, "Not everybody is so fortunate as to have two moms."

Jezzy asked, "Can you go by Kroger's on the way home and get some skim milk? I'm cooking pork chops for tonight. Oh, and there is plenty of food if you want to invite a friend, preferably female."

"I'll get a half-gallon of milk, Jezzy. You know it's a little late in the day to invite anybody home. I'm leaving in a few minutes."

Clarke mused, *People can't stand a man enjoying the bachelor lifestyle. I'm only 37 years old and content. Jezzy is always trying to bribe me into a date with the offer of free baby-sitting. When I start pushing 45, I'll really get serious about looking for a wife.*

* * *

November 18, 2002 (Monday)

Before he left on the errand for Jezzy, Clarke wanted to review a strange case he currently worked. He walked to his desk and sipped from a hot mug of coffee. *Nothing like a jolt of caffeine to rev my eight-cylinder brain into action,* he thought.

On Clarke's desk, aligned like a game of solitaire, sat six abbreviated incident reports and supporting data, prepared by a special unit of the National Center for Analysis of Violent Crime (NCAVC) using IMPS. Identical Murder Pattern Search was a computer program designed by Clarke in collaboration with the NCAVC. Data from various agencies, catalogued and compared, discerned obvious and subtle similarities in the commission of unsolved murders, murders with similar signatures placed in a grouping. Each group was given one of four regional designations: Northeast, Southeast, Northwest, or Southwest. Occasionally, a grouping could also be designated National as in the case of the notorious Unabomber.

IMPS claimed moderate success in the prompt recognition of serial killers and serial killing teams. This early warning system helped reduce the numbers of victims by apprehending the murderers at a less frenetic stage of career activity. Unfortunately, a number of murders needed to occur to detect the serial nature of the crimes.

Clarke, lead criminologist in the program, was disappointed that, since the inception of IMPS, the program only discovered 22 serial killers and ended their crime sprees. A disappointing capture rate of 5 percent endangered the program's funding. The one positive element was the isolation of a benchmark case that developed over a six-year period. Clarke, with the patience of a Red Sox fan waiting for a World Series appearance, monitored the movements of what he considered a new type of serial killer, who was patient and principled. A selfish thought, like a flash of lighting, struck Clarke's cerebral landscape. *This case study and successful conclusion could bring me the same national notoriety as Bob Ressler.*

Ressler's casework at BSU laid the background for several highly successful novels and movies. Hence, in the back of Clarke's mind, he could eventually fulfill his desire to write.

The transient thought of fame and fortune caused Clarke to ponder why an eccentric American public was always fascinated with gangsters and serial killers. At times, this fascination reached the point of adulation, not an admirable societal trait. Clarke resisted being condemnatory, since he admitted openly to the same fascination. He was amazed that the epitome of organized crime, Al Capone, still had box office draw. Like most of his colleagues, Clarke was intrigued with two famous serial killers: one real life and the other fictional. Jack the Ripper disemboweled at least five London prostitutes in 1888. Exactly a century later, Dr. Hannibal Lector cannibalized his victims.

Let me get back on track, Clarke thought. *It's time to channel this predilection for gangsters and serial killers into some scientific reporting. The brass wants a Track and Capture Protocol (TCP), and a Case Profile Analysis (CPA). Maybe if I peruse these incident reports one more time, it might trigger some new ideas.*

INCIDENT REPORT 97-106

VICTIM:	Cantrell, Bobby Dan
DATE OF INCIDENT:	January 9, 1997
PLACE OF INCIDENT:	Tipton, Mississippi
M. E. REPORT:	Body not found
AREA:	Southeast
CRIME RULING:	Probable homicide, suspicious disappearance
WITNESSES:	None
STATEMENTS:	Gas station owner saw victim talking with two out-of-town customers, male & female
SUSPECTS:	None
MOTIVE(S):	Possible revenge related to 1966 slayings
MAJOR PERSONAL EVENT(S):	In 1966, Cantrell found not guilty in the murder of three black teenagers.
DISPOSITION:	No active investigation. Case closed pending discovery of bodies or reliable evidence.

INCIDENT REPORT 98-211

VICTIM(S):	Collins, Irene Day and John Mark
DATE OF INCIDENT:	February 12, 1998
PLACE OF INCIDENT:	Alachua, Florida
M. E. REPORT:	Female: Shot in chest. Male: Shot in head. No signs of drug abuse.
AREA:	Southeast
CRIME RULING:	Homicide-suicide or possible double homicide
INSTRUMENT OF DEATH:	S&W .38 revolver
WITNESSES:	None
STATEMENTS:	Sister of female states that male and female IRS Agents visited the victims prior to deaths. IRS denies allegation.
SUSPECTS:	IRS Agents / Sutter's Hill Community Church member
MOTIVE(S):	Despondency over IRS legal action. Embittered church member upset over local pastor's suicide.
MAJOR PERSONAL EVENT(S):	Victim embezzled funds from the wealthy church. Pastor committed suicide.
DISPOSITION:	Case remains open pending clearing the IRS of criminal involvement.

INCIDENT REPORT 99-237

VICTIM(S):	Forrest, Andrew Jackson; Governor of Tennessee
DATE OF INCIDENT:	March 14, 1999
M. E. REPORT:	Stab wound made by thin pointed instrument entering above thyroid cartilage, passing into buccal cavity, coming to rest in the Broca's area. Death by rapid massive blood loss.
AREA:	Southeast
CRIME RULING:	Homicide
INSTRUMENT OF DEATH:	Ice pick or similar instrument
WITNESSES:	Female companion saw unknown male and female at the crime scene. Did not witness attack.
STATEMENTS:	None
SUSPECTS:	Pro-death penalty extremists or jealous wife.
MOTIVE(S):	Citizens angered over governor's policies on prisoners. Wife's reaction to estrangement caused by affair.
MAJOR PERSONAL EVENT(S):	Last hour clemency created political firestorm.
DISPOSITION:	Cold case file.

INCIDENT REPORT 00-335

VICTIM(S):	Shotz, Thomas R.
DATE OF INCIDENT:	April 6, 2000
M. E. REPORT:	Massive head injury, blunt trauma to pelvic area and lower extremities, spine broken at C-5 vertebrae. Victim died instantly.
AREA:	Northeast
CRIME RULING:	Homicide / Hit and run
INSTRUMENT OF DEATH:	SUV type vehicle
WITNESSES:	None
STATEMENTS:	Paper delivery boy saw two people parked in SUV near scene. Male and female strangers engage wife in conversation morning of husband's death.
SUSPECTS:	None
MOTIVE(S):	Victim's womanizing may have incited wife, relative or boyfriend.
MAJOR PERSONAL EVENT(S):	Received $8 million in drug side effect case.
DISPOSITION:	Case open. Ongoing search for vehicle.

INCIDENT REPORT 01-470

VICTIM(S):	Magruder, Marlene
DATE OF INCIDENT:	May 3, 2001
PLACE OF INCIDENT:	Madisonville, Alabama
M. E. REPORT:	Body burned beyond visible recognition. Identification made by dental records. Cause of death: Smoke inhalation.
AREA:	Southeast
CRIME RULING:	Arson / Homicide
INSTRUMENT OF DEATH:	Entrapped by house fire
WITNESSES:	None
STATEMENTS:	Local waitress stated male and female overly interested in victim.
SUSPECTS:	None
MOTIVE(S):	Anger at lack of care of children.
MAJOR PERSONAL EVENT(S):	Negligence resulted in the death of all four of victim's children.
DISPOSITION:	Cold case file.

INCIDENT REPORT 02-385

VICTIM(S):	Claxton, Rev. J. Oliver
DATE OF INCIDENT:	June 14, 2002
PLACE OF INCIDENT:	Dallas, Texas
M. E. REPORT:	Rifle shot wound to chest. Bullet shattered the sternum, severed aorta, causing the chest cavity to fill with blood. Died instantly.
AREA:	Southeast
CRIME RULING:	Homicide
INSTRUMENT OF DEATH:	High caliber rifle
WITNESSES:	Neighbor, Jose Cortezzo, saw man and woman in vehicle across street.
STATEMENTS:	None
SUSPECTS:	White supremacist group. No one has claimed responsibility.
MOTIVE(S):	Damnation for vicious verbal attacks on white community.
MAJOR PERSONAL EVENT(S):	Falsely accused a white school principle of raping a student.
DISPOSITION:	Cold Case File.

After Clarke scanned the material, he put the six reports in the upper left desk drawer and locked it. *If this serial killing spree is solved after only six incidents, we've made a monumental leap in crime prevention.* Lost in one of his working trances, he got up, put on his overcoat, took the elevator to the ground floor and walked to the parking lot. His colleagues, recognizing the signs, knew not to disturb him as he walked by, not even to say goodnight.

He forgot to pick up the milk.

CHAPTER 3
October 4, 1966 (Tuesday)
Tipton, Mississippi

In 1966, Bobby Dan Cantrell was 27 years old, three years older than his brother Carter Lee. Carter, broad shouldered and exceptionally strong for his size, stood 6 feet even and weighed 175 pounds. His older brother, shorter at 5'10", weighed a little less (164 pounds) and had the same general physique. The unmarried brothers contented themselves with drinking and chasing skirts. They considered themselves equal opportunity lovers, since they bedded white and, on occasions, black women, young or old, pretty or ugly. The Cantrells never used protection, figuring antibiotics would cure any STD. Arrogantly, they proclaimed, "If one of the stupid bitches gets pregnant, she's shit out of luck. She couldn't prove who the father was. No way!"

Bobby Dan and Carter Lee worked steady nine-to-five jobs in Tipton at the H.W. Wilkes and Sons sawmill. The mill had not converted to a sprinkler system, which used a constant spray of water to keep the logs moist, eliminating damage from dry rot, insects and fire. Instead, Wilkes and Sons used the outdated method of storing fresh cut logs in a pond adjacent to the mill. Carter Lee, a Boom Man, walked across the logs with spiked shoes and used a pike to separate and pole them toward the mill chute. The chute delivered the logs to a head saw that cut them into boards. If Carter Lee wanted to develop superb agility and a sculptured body, he had the right job. Like Narcissus, he loved his muscled body. He believed that any sane woman would consider him, like the fancy restaurants say: "The catch of the day."

Carter Lee idolized his older brother, but felt sorry for him. Without fail, when the brothers picked up a pair of broads, the uglier one invariably latched on to Bobby Dan.

Bobby Dan worked at the back-end of the sawmill process as a Lumber Inspector. Under his supervision, he and several other graders sorted cut boards into size and quality. The work was demanding, but not strenuous. He did not like to compare his fitness with his younger brother.

The brothers liked to refer to themselves as the Cantrell Boys. They thought the name conjured up images of the Clantons or Butch Cassidy and the Sundance Kid. The town's people tolerated the Cantrell Boys, giving them wide latitude in acceptable behavior. Most of the towns people logically assumed that Bobby Dan and Carter Lee were members of the Ku Klux Klan. Even the Klan thought them overly outspoken and obnoxious. Bobby Dan and Carter Lee never realized that Tipton held them in less than high esteem.

Besides the sawmill, the unincorporated village of Tipton boasted a two-pump gas station, a movie house, cotton gin, general store, one all-purpose church, and a juke joint, affectionately called Cotton's. Cotton's had the standard juke-joint equipment: a worn pool table; a juke box containing only country and western songs; five tables with oil cloth covers, and rough straight-back chairs. The building, made of sturdy cypress planks, rested on two-foot-high brick pillars. Wooden steps led to the front door and only the overhang from the tin roof gave the entrance protection from the weather. The interior was divided into the main room, where the tables and the bar were located, a kitchen, an office and a bathroom. Harold "Cotton" Herbert allegedly made the best hamburgers in the South. It was rumored, but not widely believed, that Cotton flattened the ground beef patties under his armpits.

On Tuesday night, things at Cotton's were slow. Cotton's barmaid only worked on Friday and Saturday nights. Bobby Dan and Carter Lee sat at a corner table sipping their beer. Carter Lee dropped a quarter in the jukebox and the first refrains of Patsy Cline's "I Fall to Pieces" broke Carter Lee's heart. He knew she died in 1964, but he still loved her music and considered her the greatest female country singer ever to hit Nashville. Cotton, behind the bar watching Captain Kirk order Scottie to beam him up to the *Enterprise*, paid no attention to his two customers.

"I worked my butt off today poling those damn logs around," complained Carter Lee. "I'm hitting the sack early."

"I made sure a couple of the black yard men also worked their butts off today," said Bobby Dan. "I overheard them say if they didn't get treated better and get better pay, they were going to burn the sawmill down."

A half-drunk Carter Lee piped up, "Well, if they get too wise-ass, they may just disappear like that Chaney and his two white buddies south of here in Philadelphia. Instead of burying them in a levee, we'll put 'em under that mountain of sawdust by the mill."

Bobby Dan laughed at his younger brother's serious tone and commented, "These niggers sure are getting out of hand. It's time to step on 'em before they get too brazen. I wonder if the Delta Guardians are up to anything."

The Delta Guardians, a Northeast Mississippi Ku Klux Klan organization with membership from the small rural communities of Meriwether, Greentown and Dansville, strutted like bantam roosters and bragged about their participation in the 1962 riots at Ole Miss.

Bobby Dan ordered two more beers and lamented, "I wanted to be a member of the Guardians, even dropped a lot of hints, but no one ever asked me to join. It got back to me that they considered us Cantrell Boys unfit, contaminated by fraternizing with black women."

Carter Lee said, "Hey, no big deal. We don't need some out-of-town, white-sheeted jerk-offs telling us what to do. You and I can handle any problem ourselves."

Carter Lee was a notorious hot head, and more than once his older brother had to talk him down. One night, Carter Lee made a loud comment referring to a certain lady: "No girl with pool-table legs should wear short skirts." This particular woman's escort took umbrage and a fight ensued. If the older brother had not intervened when Carter Lee went crazy, he would have beaten the semi-conscious boyfriend to death.

"Let's call it a night. We're both tired and we need to rest up for the weekend. There are a couple of sisters, Jackie and Linda, coming down from Meriwether, and we need to be in top form," said big brother Bobby Dan. "By the way, Jackie is *my* date."

Carter Lee wondered if she was the uglier one.

CHAPTER 4
October 15, 1966 (Saturday)
Near Tipton, Mississippi

Bobby Dan and Carter Lee's white Ford pick-up was perfect for an editorial cartoon; a Rebel flag flew from the antenna, the front windshield was cracked from driver side to passenger side, a shotgun rested in a rack and there were only three hubcaps. One week after the sisters came down from Meriwether, the Ford bounced along a rutted gravel road leading to the home of Chester Archer Cantrell. Uncle Chester owned 640 acres, mostly timberland, well posted against trespassing. He resided in a doublewide—all he and his wife Casey needed. An ex-Army Ranger and a World War II veteran, Chester Cantrell's Army career was cut short at Omaha Beach on D-Day when a Nazi shell blew his right leg off below the knee. The veteran got by on a meager disability pension and small timber sales.

To offset their Uncle Chester's limited income, the two nephews took him supplies and groceries once a week. The threesome drank a couple of six-packs of beer and told war stories; Chester's stories were authentic.

They came upon a rusty, dented pick-up parked beside the dirt road. The brothers decided to stop and see if somebody needed help.

"That truck is in worse condition than ours," commented Bobby Dan.

The empty truck with the tailgate rusted, blue paint bleached white and peeled, no tag, and one door white in stark contrast to the rest of the truck made the Cantrell boys wary. The sign at the turnoff read in clear print: PRIVATE ROAD. Chester and his wife lived only a mile down the road.

"Looks like someone may be up to no good," offered Carter Lee in a soft voice.

The abandoned truck was parked perpendicular to a trail through the dense woods, the narrow, decades-old wagon trail winding through cottonwoods, red oaks, slash pines and dogwoods. The path led to an abandoned shotgun shack where kids sometimes went to drink beer and smoke pot.

Carter Lee carried his Browning 12-gauge double-barreled shotgun in his left hand while he pushed small limbs aside with his right hand. Bobby Dan had a Swiss Army pocketknife in his pocket.

One of those oddities found in the Southern woods, the narrow three-room shotgun house, rose from a sea of dense forest like the ghost ship *Flying Dutchman.* The long abandoned shack had shattered windows, rotten and unsteady porch and steps, a tin roof totally covered with rust, and only one hinge keeping the front door from falling.

As they approached, they heard grunts and moans emanating from the front room. The Cantrells, familiar this with part of Chester's property, stalked with the dexterity of two Apache warriors. Approaching undetected, the Cantrells halted and crouched just below a broken front room window. Slowly they rose up and peered into the dim room where they glimpsed four colored teenagers. Carter Lee tagged the three boys as "Skinny Kid," "Short Kid," and "Muscles". Two boys dressed in jeans and T-shirts waited their turn. They watched naked Skinny Kid do his thing, the prone black girl protected from the rough-hewn floor by a worn Army blanket.

Bobby Dan held his finger to his lips, pointed to himself, and then to the front door ajar on its single hinge. He motioned Carter Lee to the back door. They both thought: *These black bastards have a hell of a nerve getting down and dirty on Uncle Chester's property.*

Bobby Dan picked up a round, two-foot long spoke carved from oak, the remnant of some sharecropper's wagon wheel. He moved up the front steps and across the porch, careful not to step on any boards that might collapse. An occasional plank creaked under foot, but the sounds of pleasure drowned out any noise he made.

Bobby Dan inhaled deeply. Adrenalin coursed through his body. His heart pounded. He felt fear, excitement and malice. He propelled himself into the shack, and raised the makeshift club.

Skinny Kid, smiling with satisfaction and accomplishment, suddenly faced the menacing apparition, and managed to utter, "What the. . ."

Bobby brought the club down. It penetrated just above the forehead. Splintered bones drove into the skull cavity. *Oh damn*, Bobby Dan thought *I didn't mean to hit him that hard.*

The startled girl screamed and rolled to free herself. Muscles and Short Kid forgot about protecting their plaything and ran through the two remaining rooms to the back entrance.

At the back doorway, Carter Lee heard screams. He leapt up the cinder block steps. The rushing teenagers collided with him. Off balance, he fell backward but never dropped his weapon. As he rolled over, he fired at Muscles, the nearest target.

Muscles' head disintegrated in a spray of blood, bone and cerebral tissue. His headless body convulsed in the leaves.

Short Kid stopped, turned to face his executioner, and held up his hands. "Please, Mister, we didn't mean no harm to anybody."

"Yeah, well you picked the wrong land to trespass on."

Short Kid knew he was going to die. The big white man applied pressure to the trigger. He wanted to say a prayer, but the words would not come. The blast hit Short Kid in the chest. Blood sprayed from his mangled heart as his body thumped the ground.

Pumped up, Carter Lee rushed into the front room of the shotgun house where the black girl cowered and sobbed. Standing mutely over the dead boy, Bobby Dan's glazed stare focused on the crumpled heap.

"Snap out of it, Bobby Dan. We just killed three blacks and we got a witness left alive. We need to figure something out, big brother. And quick."

"We're through killing for the day," Bobby Dan finally answered. "Three dead blacks ought to be our ticket into the Delta Guardians. No need to go crazy!"

Carter Lee, mind in low gear, ogled the naked girl. Her slender figure, taut muscles, small bosom, tiny waist and cute backside aroused him. Then he noticed the puddle. The poor girl lost control of her bladder, and the younger Cantrell gained a measure of human pity.

"What's your name?" Bobby Dan asked in a throaty growl.

"Georgie Ethel."

"Georgie Ethel, what?"

"Georgie Ethel Jackson."

In what he considered a supreme act of kindness, Bobby Dan told Georgie Ethel, "We're not going to kill you. Clean yourself up and get dressed. My brother will drive you home in our truck, and here's the kicker. If you ever tell anyone about what happened here, the Cantrell Boys will come visiting you, your brothers and sisters, and your Mammy and Pappy. I don't have to write it on a nail and drive it into your head, do I?"

"I won't say nothin' to nobody. Please don't kill me. I'm only fifteen."

"When folks start asking about your missing friends, here's what you say: 'I surely rode around with them, but then they dropped me off at home. Said they were going out in the woods and smoke some pot.'

"Carter Lee, you drive her back to Tipton. She stays on the floorboards where no one can spot her. Drop her off maybe a mile from her place and make sure no one is around when you kick her out. On the way back, pick up some bleach, shovels and rakes. Get movin'."

* * *

As Carter Lee stumbled down the trail, Bobby Dan glanced at his watch. *Already 2:00 p.m. Four hours until dark.* "We need to find us a dried-up creek bed. Should be several around here. We gotta get things wrapped up before dark," Bobby Dan explained.

A half-mile from the shotgun house they discovered a gulch seven feet wide and four feet deep carved by an intermittent stream. The bed was a mixture of sand, small pebbles, rotting leaves and siltstone.

"Okay, this is the spot. I'll dig the grave and you go back and drag the bodies back here," Bobby Dan commanded.

"Why in the bottom of this creek bed, Bobby Dan?"

"If the grave settles, nobody will spot it, or they'll think it's a natural depression. Besides, when the stream starts flowing in the late December, it will grade itself and fill up any low spots. It'll be decades, if ever, before the stream erodes down to the bodies."

The brothers crammed the three corpses, Skinny Kid's clothes, and the spent shell casings in the pit and then filled in the mass grave. The excess dirt they raked smooth and covered with gravel and leaves to give it an undisturbed appearance.

They trudged back to the shack, where Carter Lee thoroughly policed the area. The blood splatter in the shack was minimal, but Bobby Dan poured bleach on the stains. The weather forecast predicted thundershowers for the next three days. The rain would wash away the gore behind the shack from Short Kid and Muscles.

West of Chester's place, they hit the main county road and traveled three miles south, crossing the lazily meandering Tupelo River. Bobby Dan drove his truck while Carter Lee followed in the kid's truck. One mile past the bridge across the Tupelo River, they found an old, barely noticeable logging road. They turned west on the unused road until they came to a dead end and parked the junker under a canopy of tall oaks to prevent immediate detection by air search. The murderers carefully wiped surfaces to obscure fingerprints. The Cantrell Boys were not worried about the truck's eventual discovery; people would suspect the clandestine Delta Guardians of foul play. The brothers agreed that the DGs deserved the blame in retaliation for not offering them membership. The girl was scared enough to keep her mouth shut.

An unremorseful Carter Lee attempted to lighten the mood. "Well that was a good day's work."

Bobby Dan ignored the remark. "There will be some tears shed at the Mt. Nebo Baptist Church. That's three blacks won't grow up to be Civil Rights workers."

CHAPTER 5
January 6, 1997 (Monday)
Greenstown, Mississippi

Mike and Tess drove north on Interstate 55 planning to stay at the Greenstown Motor Lodge. Cloudy weather kept the outside temperature at 50 degrees. Inside, the Ford F-150 was a comfortable 70 degrees. Mike, a Ford man, bragged on the comfortable ride and good gas mileage.

The radio tuned to FM 91.3, M.P.R., Mississippi Public Radio, volume low, Mike listened to "All Things Considered." Another white Ford F-150 passed, triggering a thought that Mike considered important enough to mention. "This pick-up looks just like a thousand others on the road. We'll blend with the locals in Tipton." Mike glanced at Tess and asked, "What are you reading that's so interesting?"

"I pulled an article off the internet that appeared in the August 1, 1967 issue of the *News Report*. I'll read it to you."

NOT GUILTY!
Brothers get a free pass!
By Sam Langford

The seats in the Longstreet County Court House were packed with reporters, red necks, ruffians and relatives. They sat quietly as the jury foreman handed the verdict to Judge R. John Marten, II. The white haired, black robed judge studied the verdict for a minute, and without expression asked the jury foreman, "How find ye?" The foreman said, "We find the defendants NOT GUILTY, your Honor."

Few in this rural area expected the all-white jury of men to find Carter Lee and Bobby Dan Cantrell guilty of murder. The District Attorney, Granville Smith made a valiant effort, to no avail, to uphold the dignity of the State of Mississippi and to punish the brothers for the alleged mass murder of three innocent teenagers on October 15, 1966.

The State based their case on the eyewitness testimony of Georgie Ethel Jackson. She described how the Cantrell Brothers took the lives of three teenagers Eddie Herbert, Elijah Handy and Benjamin Stevens. Pointing to Bobby Dan, she shouted with hatred, "He's de one that clubbed Benjamin to death. Then I hears the shotgun go off twiced a few seconds later and I know Eddie and Elijah are gone. The Cantrells talk a little and then theys threaten to kill me and my family if I tell what I seen and heard."

Georgie, in tears through most of her testimony, told how she was forced to look at the bodies of Eddie and Elijah, one with his head blown off and the other with a gaping hole in his chest. "Theys told me that was how my family and I would look if I talked."

The State had little corroborating evidence. A Tipton General Store clerk testified he sold Carter Lee two shovels and two gallons of bleach on the day of the murders. Chester Cantrell ironically reported to the Sheriff that he heard two gunshots while sitting on the porch on October 15th.

In a closing statement, the smooth spoken defense attorney, Russell Smoot, described Georgie Ethel Jackson as a teen alcoholic, sexually promiscuous and mentally deficient. He then continued his glib delivery by stating, "Now on the other hand, the defendants, Carter Lee Cantrell and Bobby Dan Cantrell are hard working upstanding citizens. Why had it taken Georgie Ethel Jackson three months to come forward to describe the alleged crime? After all, no bodies have ever been recovered, so we can only speculate on foul play." Smoot ended his dialogue by stating: "I suggest that if three teenage black boys have been murdered, it was the work of the Delta Guardians whom we all know as the local branch of the Ku Klux Klan. My clients are not members of that organization."

"That's enough, I get the picture," Mike commented. "You know that traumatized Georgie could not make up an account or story that vivid. The Cantrells killed those boys."

They pulled into the Greenstown Motor Lodge and registered as Teri and Frank Beard. The lobby empty, Mike took the opportunity to speak with the lone desk clerk. The gold lettering on the black name badge read Finley Ferris.

"My wife and I are reporters for the *Jackson Morning Chronicle*. Our editor sent us up here to get an update on Bobby Dan Cantrell. The Cantrel Boys made quite a stir in these parts thirty years ago. Do you ever hear any scuttlebutt about him?"

The clerk looked like a bowling ball with ears. A wrinkled gray suit with outdated wide lapels did little to disguise the short, dumpy body. The white shirt back dropped a striped blue and red tie.

"The Cantrells and other fanatics like them sure gave Mississippi a bad reputation," said the clerk. "The past is always dragging us under water like a 300 pound millstone tied around our necks." The clerk didn't mind talking truth to another Mississippian about the dark period of the sixties.

"Don't hear much about the Cantrells," he continued. "Carter Lee and Bobby Dan were big news 30 years ago. My sister, who lives in Tipton, told me that Bobby Dan doesn't do much anymore except stay drunk. He married some girl named Jackie from Meriwether, but she left him after five or six years of getting beat up. He had one kid, a cute little boy, but I heard the mother got custody and moved up to Memphis to get completely away from Bobby. My sister said you can find him most every day at Cotton's getting himself tanked. I'll give you my sister's phone number. She knows everybody and everything that's going on in Tipton."

Mike thanked the clerk and mentioned, "You have made our job a little easier. Thanks for the help."

Room 1304 was on the first floor, back side parking at the entrance door. It was a secluded section away from the constant front side traffic.

Tess unlocked the door with her key card while Mike carried two small black leather suitcases.

Inside their room, both kicked off their shoes and unpacked the suitcases. Mike made two cups of instant coffee to give them a little energy boost.

"That desk clerk volunteered a lot of information about Cantrell," Mike drawled. "Should give our venture a jump start."

Tess sipped some of the hot coffee and asked, "What are we going to do tomorrow?"

"We drive to Tipton. Get some road dust on the truck so it fits in with the local scene. Bobby Dan hangs out at Cotton's, probably in the late evening. We'll check and see if he is still working at the lumber mill. We'll follow him around until we know his daily routine and where he lives. After we case his residence, we can decide how to eliminate Mr. Cantrell."

"Are we going to talk to the locals?"

"I haven't decided yet; we'll play that by ear. We don't need to risk recognition."

CHAPTER 6
January 7, 1997 (Tuesday)
Tipton, Mississippi

Mike pulled into DeMarco's Quik-Fill station at Tipton pissed off at the invisible sharpshooter firing gravel pellets at his car. The first rock hit the windshield causing a glass bruise the size of a half dollar. Mike just finished saying, "Oh shit," when the phantom sniper fired again. The second gravel bullet hit the windshield, instantly creating three cracks radiating from the point of impact. There were no self-serve pumps, so Mike and Tess waited in the pick-up for the attendant.

An older version of Bobby Dan, dressed in gray coveralls, came out the front door and sidled up to the driver's side window. "What can I do ya for?"

"Ah . . . fill it up with regular and check the oil, please."

Bobby Dan removed the gas cap and flipped the pump handle to start the gasoline flow. Mike, a little nervous at this unexpected meeting, got out of the car; it was an opportunity too good to waste. Mike started the conversation. "We were on our way to the State Prison at Caseyville and must have made a wrong turn somewhere. My wife has a brother in there for murder."

"Yeah, who did he kill?"

"He and another guy were robbing a bank when a black bank guard pulled a gun and Joey, my wife's younger brother, dropped him with three shots from his nine millimeter. He was lucky to get life without parole." In an attempt to befriend Bobby Dan, Mike in a conspiratorial manner, whispered, "Nobody should go to prison for shooting a nigger." *Damn, I hate using the n-word even if for a good cause.*

"The world has changed a lot, my man. Back in the sixties my brother and I killed three black kids and never spent a day in jail."

The pump clicked off, Bobby Dan removed the nozzle and latched it back on the pump. He opened the hood and checked the oil. *It must be okay*, Mike thought. *He returned the dip stick without any comment.*

"That'll be $18.50."

Mike handed him a twenty and said, "Keep the change. Wasn't your case on Jackson TV a couple of months ago, the thirtieth anniversary of the triple slaying? Are you Bobby Dan Cantrell?"

"Yeah that's me. Thirty pounds heavier, most of it on my beer belly. I've lost a lot of hair on top, but yeah, that's me."

"No one ever found the kid's bodies in thirty years. You must have hidden them pretty good." Mike knew he was pushing the conversation, but Bobby Dan did not seem suspicious or unfriendly.

"My brother died of emphysema a few years ago. The cigarettes finally got to him. He and I were the only ones who knew the location of the grave site. Now it's just me. I guess that ain't no big deal."

"Well, I've got to get going. Thanks for the chit-chat."

Mike got in the pick-up, cranked the engine and waved to Bobby Dan.

"That was the damnedest conversation I've ever heard," said Tess. "Thanks for saying I had a bank robbing brother."

Mike chuckled. "Pretty cool, huh? It got him talking. Lucky we were low on gas. What a break, locating him on our first day in Tipton. Let's drive to Memphis and get some barbeque ribs at Corky's."

That evening at the Greenstown Motor Lodge, Tess decided to call the desk clerk's sister. She dialed the number and listened to the ring.

"Hello."

"Mrs. Crandall, my name is Teri Beard. I'm a reporter with the *Jackson Morning Chronicle* and I'm staying at the Greenstown Motor Lodge. The Jackson TV station ran a story on the Cantrell Brothers a few months back, and my editor wanted a 'What's he doing now?' type of story on Bobby Dan. Your brother Finley, who works here, gave us some info and suggested we call you. Little things are important."

"I'll be glad to help, but please keep the source confidential. In a small bump in the road like Tipton, you gotta live with everybody. Bobby Dan lives in an old trailer on his Uncle Chester's place. The shotgun house where the murders were committed burned to ashes. Bobby Dan used the clearing to park his trailer. After the saw mill closed, he got a job pumping gas and doing minor car repairs at DeMarco's service station."

I already know that, thought Tess.

"Bobby Dan pretty much keeps to himself. He likes to drink beer and play cards at Cotton's a couple nights a week. Following the murder trial in 1967, things kinda went downhill for Bobby Dan. Lost his good job at the sawmill when it closed, got divorced and hasn't seen his wife or kid since. The big blow was losing his brother. Of course, the reporters are long gone. There has been some talk by the Feds initiating a Civil Rights case, but unfortunately, there is no new evidence. The bodies have never been found. Most people want to forget about those awful murders."

"What about the families of the victims? They must want Bobby Dan punished," Tess asked.

"All four families involved in the case either moved to other parts of Mississippi or out of state. Occasionally they'll write a letter to the *Longstreet County Gazette*, our weekly paper, complaining about a legal system that allows killers to walk around free."

"Okay, thanks for the info and I appreciate your help. Could you give me directions to where Bobby Dan is living?"

"No problem. Go south from Tipton until you hit the first bridge across the Tupelo River. Continue for another three miles or so where you'll see a sign to your left marked Chester Archer Lane. Turn there and go about a half-mile to a narrow dirt road to the right. About 500 or 600 feet down this road is a clearing with Bobby Dan's trailer. By the way, if you come to the second bridge across the Tupelo River, you've gone too far."

"Thanks again. I'll keep you and your brother's name confidential. Good-bye." Tess hung up the phone.

"Mike, can you believe that in two days, we've been face-to-face with Bobby Dan and know where he works and lives?" Tess said.

"What a travesty that it's taken 30 years for justice to show up," Mike said. "Tomorrow we inspect this trailer and figure out how we're going to remove him from the living. Are you hungry? This detective work is making me hungrier than a junkyard dog."

* * *

January 8, 1997 (Wednesday)

The pair arrived in Tipton at nine o'clock. They spotted Bobby Dan in his coveralls at the Quik-Fill station cleaning a windshield. Heading south on the main gravel road, they pulled up to Bobby Dan's trailer 20 minutes after leaving Tipton.

Mike climbed the cinder block steps, tugged on latex gloves and opened the unlocked front door.

"I guess he doesn't have anything worth stealing," Tess quipped.

Inside they made a quick survey. The master bedroom with bath, located at one end of the trailer, boasted an unmade double bed, chest of drawers and a cedar chest. The opposite end of the trailer had a smaller bedroom and attached bath. This second bedroom contained a student's desk and chair. The small bedroom closet was full of clothes rank with the unpleasant odor of soil and sweat. A worn sofa bed, a lounge chair, a 19-inch TV on a metal stand, an end table with a ginger jar lamp and a coffee table formed a grouping in the living room. The kitchenette was big enough to accommodate a small chrome legged table with only three chairs. The stove operated on butane gas. The apartment-size refrigerator contained beer, lunch meat, a few apples, mayonnaise, fruit juice and some frozen dinners in the freezer compartment. The paneling exhibited dark amoeba-shaped water stains from roof leakage. In the master bath, the ceiling sagged, probably from a large leak over time that was never repaired. Dirty work clothes were piled up in the corner. The stacked washer and dryer looked like they still worked.

"Let's check out all drawers, shelves, cabinets and whatever to see what turns up," Tess suggested.

Mike rummaged through the desk drawers in the small bedroom. They contained mostly bills, pencils, pens, tablets, loose change and stamps. In the bottom drawer, he found a folded, white, letter size, blue-lined piece of tablet paper. On one side a crude map showed a route through the woods, describing right and left turns at certain markers and distances. *Those markers are long gone*, he thought. At the end of the map were three small crosses in what appeared to be a gulch or creek. Mike, moved to sadness by what he just discovered, refolded the map and put it in his shirt pocket.

"Tess, I know the proper treatment for Bobby Dan."

"What?"

"He has an old, double-barrel shotgun in the bedroom closet with some outdated boxes of ammo. It may be the same weapon used by his brother to kill two of the black kids. We'll gun him down the same way. Likewise we'll bury his body so no one will ever find it."

Tess frowned and asked, "What's the point of a hidden burial?"

"I accidentally found a crude map indicating the burial site of the three teenagers. Maybe Bobby Dan was going to reveal the map on his deathbed. Probably just a few bones left, but identification through DNA can be made. To answer your question, burying Bobby Dan is poetic justice. Tomorrow we finish the project."

* * *

January 9, 1997 (Thursday)

They parked behind the dilapidated trailer. The mobile unit was anchored perpendicular to the entrance road, making it easy to hide the pick-up from someone approaching the front.

Mike unloaded the truck. That morning in Greenstown, they purchased a sack of lime, orange flagging, two pairs of nine dollar rubber boots, a couple of flashlights, a rake and a roll of tape. On the way to the trailer, passing through Tipton, they again saw Bobby Dan working at the station. His being at work would reduce the chance of interruption during their operation.

"Tess, you follow me through the woods and tie a piece of flagging on a branch every 20 yards so we can find our way. Make the knots loose so they'll be easy to untie and retrieve later."

Navigating through the trees and underbrush, they stopped about 300 yards from the trailer. The spot was ideal for the intended purpose. The small opening in the forest growth was large enough to dig a grave.

Mike laid out the shape of the grave and started digging. On occasion, he hit a root too thick to cut with the shovel and used the pickaxe to break through the impediment. Mike dug for 15 or 20 minutes then rested while Tess took over. The top three feet was loamy, except for the roots, so that progress was rapid. The loam was underlain by yellowish clay, which required more pickax work. Mike figured the grave was deep enough at five feet. It had taken three hours to dig the pit, but there was no need to hurry.

"It's four-fifteen and should be dusk in another hour," Tess cautioned. "If Bobby Dan doesn't stop off for a few beers, he should be home around five-thirty or six."

As they walked back to the trailer, a slight breeze began to stir the leaves. Without the heat exerted from digging, they felt their bodies cooling. The setting sun and deepening shadows accented the chill that penetrated their minds and bodies.

Tess murmured, “I’m excited and scared. We need to do this job right.”

“No sweat,” Mike replied. “Everything is falling into place; maybe the God of Justice, whoever he or she may be, is helping us.”

* * *

The electric company had installed a post with a halogen light that automatically came on at dusk. At six o’clock the shadows began a macabre dance as the tall pine trees swayed in the breeze.

Earlier, at five o’clock sharp, Mike donned gloves, went into the trailer, retrieved and loaded the shotgun. He also took the precaution of putting a few extra shells in his pocket. He pocketed a spare set of Bobby Dan’s truck keys hanging on a brass hook next to the door. Mike rejoined Tess outside to await the arrival of their prey. Justice, in the form of retribution, would be delayed for a short time if Bobby Dan stopped for a few beers. But there would be no last minute reprieve and no hymn singing, candle-burning, anti-death penalty crybabies.

The headlight beams and the hum of the V-8 engine gave warning of the arrival of the late model Bronco. Despite the cold, beads of sweat dotted Mike’s forehead. Barely breathing, the two figures stood immobile at the side of the trailer. Bobby Dan pulled up, put the gear lever in park, got out and started for the door.

“Just stand where you are,” Mike commanded.

“Who the hell is way out here on a cold night?” Bobby Dan said, uncomfortable staring into the muzzle of his own shotgun.

“We are just two citizens about to do what the State of Mississippi should have done 30 years ago,” replied Tess.

“I recognize you two. Came into the station a couple of days ago. Told me you had a relative locked up in Caseyville for murder. Gimme my shotgun and get the hell off my property!”

“You make any sudden move; you won’t be going to the Quik-Fill tomorrow. If you don’t mind taking a walk in the woods, I want to show you something.”

Bobby Dan figured, *This pantywaist somehow found the 1966 grave site. Why else would he be forcing me to go there?*

"If you're gonna kill me, it might as well be here," Bobby Dan said. "Besides, you and your lady friend don't strike me as cold-blooded killers."

"Your choice, Buddy. There are a couple of dead gooks in Nam that thought the same thing," Mike lied. "Follow my wife through the woods; it may give you a few more minutes to think of a way to save your life."

Tess turned on the flashlight and started walking toward the orange flagging.

"Walk about 10 yards behind my wife and don't do anything stupid," Mike ordered. "That's if you want to live a little longer."

"Okay, okay, listen," pled Bobby Dan. "Those kids were trespassing and using my uncle's shack to screw their curly little heads off."

"You didn't need to kill them to teach them a lesson," Tess parried, continuing to follow the reflective orange flags.

Bobby Dan reluctantly trudged after Tess. *Why would white people want to kill me for getting rid of three worthless niggers?*

"Listen, the State found me not guilty. You're taking the law into your own hands. My friends will hunt you down, you hear me?" Bobby Dan threatened.

"You ain't got any friends," Mike retorted.

Thoughts raced through Bobby Dan's mind. *Is this the way to the old burial site? It's been 30 years since I walked to the grave site of those stupid kids. Maybe this is the way. With this bright moonlight, it would be easy to follow the path without the flashlights. I wonder if this guy is alert and a good shot.*

Tess stumbled on an exposed tree root. She dropped the flashlight, fell forward, and hit the path with a thud.

Seizing his opportunity, Bobby Dan leaped over Tess and ran for his life. He had had the foresight to keep one eye closed so Tess's flashlight would not totally impair his night vision.

Mike saw Tess fall and Bobby Dan escape. He aimed and pulled the front trigger of the double-barrel Browning shotgun. The response was a sharp click. No ear splitting boom, no muzzle flash and no shoulder slap from the violent recoil. "Damn those old shells," Mike said. *I guess a misfire is a misfire no matter what the reason.*

Mike lifted Tess to her feet and commanded, "Follow me. I don't believe Mr. Cantrell is going to get very far if he stays on this path."

Bobby Dan never saw the freshly dug pit. He sensed free-fall. He heard his right knee pop as he landed. He saw the far side of the pit slam into his face. He twisted his body to face upward. His dazed condition mercifully dulled the pain from the fractured knee.

"Hey brother, what you doing in that pit?" quizzed Carter Lee.

"You're dead. So how'd you get up there, little brother?"

"Well, I run that little nigger gal home like you told me and picked up some tools," answered the image manifested in Bobby Dan's mind. "I'll help you out of that hole so we can bury those three bodies."

"Quit shining that damn flashlight in my eyes, Carter Lee," Bobby Dan demanded.

"Don't you wish I was your brother? Bobby Dan, just so you know, you're being executed for murdering those three kids; it's not personal."

Mike aimed and pulled the trigger. This time the shotgun belched the double-ought buckshot.

Bobby Dan's abdomen ripped apart. He groaned.

The sight of the entrails nauseated Mike. The man he hated moments ago, he now pitied. He mercifully fired a second shell into the brain of Bobby Dan.

Mike threw the shotgun in with the dead body. He slit open the 50-pound sack of lime and covered the corpse with the powder, then tossed in the sack. He read somewhere that lime will help decompose the body and possibly eliminate detection by cadaver dogs. Mike and Tess worked hurriedly to refill the grave. The humped surface would eventually flatten as compaction took place during settling. Mike raked back leaves and decayed debris over the bare ground. He found some rotten branches and scattered them across the grave. If the site was not discovered immediately, it would vanish in the undergrowth within a few weeks.

Slowly they made their way back to the trailer, careful to collect the orange flagging. Mike raked the ground where tracks matted weeds and grass.

"Let's check the area very carefully," Mike told Tess. Then he loaded the rake, shovels and pickaxe.

"Tess, you drive the F-150, and when you hit the main gravel road, go north toward Meriweather. I'll follow you in the Bronco. We can locate a store staying open all night. The parking lot is a great place to ditch the Bronco."

CHAPTER 7
January 10, 1997 (Friday)
Greenstown, Mississippi

They slept late on their last morning at the Greenstown Motor Lodge. After a shower, Mike and Tess breakfasted on a three-cheese omelet. With their first mission successfully completed, they checked out and headed south to Jackson.

On Interstate 55 South, Tess began the conversation. "For amateurs, we did pretty well. I don't think there are any witnesses to our hanging around Tipton."

"The desk clerk and his sister might eventually connect our conversations with the disappearance of Bobby Dan. I doubt it will help the cops," Mike concluded.

"It's a tough responsibility being the judge and executioner," said Tess. "It was sickening to see Bobby Dan's intestines spread out in his own grave." They both sat speechless reflecting on the mental image that gave a new meaning to spilling one's guts.

Tess laughed. "We almost blew our first adventure. At the most inopportune time, I tripped and went sprawling, and that old Browning shotgun misfired. If poor old Bobby Dan didn't fall into his own grave, we would still be out there with flashlights looking for a 58-year-old meathead. Do you think we can ever prime ourselves again to do another crazy stunt like that one?"

Mike concentrated on the heavy truck traffic, but he answered after some thought. "Our guidelines called for one project per year. A year will give us time to recharge and perhaps find another worthwhile target. Our first job was easy. Bobby Dan was a real horse's butt right up to the end. I can't feel any remorse for murdering that slob. Sometimes good people have to do bad things."

CHAPTER 8
February 14, 1997 (Friday)
Jackson, Mississippi

Farley Winston and Rolanda James, the white and black co-anchors on CMTV, Channel 12, were reporting a missing person's story.

Winston announced, "Bobby Dan Cantrell has not been seen for a month. Mr. Cantrell and his brother were accused of killing three black teenagers in 1966. The Longstreet County Sheriff suspects the disappearance may be tied to black radicals or remnants of the Delta Guardians."

James commented, "Mississippi has changed radically from the sixties. Bobby Dan Cantrell and the turbulent Civil Rights movement are almost forgotten." She then turned to her co-anchor and said, "On a lighter note, Happy Valentines Day, Farley."

* * *

June 19, 1997 (Thursday)

Mike drove to his office, a functional conversion of a Victorian home located in the 600 block of North State Street. It was 7:00 p.m. and the staff had already departed. He unlocked the front door, disarmed the alarm and went to the copier. Slipping on latex gloves, Mike opened a new package of copier paper and inserted a few sheets in the feeder. As soon as the machine warmed up, he made a copy of the yellowed burial location map of the three teenagers. He examined the copy for clarity and then folded it. Mike took one 6 x 10, self-sealing envelope from a newly purchased package of 12 and inserted the map into the envelope.

Next, Mike took a copy of the *Jackson Morning Chronicle* and opened the paper to page two. He carefully cut out the address at the bottom and taped it to the envelope. He thought, *Tomorrow I'll drive up to Greenstown and mail the letter to the* Chronicle. *The editor will go crazy speculating on who sent the map. Could it be Bobby Dan himself? If the* Chronicle *does its part, the parents of Eddie, Elijah and Benjamin won't have to wonder where their kids are. Maybe there will even be enough remaining bones to have burials. That would be a blessing.* Mike smiled with satisfaction.

* * *

July 1, 1997 (Tuesday)

Mike was on a business trip allowing Tess to enjoy complete solitude in the small bedroom. The crewel comforter and top cover were neatly folded accordion-like at the base of the pencil post, king size bed. Three elephantine Audubon reprints of the Amsterdam Series pictured southern birds in a vibrant array of colors.

Head propped up by two pillows, body sunk into the softness of a feather mattress pad, Tess felt as if she were floating on a fluffy cloud. She was engrossed in a book entitled *Doc Susie* by Virginia Cornell, a biography about Susan Anderson, M.D., 1870-1960. Doc Susie dealt with prejudice, deplorable weather conditions and a lack of resources to bring medical care to silver miners, loggers, and residents in the mountainous terrain surrounding the Granby-Fraser area of Colorado.

As a teenager, Tess had thought she would make a great doctor, but school advisors counseled her about the constant problems she would face in a male dominated profession. Tess mistakenly listened to her advisors and not her heart and opted for nursing school instead. With complete empathy Tess read that the diminutive woman doctor's only offer of employment was as a nurse in the town of Greeley, Colorado. Doc Susie, too, was the victim of the widespread disrespect for women who dared to be doctors.

Tess sobbed when she read that Doc Susie's brother John was a victim of pneumonia. It was easy for Tess, being a nurse, to imagine John's temperature spiking to a dangerous 104 degrees and feel his distress from severe chest pain. Tess could hear the hacking cough and see the thick brownish-red phlegm spewed into the already stained cotton rag. Tes thanked God that she did not live in the early 1900s when no doctor had a miracle antibiotic to fight disease.

As the captivated Tess assimilated the rugged experiences of this unsung heroine, a kaleidoscope of suppressed memories invaded her thoughts. How marvelous and unpredictable is the human mind demanding to be heard on its own time and terms.

Five-year-old Tess dreaded leaving the safety of her home to enter the vast unknown called kindergarten. She still reeled from the shock of her father dying of peritonitis because a lovable country doctor misdiagnosed a ruptured appendix as an upset stomach. Her mother, lonely and desperate for a provider, remarried one year later. Frank raised Tess and her older brother with the same love and enthusiasm as if he had been their biological father.

Although she knew it should not have been a big deal, the sensitive Tess was embarrassed at having a different last name from her mother and stepfather. Some of her classmates teased her about not having a "real father." So Tess compensated by being physically tough. Though not a bully, if someone pushed the right button, they usually got knocked on their butt. She grew up on a 65-acre farm just a few miles west of Sweet Gum, Mississippi on State Highway 35. Thirty-five acres, tired from lack of crop rotation and fertilization, were cultivated year after year. The remaining thirty acres provided pasturage for the family's lone cow. Tess and her brother, after hoeing, picking, feeding, milking or some other chore, came home tired. The Presley family was dirt poor, but the farm kept them from starving. Despite the poverty, Frank made sure his stepchildren had music lessons. He believed that the ability to play a musical instrument built character.

Tess's brother grinned when little Tess promised to rescue them from backbreaking work and poverty.

In high school, Tess won the admiration of her classmates. She altered her thrift shop clothes and was voted best dressed. She sang with a trio, accompanied the church choir on the piano, and played the alto sax and the French horn in the school marching band. She also excelled at basketball. Hardship molded a mentally and physically tough Tess. Talent rounded off the edges.

Tess forgot many of the good and bad times in high school but never one particular tragic episode. Doc Susie lost her younger brother to pneumonia. Tess lost her older brother to a drunk driver. Her belief in a just and merciful God was challenged when He took her father and then her brother from her.

In that pivotal moment, she decided to dedicate herself to saving lives. Tess applied to the University of Mississippi School of Nursing and was accepted on a full scholarship.

Piano lessons taught Tess hand-eye coordination and dexterity. The hard work on the farm gave her the strength to easily handle the heavy instruments sometimes used in surgery. Both patients and doctors liked her.

Tess's temperament reflected both gentleness and vindictiveness. During her senior year as a nursing student, she had a patient named Mrs. Helene Granger, on the third floor, west wing, room W-306, who was slowly dying of heart failure. The onset of pulmonary edema caused Mrs. Granger to constantly gasp for air and keen from severe pain. The protocol of high morphine dosage under normal circumstances would have been lethal, but Helene Granger was an alcoholic. The morphine injections were not alleviating the suffering. The Granger children begged for someone to terminate their mother's suffering. Tess removed a vial of promethazine HCL from the medicine room. The non-controlled substance, usually given to patients, prevents nausea and vomiting after surgery. She intravenously injected 1 cc of the clear liquid. At the same time, she also injected the dosage of morphine prescribed by the attending doctor. The two drugs given concomitantly severely depressed the central nervous system causing death. Tess did not feel guilty when Mrs. Granger died. "I have played God for a moment, but I used my power mercifully," she whispered to herself. *HE will forgive me for that trespass*, she thought.

She recalled a second incident in which she exhibited her vindictiveness. She was a clinical manager, counseling a 23-year-old named Ted Daws, a closet homosexual admitted to the hospital feeling lethargic and exhibiting mouth sores. The diagnosis: HIV, tantamount to a death penalty, caused the patient to become depressed and bitter. However, this mental state did not warrant his perverse hostility and contempt toward the doctors and nurses.

Tess explained, "You need to be careful not to infect others. Be careful with your body fluids."

Daws propped himself on one elbow and spit in her face.

She ran to the nearby sink and washed her face with antiseptic soap. At the nurse's station medicine cabinet, she grabbed a bottle of saline solution and doused her eyes. The solution splashed the front of her uniform. She dried her face and wrote an incident report. She decided Ted Daws was not going to die from AIDS.

An hour later, Tess entered Daws's room. She said, "You need this injection. It's a new medicine called Kaposol that retards the HIV virus." In a large vein just above the watch imprint, she inserted the syringe. "There'll be a little sting."

The lights were dimmed since Daws complained his eyes were sensitive to light. He never noticed the syringe was empty.

She depressed the plunger injecting air bubbles into the vein. Tess left the room, as the air embolism caused a thrombosis, the prelude to cardiac arrest.

I played God for a second time, Tess thought, *but this time I enjoyed being the instrument of death. I put two people to death. Mrs. Granger was a mercy killing. Ted Daws was a merciless killing.*

In a moment of serious introspection, Tess questioned whether the Ted Daws incident and the laughable handling of her brother's death were the precursors to the execution of Bobby Dan Cantrell? She thought, *It's time to tell Mike the full story.*

Tess shut the door on memories and went back to reading *Doc Susie.*

* * *

July 3, 1997 (Thursday)

Mike Miller returned from his week-long business trip to Houston, and he and Tess lounged in their spacious sunroom. Because their home was built on a shoreline point, the sunroom offered a non-obstructive view of the Barnett Reservoir. Sailboats already skimmed across the water like water skeeters. The bamboo furniture was constructed and padded to give the comfortable sensation of sitting in a bucket seat.

Mike was nose-deep in the Sunday sports section of the *Jackson Morning Chronicle.*

Tess was enjoying her favorite comic strip, "Prince Valiant," who, with his son, Arn, was trying to rescue the kidnapped Aleta from a marauding band of Vikings. Tess liked to imagine the impetuous handsome Arn. She wondered if his first name was in fact Arnold like her brother. *Arn must be the diminutive for Arnold. Well maybe not, but I like it.* "Mike, can you give me a few minutes of your undivided attention?" she asked.

"Yeah, sure," he answered. "I'll even lay down the paper to prove I'm listening."

"I've never told you about my big brother," she said. "It's a sad story. But I think the story will help you realize why I'm such a nutcase that doers of bad deeds deserve hard punishment."

"I'm all ears, honey. Take your time. We have all day," he said.

Tess closed her eyes and bowed her head. She visualized a small brass key. She mentally took the key and unlocked a small oak chest. In this imaginary chest, her most painful memories were stored.

CHAPTER 9
March 22, 1969 (Saturday)
Sweet Gum, Mississippi

Arnold James Taylor, had he lived, would have either been the President of the United States or a first-round draft pick in the NFL. In his sophomore year at Longstreet County High School, he stood 6'5", weighed 235 pounds and ran 100 yards in 10 seconds. He preferred being called Jimmy, his middle name. Old timers called him a throwback to ’40s football, since he played right-end on offense and defense. On the basketball squad, he played center averaging 27 points and eight blocked shots per game.

In academics, he carried a 97 percent average in the college and career curriculum. To round out his high school activities, he joined the Glee Club, French Club and Drama Club. The likeable teenager, the new breed of Southerner, thought people ought to get along, no matter what their color.

Baby Tess could not pronounce “Arnold” when she started muttering at 18 months old, transforming Arnold to Jabo. As they matured, Tess did not embarrass her sibling by using the nickname, but occasionally in a time of stress at a basketball or football game, she would blurt out, “Go get ’em, Jabo.”

Jimmy thought Tess was a pest, but she absolutely adored her tall, athletic brother. She even fantasized a few times that her Jabo was her boyfriend. She knew the concept was ridiculous, but dreams have weird twists.

Chilly weather but clear skies made for a beautiful March Saturday. High school basketball season had ended. Tess’s mother and stepfather drove to Memphis to do some shopping. Tess worked on her science fair project cataloging grave markers into various types. Outside, Jimmy waxed the family pick-up truck to impress a date that night.

The rural postman delivered the mail about 12:30 p.m. A little after one o'clock, Jimmy finished waxing the pick-up and decided to walk down the short gravel driveway to the mailbox. He hoped for a letter from a girl he met at a church retreat the previous summer. Jimmy shouted in the direction of the house, "Hey, Tess, I'm going to get the mail."

Jimmy walked toward the mailbox. A 1966, four-door Ford Country Squire station wagon kicked up dust traveling east along the gravel road. *The fool is traveling too fast*, Jimmy thought. The wagon's gravel and dust cloud billowed across the open unplanted cotton fields. Disgusted, he thought, *That dust is going to settle all over my clean pick-up truck.*

He grabbed the mail, turned his back to the oncoming vehicle and sorted through the letters and magazines. The brakes made a shrill squeal. He froze instinctively. The driver lost control and veered off the gravel road. The station wagon plowed into the tall teenager, propelling him through the air.

Tess, at her maple wood desk, heard the screeching car and the loud thump. She recognized the sound—the same sound as when her stepfather hit an 80-pound Labrador that had bounded in front of his car. Filled with dread, Tess ran down the stairs, down the hallway and through the front door. As she raced down the driveway, she saw a boxy shaped green vehicle barreling in the direction of Sweet Gum. She screamed as she saw her beloved Jabo lying on the ground face up.

Jimmy made no visible movement. Tears running down her face, Tess asked, "Where are you hurting, Jimmy?" A glassy stare and shallow breathing were his only response. "I'll be right back in a minute," Tess assured him; "I'm going to call for an ambulance."

Tess dialed the number for the Sweet Gum Community Hospital from a list of emergency numbers above the telephone. A female voice announced, "Sweet Gum—"

Tess interrupted, "Marge, this is Tess Taylor. A car just hit my brother. He's in bad shape, but not bleeding badly." Frantic, she shouted, "*Please* send an ambulance to our place and call Sheriff Ashley." Before Marge could say anything, Tess hung up the phone and ran upstairs. She yanked a blanket from her bed and ran outside. She knew the blanket would not delay the onset of shock but it would help with the cold.

Trying to be brave, Tess sat beside her Jabo and tenderly held his hand. "I called the hospital. An ambulance will be here in a few minutes. Hang on big brother; you're going to be okay."

The ambulance arrived in 7 minutes, 40 seconds. Two EMTs moved quickly to Jimmy's prone body. The younger EMT applied a blood pressure cuff. After taking a reading, he said, "John, he's 86 over 60— not good." John administered a glucose IV.

"Thanks Mickey," said Jack, "Get the girl to help with the gurney. We need to get out of here."

Together, John, Mickey and Tess performed a three-man lift to get Jimmy onto the gurney then Mickey loaded him into the ambulance.

Tess asked, "Can I ride to the hospital with him?"

John nodded, and Mickey helped Tess into the ambulance. She would call the house periodically until her parents got home. She figured the sheriff would catch up with her at the hospital.

X-rays and palpitation determined that Jimmy sustained a ruptured spleen and bled internally. In addition, three ribs were fractured and both legs were broken below the knee. The doctor performed a splenectomy to stop the internal bleeding. He reset the broken bones and taped the rib cage, but one, bright young doctor worried about possible cranial contusions. He ordered the patient sent to Methodist Hospital in Memphis.

Longstreet County Sheriff Aaron Ashley pulled into the emergency parking space at the Sweet Gum Community Hospital, rushed through the emergency entrance and found Tess sitting in the waiting room.

"Tess, is Jimmy okay?" the Sheriff blurted out.

"He's alive, but the doctors are worried about swelling in the brain. I need to get a ride home. Mom should be getting back from Memphis and may possibly have passed Jimmy on the road going there."

"I'll drive you home and you can answer some questions. I know it's a bad time to ask, but we need to act as quickly as possible."

Tess described the events of the past two hours. Sheriff Ashley listened intently without interruption. He did not want to influence her recollection. If she rambled, remained silent, or just cried, that was fine. When she said, "I couldn't see the license plate for the distance and the dust, but it was a green vehicle, longer than a car, probably a station wagon."

Oh my God, Sheriff Ashley thought. *A green station wagon with an erratic driver. I know the lowdown son of a bitch.*

* * *

June 11, 1969 (Wednesday)

Though not newsworthy for the *Jackson Morning Chronicle*, the trial made headlines in the *Longstreet Sentinel.* The police arrested Forest "Buddy" MacFoster, indicting him for the less serious offense of driving while intoxicated and leaving the scene of an accident. However, the indictment carried the felony charge of vehicular homicide. The defendant waived his right to a trail by jury and requested a bench trial. The facts of the case not in dispute, it was obvious that "Buddy" and his court-appointed public defender thought the presiding judge would be more understanding than a panel of his peers.

* * *

The crucial testimony for the prosecution was that of Sheriff Aaron Ashley, elected four times as sheriff of Longstreet County.

The testimony of Aaron Ashley began:

Ashley: As soon as Tess, ah . . . Miss Taylor told me that the vehicle color was green and that it had a box-like shape, I suspected the defendant. He drives a green Ford Station Wagon. He's been arrested 12 times over the years for drunken driving or exceeding the lawful speed limit. He has caused damage to several autos and property. I phoned you, Your Honor, and you issued a search warrant and authorization to take a blood sample from Mr. MacFoster. A medical technician, a deputy and I arrived at the defendant's home exactly one hour and ten minutes after my office was notified of the accident.

Judge Scott: How are you so sure of the time?

(Judge Scott, an Ole Miss law school graduate, had left his private practice after an overwhelming vote elected him District Judge. Although he had developed an unpopular reputation of being too lenient on crime, he still won elections against mediocre candidates.)

Ashley: All calls are clocked in, Your Honor. As is my custom, I always note the time I arrive at a location and the time I leave a location. It's standard law enforcement procedure.

Judge Scott: Continue.

Ashley: After we knocked on the door several times, Mr. MacFoster finally opened it. He gruffly asked what we wanted. I handed him the search warrant and the BTA, excuse me, Your Honor, the Blood Test Authorization. He read the documents then let us in. He sat down in the living room without a word. We asked to see the defendant's car and found his green station wagon parked in the three-sided carport. There was severe damage to the grille, the right side headlights were shattered and the hood buckled. The hood felt warm to the touch. My deputy collected some bloody shards from the headlights while the EMT took a blood sample from Mr. MacFoster. Based on what we found, I arrested Mr. MacFoster on a hit and run charge and read him his rights, in the presence of the other two men who accompanied me.

Judge Scott: Did the defendant present any notable emotional response to the charge and did he make any exculpatory statements?

Ashley: He just looked dejected and held out his hands to be cuffed. He did say he didn't realize he'd hit somebody and inquired who it was. After I told him, he asked if Mr. Taylor was all right and stated that all he remembered was waking up in a field and having to swerve back onto the road. He thought his car damage was from hitting a dog.

Judge Scott: That is a critical admission. Did the defendant sign a statement, Sheriff?

Ashley: No, your Honor.

Judge Scott: Continue.

Ashley: The next day, Jimmy . . . I mean Mr. Taylor, died of a subdural hematoma. An awful shock to the community. A GLC or Gas-Liquid Chromatography was done from Mr. MacFoster's blood showing a BAC or Blood Alcohol Concentration of 110 milligrams per deciliter. At that level, I was informed that an individual's judgment and controlled responses would be severely diminished. An automotive expert confirmed that the shards found at the scene were from the headlights of Forest MacFoster's station wagon. The blood splatter on the car was the same blood type as the victim. The charge was then upgraded to vehicular homicide.

Tess vividly remembered the two main points the defense used in an attempt to free their client. She utterly despised Roger Hawthorne, Jr. of the firm Meyer, Hawthorne and Smith. Hawthorne had volunteered for service in World War II and was rejected, to his embarrassment, for *pes planus*, more commonly known as flat feet. He was relieved when the war ended and people stopped asking, "Why aren't you in uniform?" He hated it when anyone called him a draft dodger.

Roger Hawthorn, Jr., LL.D. capably presented the defense's position in summation: "Your Honor, my client is a respected and accepted member of this community. He teaches chemistry and physics at the local high school. His ex-students brag on how well he prepared them for college."

Roger Hawthorne paused, breathed heavily and then continued his presentation. "Everyone, including yourself, Your Honor, knew that Forest MacFoster, referred to as 'Buddy' by his friends, had a drinking problem. In fact, he is a victim of CAS or Chronic Alcoholic Syndrome. Despite this dreadful handicap, he still continued to make a worthy contribution to the community through teaching." Hawthorne was amused to see Sheriff Ashley nod assent.

"Your Honor," Hawthorne continued, "a verdict of not guilty in thi case is suggested by the following example: Suppose Mr. Smith ha tuberculosis and he accidentally infected Mr. Jones. Unfortunately, Mr. Jone subsequently died from the infection. The State of Mississippi would no prosecute Mr. Smith for an offense I will simply name pathological homicide. Roman law gave us the tenet: *Actus non facit reum nisi mens sit rea*. The act does not make a man guilty unless the mind is guilty. Although Mr. MacFoster's body was driving the car that was involved in this tragedy, clearly there was no intent of the mind to commit the act. Eminent psychiatrists and medical doctors have deduced that the chronic alcoholic lacks the capacity to stop both the taking of the first drink and limiting the intake of this drug. The result is intoxication. At this point, the chronic alcoholic, exampled by Mr. MacFoster, loses control of his behavior and judgment."

At this point, Hawthorne made a preemptive move. Judge Scott undoubtedly knew his argument could be stricken by present case law. He needed to be crafty.

"Your Honor, I refer you to the case of *Leroy Powell, Appellant* vs. *the State of Texas*, argued before the Supreme Court of the United States in 1968. The Court, by a split 5 to 4 decision, held that Powell, a chronic alcoholic, could not use his uncontrollable condition as a legal defense against the charge of intoxication in a public place. The decision as decreed appears to favor the prosecution in this case, but there is subtext that is relevant to the issuing of an appropriate verdict from this court.

"First: Criminal law, morality, medical advances, psychiatric view points and beliefs of the population concerning alcoholism are constantly changing. We have not arrived at any point where there is a widespread consensus in the human equation on how to deal with the disease of alcoholism. Therefore, it was premature to proclaim a Constitutional Law that would prohibit discretion of the courts to work out the penalties for this societal problem.

"Second: Mr. Justice Black, who concurred in the decision, wrote that the nation could be more tranquil and orderly if it functioned on the principle that the local communities should control their own peculiar local affairs under their own local rules.

"It is obvious, Your Honor, is it not, that the court indeed made a decision in the Powell Case that goes against my client, but it left the door open for localities to try similar cases until enough verdicts are rendered that a consensus may be established at a future date."

Hawthorne knew he was not standing before a Supreme Court Judge but a friendly District Judge, who could be persuaded to believe such specious arguments. The personable lawyer counted heavily on the "Ole Miss" connection.

Tess wanted to scream at Hawthorne, "You worthless ass-kissing Ole Miss piss-ant lawyer!" *The jerk is actually telling that decrepit, beak-nose judge to ignore the Supreme Court of the land. Instead of thinning out the deer population, we need to thin out the lawyer population. I'd throw at least half of them in the dismal swamps. The headlines would be hilarious. ALLIGATORS EAT UP SHARKS.* Tess trembled, fearing that justice might completely vanish like a puff of smoke on a windy day.

Roger Hawthorne continued to deliver his summation with clarity and intensity. The defense lawyer never bored a juror or a judge. He had the gift.

"Your Honor, it is germane, and perhaps even critical, to discuss the medical aspects of this case presented earlier in this trial in the testimony of Dr. Edward Johnson, esteemed cardiologist. My client is 63 years old. At age 56, he was diagnosed with mitral valve stenosis caused by calcification due to his advancing years. His cardiologist explained to him that his condition was like a kink in a garden hose and if you didn't get the kink out, the hose could not deliver water to where it was needed. Surgery replaced the diseased valve with an artificial valve. It was then necessary for my client to be on an anticoagulant therapy, which utilized the drug Coumadin. The administration of the blood thinner is to prevent an occlusion, or blockage, in the valve. Of course, the danger to the patient is that the blood may be so diminished in clotting factor that a fatal bleed may occur in the event of an external or internal injury. Mr. MacFoster undergoes bi-monthly testing of his prothrombin time. The PT measures whether sufficient clotting factors are present. I suggest that my client could not withstand the rigors of confinement. Any rough treatment by other prisoners or even guards could result in a hematoma. If the hematoma is not drained and the bleeding stopped, severe organ damage or death will occur. The prison is not equipped to monitor the PT nor can it quickly respond to a hematic crisis. To sentence the defendant to incarceration would be tantamount to a death penalty."

A sober Buddy MacFoster watched and listened to his defense attorney, fascinated with the performance. He thought, *Maybe I'll be found innocent I sure could use a drink. Just one would slake my craving.* He smiled wher the Judge glanced his way during the testimony, glad that his attorney wa not going to ask him to testify in his own defense. *By God, I just don' remember hitting that boy. If I could only keep from taking that first drink but nobody knows the demon that commands me to take a drink.*

The able Roger Hawthorne, Jr., cast a look at his tragic client. He was not overjoyed with having to defend a chronic alcoholic who had run down and killed a young boy. Hawthorne's father had been a sot, and he hated alcoholism. *Why did he have to beat up Mom every time he got loaded?*

Hawthorne snapped out of his mental detour and continued into the last segment of his presentation: "Your Honor, the final part of my summation is purely speculative. However, the shear plausibility of the following conjectures dictates relevancy. Mr. MacFoster told the sheriff that he blacked out and did not remember hitting a person. It is entirely possible that my client's binge drinking led to a condition called Holiday Heart in medical lingo. Holiday Heart—arrhythmia to a cardiologist—is an irregular heartbeat. This abnormal rhythmicity may have precipitated a diminished blood supply to the brain causing a gray out. During this temporary state of unawareness, Mr. MacFoster's car left the road and struck Arnold James Taylor. On regaining consciousness, MacFoster regained control of his car and remembered nothing about striking an individual. When he arrived home, he did notice the damage to the front of the car, but believed he had hit a large dog.

"Your Honor, to find the defendant guilty under this circumstance would constitute cruel and unusual punishment under the Eighth Amendment of the Constitution."

* * *

July 17, 1969 (Thursday)

Thirty-six days after the trial, Tess sat in the courtroom awaiting the decision. She had a gut feeling that unlike her brother Jabo, this sorry-ass drunk was going to walk away from the whole episode with just a slap on the wrist. It was going be another controversial finding so that Judge Scott could make a name for himself, build up his legacy.

The judge began, "There is great difficulty in emphatically stating that alcoholism is a disease. We know that tuberculosis is a disease caused by tiny microbes. The medical profession can identify the cause, the undisputed symptoms, and provide the appropriate protocol for treatment. But medical doctors, psychologists, and biological researchers cannot agree on the definition of alcoholism or how to successfully treat those with an acute drinking problem. The urge to take a drink may be so compelling that Mr.

MacFoster cannot resist taking the first drink. From that point, his continued drinking to excess is driven by an unmanageable compulsion. As Mr. MacFoster reaches the state of intoxication, his behavior becomes involuntary acts conditioned by habit. Thus, the paradox: Mr. MacFoster drives a car and is unaware that he is actually driving a car. He is totally unaware that he is responsible for the death of Arnold James Taylor, although Mr. MacFoster is cognizant of the fact that he is a chronic alcoholic and while inebriated has been involved in non-lethal injury and property damage. His drinking leads to a predictable outcome. Would it be unreasonable for Mr. MacFoster to take precautions while he is sober to prevent calamity? In this case, drinking at home or providing a designated driver would have saved a life. The Court, therefore, finds the defendant guilty as charged and sentences him to serve 25 years at the State Penitentiary at Caseyville."

Tess shouted, "Hallelujah!" *At age 63, this might well be a life sentence for the old murdering drunk,* she mentally calculated.

Roger Hawthorne, Jr., aggravated with the Judge, thought, *I presented an excellent defense and my reward was a big fat zero.*

The judge slammed his gavel twice to stop the murmuring in the courtroom and said sternly, "I have not finished rendering my decision. Mr. MacFoster has a serious medical condition that requires constant monitoring. Incarceration would most likely lead to the premature death of the defendant. Therefore, I am suspending the sentence under the following conditions: Mr. MacFoster is forbidden to drive any vehicle for a period of five years. He is to immediately enter a detoxification facility and continue psychiatric counseling for a one-year period. In addition, he must join Alcoholics Anonymous for a period of five years. Any violation of the Court's Order will immediately repeal the suspension and the defendant will begin serving his sentence."

Even now, in 1997, Tess recalled how furious and upset she became. Barely bridling her fury, she ran to the nearest restroom and vomited. No justice administered on behalf of her beloved older brother, Tess promised to make it up to Jabo. She didn't know how, but she would find a way.

In 1969, Tess knew of only one way, mentally and emotionally, to survive this dark period. She imagined putting the horrible memories in an oak chest. Then she visualized turning a key in the lock, isolating the agony from the rest of her being. It was highly probable she was not going to unlock the oak chest for years, and maybe never.

Years later, Tess would be required to take a nursing course titled "General Principles of Psychology." Tess figured old Freud was pretty smart. He segmented memory into conscious, preconscious, and unconscious. *The unconscious is where we bury the memories that are devastating, painful, embarrassing or degrading. We don't want them popping up and ruining our life. So even when I was only sweet sixteen, I was applying Freud in my predicament*, she deduced.

As Tess related the story to Mike, she saw everyone projected on a mental movie screen: Jabo, Sheriff Ashley, Forest MacFoster, Judge Scott, and Roger Hawthorne. Like a camera automatically focusing, Mike's ashen face appeared in the imaginary viewfinder.

Mike shook his head. "I never suspected you carried such a heavy burden. You are courageous beyond belief and I love you for it."

Tess and Mike sat in silence for what seemed like hours.

Finally breaking the quietude, Mike said, "Tess, I, too, had a tragic episode in my life. It involved my mom and me. My dad never knew about the events."

"Honey, don't ever hesitate telling me about anything," Tess said. "You know I'm a good listener and I promise not to bite."

Mike just smiled.

CHAPTER 10
July 3, 1997 (Thursday)
Jackson, Mississippi

Tess could not remember seeing such a forlorn expression on her husband's face.

Why is it so hard to openly deal with old painful episodes, she thought? "Come on Mike, get it out, you'll feel mentally fifty pounds lighter," Tess said.

Mike was silent, reflecting on the past. He then began to tell his story, or more accurately, the story of his dad and himself.

* * *

His name was Joe Hooker Miller, named by Mike's granddad after "Fighting" Joe Hooker. Hooker, a civil war general, was not a good tactician but liked to fight. Mike's father lived up to his namesake, earning the Silver Star for bravery during the WW II Battle of the Bulge.

Unlike his father, a veteran of WWI and a career soldier, young Joe did not want to make the Army his life. Discharged from Fort Dix in New Jersey, he had one goal in mind: he would use his G.I. Bill to go to college, major in pre-med, gain acceptance to a school of medicine and eventually become a general surgeon. Joe had seen killing and had killed others himself. "To become a doctor," he once told Mike, "is a decision to balance the scales on the side of saving lives."

In the last year of residency at the Southeast Pennsylvania Medical Center (SPMC) in Bethlehem, he unexpectedly met his future bride. A heavy snowstorm created a challenge for even the most capable driver. Joe, driving in low gear to the Medical Center, brought his car to a stop at a traffic light.

He glanced in his rearview mirror to see a car, unable to stop, sliding in his direction. Joe cursed the careless driver and braced himself for the impact.

This little fiasco is going to make me late for surgery, Joe thought. "I'm going to be polite, but somebody's going to get lectured on how to drive in the snow. I'll bet the idiot doesn't even have snow grip tires," he said.

Each got out of their automobile, hopeful that the gentle collision had not caused any real damage. The girl spoke first. "I'm so sorry. I hit the brakes, but the car just kept going forward. My mind's on my mother who's having surgery this morning at the Medical Center. I really wasn't paying attention to my driving. Can you believe my bad luck?"

Joe stared at the most beautiful face he had ever seen. All thoughts of a lecture on driving in the snow burned out like a shooting star. He quickly surmised that the only consequence of the collision was the front bumper of her car hooked onto his back bumper. "What's your mom's name," Joe stammered?

"Irene Walenska," the pretty girl replied.

"Look, your luck just changed," said Joe. "I'm the Chief Resident and I'm on your Mom's case. Before she goes under anesthesia, I'll tell her that her daughter . . . err—"

"Rhonda."

"Rhonda was held up by the snow, but she'll see you as soon as you wake up."

"Gee, I'd appreciate that," she said. "She thinks I'm a scatterbrain, but maybe she'll be impressed that I got a message to her by the Chief Resident."

Pleased at being a rescuer of sorts, he replied, "There's no damage to the cars. I'll stand on my bumper and you back up your car. We'll be unhitched and ready to go."

* * *

Fifteen months after the car accident, Michael Joe Miller, weighing 6 pounds, 16 ounces, was born on March 22, 1950. Joe wanted to call him Little Joe, but Rhonda insisted on calling him Mike. She came from a big Polish family and wanted five or six kids. Her husband was more interested in medicine than progeny. Despite vicious arguments on this subject, Mike was their only child.

* * *

In 1967, Michael Joe Miller was in his senior year of high school and the epitome of the description "happy go lucky." He was an ordinary athlete, content to be second string on the varsity football and basketball teams. He excelled in his science courses with an overall G.P.A. of 3.6 out of a 4.0. On his seventeenth birthday, he received a sleek, new, red Ford Mustang Fastback Coupe. The car, his good looks and being a doctor's kid gave Mike a big edge in getting a date with almost any girl in high school.

* * *

Although Dr. Joe Miller chose not to be a career soldier, he never relinquished the physical and mental toughness of an Army Ranger. He abided by the basic code of conduct: If threatened by an enemy don't run and let some other poor soul do your fighting; stand your ground and make the enemy pay dearly for being in your space.

Joe Miller wanted his son to adhere to these same principals. He taught Mike how to use weapons and instructed him in the art of self-defense. "Son," Joe would admonish, "in a bad situation, think quick, make a plan, put it into action, keep your head low and don't get stupid."

Mike loved to play war games with his dad. Joe would indicate a certain area in which he was going to hide. It was Mike's job to locate his father's position and then plan an attack. He was surprised at how many times his dad anticipated his moves and out-maneuvered him. Joe would say, "You've got to plan better."

Mike would say, "You're too cool for words, Dad. I feel sorry for those Germans."

Living at home, Mike was a student at Lehigh University. Lehigh offered a BA in Geology. He liked the outdoors and liked collecting rocks and fossils. Geology seemed a natural career choice. He also had a crush on a girl attending Cedar Crest College in nearby Allentown.

Mike got home a day early from a field trip to a spectacular rock hunting area in Franklin Furnace, New Jersey. The leased Greyhound bus dropped Mike off in the parking lot at the rear of Williams Hall, home of the Geology Department. He checked the time. It was 2:30 p.m. His girlfriend was still in class; he thought, *Might as well spin home and see Mom.*

He pulled into the driveway at his parents' home and saw the three-car garage doors closed with a blue Chevy in the driveway. *I'm only staying a short while before I drive to Cedar Crest*, he reasoned, *so I'll just park in the driveway. I wonder who is here. I sure don't recognize the car.*

Considering having some of his fraternity brothers and their dates over for a swim party, he walked around to the backyard to see if the swimming pool looked good. He imagined ribeye steaks cooking on the charcoal grill, served by a girl in a bikini . Mike grinned, strolled to the back door and entered the kitchen-breakfast area. He walked down a tiled hallway past the downstairs master bedroom on the left and the formal dining room on the right. At the end of the hallway and to the left, a stairway led to the second floor. To the right, one entered the foyer and front entrance. Straight ahead was the den. Before climbing the stairs, Mike glanced in the doorway. In prominent view were his rock and semi-precious gem collection in two matching glass display cases. About to climb the stairs, he heard his mother squeal, "Oh, Jerry! I'm about to explode." Shocked, he thought, *That sure as hell's not my dad's name!*

His dad's training took over. *Jerry is obviously the enemy*, he concluded. *I must back away, make a plan, and attack from another direction at another time.* Mike quietly retraced his footsteps and went back to his car. He wrote down the license number of the blue Chevy. He did not open the car and search for any identification. He would not leave any trace of his presence.

Mike had a college friend whose father was with the Pennsylvania Highway Patrol. The friend told his dad that he spotted a cute girl and got her license plate number. "Hey, Pop, I know it's against policy, but could you get me a name and address?" he asked. His father gladly helped his son in the pursuit of romance.

* * *

Mike waited in the shadows outside the duplex. At dusk the corner streetlight provided limited lighting. *It's always possible that some passerby might remember me*, he calculated. *It's an acceptable risk. Dad warned that no plan is absolutely perfect. If I wait for the perfect plan, I may lose an opportunity to strike quick and hard.*

The blue Chevy drove up to the curb, and the driver, Jerry Kellogg emerged. The man was less than 6 feet tall and thin to the point of emaciation. He reminded Mike of Howard Hughes with his handsome but siniste countenance. *What does Mom see in this jerk*? Mike wondered "Mr. Kellogg," Mike announced. It was more of a statement than a question.

Kellogg was startled by the figure of a young man approaching from behind an elm tree.

"Do I know you?"

"No sir," Mike said. "I'm Marjorie Miller's son." *This guy is way out of shape and is no match for me*, Mike concluded. He moved closer.

"Son, I have no quarrel with you. It would be best if you got out of my way," Kellogg advised.

Mike threw a punch with enough force that he heard bones breaking in Kellogg's jaw. The stunned Kellogg fell to the ground, pain not yet registering. Making a tactical mistake, he rose to his feet.

"Mr. Kellogg, can you understand what I'm saying?"

His jaw injury and pain made it difficult for him to speak, so he just nodded yes.

Mike shouted, "*Never* see my mom again! And never, *never* call her on the phone or write her a letter! If you do, *asshole*, I'll cut your balls off and stuff them in your mouth, and *then* I'll kill you! Do you comprehend what I just told you, *Mr. Kellogg*?"

Kellogg nodded in the affirmative.

Then Mike pulled his fist back and said, "Do you *comprehend*?"

Fearful of being hit again, Kellogg firmly nodded his head yes.

Then Mike kicked him hard in the groin, hoping to cause permanent damage. Before Kellogg fell, Mike applied the *coup de grace* with another punch to Kellogg's nose. Mike turned his back on the prone, bleeding Kellogg and walked to his car. *That was pure justice*, Mike thought. *It felt good.*

* * *

The next morning, after his father left for work, Mike and his mom had a late breakfast.

"Mom," Mike said firmly. "I'm going to tell you something, but do not interrupt me, and don't ask me questions even after I finish. And do *not* get up and try to leave the table until I finish."

Marjorie thought Mike was about to tell her he got some girl, some bimbo, pregnant, causing him to have to get married and drop out of college. She said with, "Mike, if you're in trouble, your dad and I can fix it."

"Mom, *I'm* not the one in trouble. *You're* the one in trouble! I'm laying out some ground rules, so you'd better just listen up."

His intensity struck her, *Oh my God, he knows!*

Mike looked her right in the eye and said, "Last night I met with Mr. Kellogg. I warned him to stay away from you and to never see or contact you again. Before I beat him into unconsciousness, I told him I'd kill him if he ever disobeyed my instructions. It's not an empty threat, Mom."

"But, Mike, let me exp—" Before she could say another word, Mike placed his index finger to his lips.

Seething, he said, "There is no defense for what you did, so be quiet. Dad's a hero, a decorated WW II veteran. He's a great surgeon, a faithful husband and the best father. You've dishonored him, and he doesn't deserve this. You're my mom and I love you, and I'm willing to put this behind us, but if you ever have another affair, I'll make you very sorry. Get my drift? This discussion is over, and I never want to speak of it again!"

* * *

The *Allentown Sentinel*, second page, morning edition, reported the beating death of a local pharmacist named Jerry Kellogg. The police could not provide any motives or suspects.

CHAPTER 11
November 3, 1997 (Monday)
Jackson, Mississippi

The sunroom, as they called it, was Tess's favorite place to relax in their large house. The room was 25 feet in depth and 40 feet in length. The floor was old brick laid in the popular basket pattern. The ceiling, conveying the shed design, sloped from a 30-foot height to 13 feet. Four skylights, five-feet square with translucent domes, provided natural lighting. Five floor-to-ceiling double-insulated windows permitted a wide-angle view of the Ross Barnett Reservoir. The effect was a bright, cheerful solarium. Four bamboo chairs with yellow leather padding were as comfortable as any easy chair. The chairs were in a grouping facing three sides of a glass top coffee table with a three-cushioned sofa facing the fourth side.

She was sipping a cup of fresh brewed coffee and reading *USA Today*. The *Today* was one of many regional newspapers that Tess subscribed to in order to locate those individuals who deserved punishment. On the third page the header read: "Church Finance Clerk Takes the Tithes." She read the following copy:

The Sutters Hill Community Church located in N.W. Gainesville, at the intersection of N.W. 39th Avenue and 83rd Street, has a congregation of over 1,500 worshipers. Most of the members are educated upper middle class with substantial incomes. The Pastor, Reverend Gerald K. Sparks and the Church Directorate continually wondered why the church's finances were always in the danger zone. The mystery was solved Friday when a forensic accountant revealed that the church secretary had embezzled at least $900,000 over a period of years from the church.

Pastor Sparks apparently was so distraught that this theft occurred during his tenure that he committed suicide with his own hunting rifle. In tears, his wife said, "He shot himself in the backyard so he wouldn't mess up the house or disturb the kids." Sadly, there was no farewell note to his family.

Karl Younger, with the accounting firm of Younger, Dean, and Edwards, stated that he was not in a position to release any details of the alleged theft. However, several church members, who did not want their names published, said that the church records only went back five years. After five years, the church routinely destroyed the financial records to save storage space. Since Mrs. Collins has been employed for 15 years in the capacity of Finance Clerk, one can only speculate on the total amount of funds taken from the church.

The Finance Clerk, Irene Day Collins, and her husband, John Mark Collins, were long-time members of the Sutter Hill Community Church.

In a truly Christian display of "turn the other cheek," the Church Directorate voted not to press any charges. However, about one-third of the church membership were furious that their tithes and offerings went into the pocket of the Finance Clerk.

An unnamed member asked the question, "What does this kind of response teach our kids? You can steal a lot of money and walk away with no punishment! A lot of the members are going to move their letters to another Church."

When contacted, Donald Dudley, the Chairman of the Church Directorate, stated that the church was "seeking some restitution." He further stated that, "It was just a bad situation that was splitting up the church. Time and the good Lord will resolve the predicament."

Tess lowered the paper into her lap and hollered, "Mike come here a few minutes!"

Mike, lounging in the nearby den, watched a book review program on C-SPAN. "This better be good."

"Hon, I just read in the *USA Today* about a church finance clerk who got away with embezzling almost a million bucks. The theft pushed the pastor over the edge and he ended up committing suicide. His death almost makes her a murderer.

"Whadda you mean, got away with?"

"The Church didn't press charges, and she probably can only make minor restitution. Another case of big crime, little punishment," Tess grumbled.

"It has been ten months since Bobby Dan Cantrell went missing. guess it's time to choose a second offender if we intend to go forward with the plan," Mike said.

"Let's fly down to Gainesville this weekend and snoop around fo information," Tess suggested. "We can make a final decision after we d some investigating on our own. If it was just the embezzlement, the crime might not fit the punishment. In my way of thinking, two crimes were committed: embezzlement and murder."

CHAPTER 12
November 8, 1997 (Saturday)
Gainesville, Florida

They landed at Gainesville Regional Airport Saturday afternoon and checked into the Traveler's Inn located at the airport. The inn was conveniently located in northeast Gainesville only seven miles from the Sutters Hill Community Church. They rented a Ford Taurus at the airport.

* * *

November 9, 1997 (Sunday)

The next morning, the sky was clear and the temperature near 70 degrees, as they pulled into the blacktop church parking lot at 10:30 a.m. The Gainesville telephone book showed that the worship service began at 11:00 a.m. Mike and Tess hoped to engage some church members in conversation either before or after the service.

They entered the massive front door into a vestibule carpeted with three oriental rugs, each one centered under an immense chandelier. Three doors allowed entrance into the sanctuary. On each end of the vestibule, a stairway led to the balcony section.

A greeter approached them, offered them a church bulletin and announced, "Welcome to the Sutters Hill Community Church. The ushers are not here yet, so just go inside and seat yourselves anywhere you like."

Tess took the bulletin and said, "We are new in town and looking for a home church. I've heard some good things about your church, so my husband and I thought we would visit."

The greeter, thirty-fivish, dressed in a dark blue cotton suit, white button-down shirt and a red and blue striped tie, replied, "Like Gainesville, the church is growing in membership every week. We are a friendly church." The greeter turned away from Mike and Tess to welcome another couple, who also entered the front door.

Mike followed Tess through the center door into the sanctuary, where three sections of pews tapered downward to the pulpit and choir loft. Behind the choir loft, in typical church architecture, was a water-filled tank used for the immersion ceremony that represented burial and resurrection. Each side of the church had six enormous, leaded, stained-glass windows. The windows, measuring 5 feet wide and 25 feet high, depicted eleven disciples and Jesus. Judas, the betraying disciple, was not pictured. The scenes seemed to come alive as sunlight glowed through the glass, creating an almost magical effect.

They sat on the right side, halfway down the aisle in the middle of the pew. This seating would allow Mike or Tess the opportunity to converse with a church member who might sit on either side of them.

Tess whispered, "What do you think the Lord's reaction might be to our sitting in his house contemplating the murder of one of his children?"

Mike thought for a moment and then whispered, "People believe in a meek and mild God, who overlooks all our sins like a permissive parent. But God has always brought retribution on the unjust. Perhaps He is using us as His instrument to punish Irene Day Collins. Look what happened to Ananias and Sapphira for lying about their possessions at the altar of the Lord. They died at the feet of the apostle Peter, but we're not informed exactly as to what caused their death. It could have been a believer led by God to strike them dead with a sword for their dishonesty."

"You're so full of it, Mike. People are coming in now; we'd better change the subject."

The locally televised service timed exactly one hour. The Assistant Pastor, substituting for Sparks, used the time-honored technique of three points, a poem, and a prayer to deliver his homily on how divisiveness can destroy a church.

After the invitation and benediction concluded, an elderly lady sitting next to Tess, said, "Hello, I'm Martha Tynesdale. Thank you for coming to our church. I saw you raise your hand as a visitor. Are you looking for a church home or are you just passing through Gainesville?"

"Thank you for asking," Tess said. "We're looking for a church, and we certainly enjoyed your choir and pastor. We haven't made a decision, yet, due to the conflicts facing your assembly."

"Oh, dear me! That embezzlement thing and the suicide were such a shock to everyone. Of course, the Collinses cancelled their membership in our church and moved to Alachua. It's a small town a few miles northwest of here. She stole a lot of money from our church, but fortunately, we're not in debt. We have a good Church Directorate and they have the support of most of the congregation. Just a few hotheads want to prosecute the woman. So please consider coming back again and joining this church."

"You are a good sales lady. I may take you up on your suggestion."

* * *

Mike sat in their motel room looking at the bulletin he received at the Church. He noticed that the name of the Associate Pastor was Daniel K. Stevens. Looking in the Gainesville phone book, he found three Daniel Stevens but, fortunately, only one with the middle initial K.

"What are you doing, Mike?" asked Tess.

"I'm thinking about calling this Daniel Stevens and see if he'll tell us more about the embezzlement."

"You're a stranger on the phone. You're going to have to be subtle and persuasive," she warned.

"No kidding. Just listen to a pro."

Mike dialed the number and on the fourth ring, a pleasant voice said hello.

"Is this Daniel K. Stevens, a minister at the Sutters Hill Community Church?"

"Yes. Who is this?"

"My name is Frank Beard," said Mike. "I've been attending your church for a couple of weeks and my wife and I are looking for a home church." Mike paused, waiting for a reply.

"Sutters Hill is a great church,". Stevens stated. "The church staff is wonderful and I'm sure you observed that." Stevens sounded like he was delivering a canned spiel.

"I was talking to one of your members, a lovely elderly lady, named Martha Tynesdale. She suggested I talk with you," Mike lied.

"Martha is a gracious and faithful member. I know she spoke well of the church. What is it you need to know?"

"The good Lord has blessed my wife and I economically," Mike said. "We've worked hard and have tried to be faithful stewards. Your church has had some bad publicity this past week. What I'm driving at is, my wife and I want to make sure our tithes and offerings go to the right place."

Tess winked at Mike and silently mouthed, "Atta boy."

"I appreciate your concern," said Stevens. "The church, I suppose, was just too trusting of one individual. The whole episode demonstrates the power of the Devil and his commitment to destroying the Church."

Mike sensed that Daniel Stevens, although talking to a stranger, needed to unload a heavy burden. He waited patiently, but Stevens remained silent.

"Have you instituted some safeguards?" Mike asked.

"You bet. We've put in place a good check and balance system. One employee totals the loose cash and checks then gives me a report. The cash and checks, turned over to a second employee, are re-totaled and the amounts entered into the computer. That employee also gives me a report. Both these reports must match each other. A third employee reconciles these reports with the bank deposit statements. Quarterly, we send out statements to all members, and then we select a few members at random and ask them if their gifts, as recorded by the church statement, match their personal records."

"Well that satisfies me that my offerings will go to the church and not some conniving thief," Mike declared. "Do you mind if I ask you one more question?"

"No, go right ahead."

"How does someone steal a lot of money over years and not get caught?"

"As in the case with many embezzlers, Irene kept two sets of books," Stevens said. "The false set she showed the church. The second set was the actual complete record of transactions. If John Jones and John Smith each gave $3,000 to the church in the first week of June, she would record those amounts only in the second book in order to issue them a bogus receipt. The John Jones and John Smith gifts never got recorded in the false set of books. She would then issue two checks to herself in the amounts of $3,000 each and then cash them at the First Regional Bank of Florida. She visited different branches of that bank and used various tellers. No one teller ever got suspicious. In this fashion, it is supposed, she took anywhere from $7,500 to $10,000 a month. John Jones and John Smith would receive a quarterl statement showing their correct giving, so they were satisfied. The church never verified these statements by contacting any individual. Irene would not let anyone else work on the books or statements saying, 'I don't want the books messed up—'"

Mike interrupted, "I hear what you're saying, but it's still hard to grasp. What did Mrs. Collins do with the money?"

"First, let me say that Irene and John Mark were extremely private people who did not socialize with other church members. This lack of fellowship made it difficult to get to know them or their lifestyle. We did know they owned a home in Gainesville and a condominium at Sand Piper Cove in Destin, Florida. Their five children always were dressed in designer clothes and drove nice automobiles. Mr. Collins was a community college teacher probably making $60,000 a year, and his wife made $36,000 here at the church. Now in retrospect we should have recognized this anomalous life style. Before we became aware of the theft, everyone assumed either Mr. Collins or Mrs. Collins had an independent income or had inherited a great deal of money."

"Mr. Stevens," asked Mike, "don't you think the church has sent the message that crime does pay by not prosecuting Irene Collins? What must the young people of the church believe?"

"There was just no good answer. If we went to trial, this sore would be around for years. We excised the malignancy so that the healing process could begin. The church did negotiate a decent restitution. Both homes were sold, along with some antique furniture and valuable oil paintings. The proceeds went to the church. The church recovered $425,000, which we would not have recovered if we had prosecuted. The legal costs would have been staggering for both sides. Irene and John would have been destitute. Even with a favorable verdict the church would have received nothing. Our loss was perhaps $900,000. We did pretty good to recover almost half that amount. Of course, many people, including myself, believe she may have taken more than a million."

"Mr. Stevens, I've taken up enough of your time. I appreciate the conversation. Oh, and by the way, what happened to the Collins woman?"

"After they sold their homes, they moved up the road to Alachua. Irene's widowed sister, I believe her name is Mrs. Eddiceston, lived alone in a large house. It was a break for both sisters; one got a place to stay, the other companionship."

"Again, thanks for answering my questions. Good-bye and I'll pray for your church." Mike hung up.

He turned to Tess and relayed the conversation. Not wanting to sit around until the 7:20 p.m. departure time, he suggested they drive the 16 miles to Alachua and find the home of Mrs. Eddiceston. Mike checked the phone book and found a Mrs. Robert L. Eddiceston at 1734 L.N. Pearce Street. He wondered why L.N. Pearce deserved to have a street named after him. It only took 25 minutes on U.S. Highway 441 to reach Alachua.

They stopped at a quick stop in Alachua and Mike bought two diet cokes. He asked for directions to L.N. Pearce Street. The attendant gave him some easy-to-follow directions.

As they turned onto L.N. Pearce Street, Tess advised, "It looks like the even numbers are on the right side, so you keep your eyes on the road and I'll find the house."

The brass plaque on the mailbox glimmered with the number 1734. The structure was an elegant three-story Victorian home. Tess exclaimed, "What a beautiful, beautiful house." The steep, irregularly-shaped roof, the gables, the decorated queen-post trusses, a lower wrap-around porch, gingerbread, ornate spindle work, corbelled chimneys, and the turret with a conical roof were all typical Queen Anne. "It was worth the trip just to see the Victorian Lady." Tess averred, "That thieving harpy doesn't deserve to be living in a place so elegant and regal. But we're going to take care of that situation."

Mike had to smile. He loved the house and his wife, both queens.

* * *

November 9, 1997 (Sunday)

The Millers flew from Gainesville Regional Airport to Hartsfield in Atlanta. With 33 minutes between flights, they barely made the transfer from the commuter flight to the Delta 747. Mike always felt strange taking the flight from Atlanta to Jackson. Like this night, taking off at 9:05 p.m., cruising for an hour then landing at 9:05 p.m.

Mike watched a stewardess in a blue uniform walk the aisle checking seatbelts.

"I'm beat," groaned Tess. "I'll be glad to sleep in my own bed tonight."

"That makes two of us. In fact, I may nap a little on the flight," Mik said.

When the jet reached a cruising altitude of 32,000 feet and leveled off, Mike adjusted his seat backward and closed his eyes.

The image of Bobby Dan Cantrell appeared in Mike's head. *Gee, what triggered that memory?* Mike wondered. *The law really screwed up in not prosecuting old Bobby, so we had to do the job. We ought to send the State of Mississippi a bill for our expenses. This business with the Collins woman is going to be a little more complicated. I've got to figure a way to set her up for the elimination. I actually enjoyed putting Bobby Dan down, but I'm going to need to pump myself up a little on killing a church person.*

Mike's mind rolled into high gear. *How did a nice kid from Bethlehem, Pennsylvania, get involved in doing the law's job of dispensing justice? It's going to cost plenty to go forward with our plans. Well, I made it big and I can't take it with me, as the saying goes. I must be the proverbial means that justifies the end.*

* * *

Mike had been an independent geologist for several years. Trans-American Petroleum Company trained their geologists to be good oil finders and good managers. He used that expertise to establish himself in the oil and gas community, believing that a person should always position himself or herself so that if a great opportunity arose, they could grab hold. The "lucky break" wouldn't happen while working for others.

In the '80s, many major American oil companies divested their stateside onshore properties and concentrated offshore or in foreign countries. Trans-American wanted to sell one of their properties, the Frenchville Field in Point Coupee Parish, Louisiana. A vice-president who liked Mike called him and inquired if he would be interested in acquiring the Frenchville Field. The asking price was $1.5 million.

It was the very opportunity Mike was looking for; he borrowed the purchase price and an additional $500,000 for operating expenses. There were 42 oil and gas wells ranging in depths from 2,000 to 4,500 feet. The wells were fully equipped but shut down because of low profit margins. Mike knew most major oil companies were plagued by massive overhead. Big companies were also guilty of flowing wells at excessive rates to establish quick payouts and large cash flows. This practice caused pay zones to turn to saltwater or oil rock to crumble and plug the well with sand. Mike knew these bad oilfield practices prevented recovery of all the producible oil trapped in the reservoir rock. A small independent company could reduce the overhead and redrill wells to capture the oil left in place. In addition, many of the wells had thin pay zones, bypassed by Trans-America as marginal in the amount of oil produced. These “behind pipe pays” were money in the bank for an independent oilman. All Mike had to do was perforate and produce these zones without redrilling, reworking, or reequipping.

His workdays were 10 to 12 hours, and Saturdays and Sundays were part of the work schedule. The technical skills and business savvy garnered at Trans-American guided Mike toward success. After one year, there were 22 pumping oil wells and 16 flowing gas wells in Frenchville Field. The price of oil went from $9.00 a barrel to $31.00 a barrel, and gas went from $1.15 per million cubic feet (mcf) to $4.35 per mcf. Mike’s company, named Tessco after his wife, grew to nine employees. Two pumpers and a mechanic operated the producing wells. The office manager, accountant, and two secretaries kept the paper-shuffling running smoothly. A petroleum engineer, a geophysicist and Mike, the geologist, provided the science. The net monthly income, after landowner’s royalty, state severance tax, operational costs, and employee overhead grew to $600,000 a month.

Mike thought the firm was indeed “getting there”. His wealth became so staggering that the amount became meaningless. He climbed the mountain, surveyed the landscape, and now looked for another mountain.

* * *

Last year, out of the blue, Tess had said, “Mike, we’re gonna get off our asses and make a difference.” Maybe this was the next mountain. He and Tess gained success by hard work and risk-taking. Only in the good old USA could an ordinary kid become the President, walk on the moon, discover a vaccine to stop polio in its tracks, create an empire by making movie cartoons, or become the wealthiest man in the world by being a computer wizard.

In addition, in the good old USA, young kids became dopeheads, adults abused and molested children, people showed disrespect for the law, and family values tanked.

Mike knew that the decline into moral chaos had to stop.

Retribution and punishment would be the major weapons to halt the decay. Mike wondered how a psychologist would react to the proposition *broke the law to enforce the law or I rejected morality to restore morality*

The old conundrum: Does the end justify the means? In some cases, the answer must be yes.

Mike decided there must be others who believed like them. He wanted to contact them and see what they did to make changes. Mike took solace from the fact that the founding fathers broke the law and rebelled to set men free of tyranny. They were patriots. *Hmmm, I wonder if Tess and I are modern-day patriots. We're simply demanding that all men must take responsibility for their actions. You don't obey, you gotta pay.*

Mike knew their apprehension might lead to maximizing the effect of their project. From a trial platform, they could speak to all America and plead their case. They did not want to ignite lawlessness, but as long as government and society tolerated moral excesses, courageous citizens needed to follow our footsteps.

Boy, this is some heavy shit, Mike thought. *I need to concentrate on how to eliminate Irene Day Collins*. Sudden revelation revealed the plan to bring about retribution in the Collins case. It always amazed Mike how the subconscious part of the brain worked on a problem. The answer would pop up in the middle of the night, like suddenly recalling a name after trying to remember it the day before.

* * *

"Hey! Wake up, mister. . . I never sleep on the job," Tess cajoled as she poked Mike in the ribs. "You have been sleeping ever since we took off from Atlanta."

"For your information, I was just thinking with my eyes closed," said Mike.

"Give me a break," kidded Tess.

Delta Flight 1372 landed without incident and all 72 passengers deplaned.

On the drive home, Tess asked, "If you were thinking with your eyes closed, did you come up with anything I should know about?"

"As a matter of fact, I did," said Mike. "First of all, I've developed a plan to entrap and eliminate Mrs. Collins. I need to work out some details before I run it by you. I was feeling a little sorry for Irene; her indiscretion hardly equals that of Bobby Dan Cantrell, but we can't get into a rut trying to quantify a wrong-doing."

Tess reached over with her left hand and massaged Mike's shoulders. "Honey, I love you and you are a good person. And a good person has a conscience, but we have to stay focused. Many people felt sorry for Forest MacFoster, even though he was a drunk and killed my brother. Feeling sorry for MacFoster and his ilk is not an option in my world. Besides, I don't call causing a suicide a minor indiscretion."

CHAPTER 13
February 10, 1998 (Tuesday)
Alachua, Florida

Tess and Mike rented a green Ford Taurus at the Gainesville airport and then checked into the Traveler's Inn. Mike decided to drive to Alachua, familiarize himself with the Collins' neighborhood, and then place a phone call to the ex-secretary of the church.

Irene Day Collins sat at the window located in the second-story tower of the old Queen Anne home. The view, no longer farmland or pine forest, but new homes and city streets, was still a restful experience and a place to reflect on the past. *I miss all my church friends*, she thought. *Nobody calls anymore; I'm a leper without the leprosy. God surely won't forgive me because I can't forgive myself. What got into me that made me steal from my Lord? My parents would be horrified.*

* * *

Dr. George Day, head of the Cardiology Department at Shands Hospital in Gainesville, was the best known and most respected cardiologist in the State of Florida. Patients included the Governor, an ex-president of the United States, and several famous big league football and baseball players. One day while walking down a hospital corridor, he spotted what appeared to be a gold coin the size of a nickel lying on the tiled floor. He stopped, picked up the object and on examination, saw not a coin but a pendant with the initials G.D. *Well*, he mused, *these are my initials, but I obviously don't wear feminine jewelry.* A small loop bent open allowed the pendant to slip off the supporting charm. Obviously, the wearer never heard the "plink" as the small pendant hit the floor. He put it in his pocket and proceeded to his office.

* * *

Two weeks later, when Dr. Day made rounds, he reached in his lab coat pocket and discovered the forgotten pendant. He finished answering a med student's question and then asked one of his own. "Does anybody here know of someone, besides me, with the initials G.D.? The person probably works here at Shands."

One of the residents said, "A good-looking gal named Ginger Degnan works in the Public Relations Department."

George went to the Public Relations office that afternoon and asked for Ginger Degnan.

"I'm Ginger Degnan. What can I do for you?" Ginger was about 5'3", thin framed and flat chested, but extremely well dressed in a tailored suit. The pretty face, framed by real blonde hair, had pale blue eyes regarding him from beneath blonde lashes.

"I'm Dr. George Day. I found this pendant. Same initials as mine, but it's not my style of jewelry." He turned red with embarrassment when Ginger did not laugh.

"Thank heavens, someone found my charm. My parents gave it to me many years ago. How can I thank you?"

George noticed that she did not wear a wedding ring. Like most doctors, he got right to the point. "Would you have dinner with me some night this week?"

"Well . . . Yes I would," she replied. *That's why I'm working here, silly, to meet rich and handsome doctors like you*, she thought.

Six months later, George and Ginger married. Eight months later Ginger delivered, what she told her friends was, her "preemie." The baby was beautiful, weighed 5 pounds 4 ounces, and was breast fed for six months. It was the first time in her life that she had a bust line. The Days had another baby girl two years later. The parents and older sister spoiled this second child named Irene.

* * *

Irene watched a green car slowly drive by the house, turn around in driveway down the block and drive by slowly in the opposite direction.

wonder what that's all about, she thought. *Probably some church members that would like to run me down if I was out on the sidewalk.*

Irene chuckled as her thoughts of the past continued. *Mom and Dad gave me a wonderful start in life. They took me on fantastic vacations, bought me expensive clothes and sent me to the best schools.* She fell in love with John Mark Collins who graduated from Florida State Teacher's College. Her parents thought he was below their station and were unequivocal in their rejection.

Irene fell into a mood of introspection. *Why have I succumbed to a life of embezzlement? "Thou shall not steal," says the eighth commandment. I loved the church, the friendly church members and my Lord. Did the Devil make me do it? Let me be honest with myself. It was about the money and what money could do.*

* * *

There was no family fortune after Irene's parents died. Her mother drifted away under the degenerative onslaught of Alzheimer's disease. The palliative treatment and nursing care became a severe financial burden. Shortly after her mother's death, George Day was diagnosed with Chronic Renal Failure. The slow, relentless, kidney function destruction by the CRF necessitated dialysis to counter the onset of uremia. Transplantation was considered, but a suitable donor was never found. George's ailment wiped out the remaining meager savings.

* * *

Irene heard the phone ring and her sister, Darlene, calling, "Irene, the phone is for you. It's a man."

Irene took the front stairs to the first floor, entered the parlor, took the phone and said, "Hello, this is Irene Collins."

"Mrs. Collins, my name is Len Dravo," Mike lied. "I hope I'm not catching you at a bad time."

"No, Mr. Dravo, I'm in between jobs and have a lot of spare time. Please call me Irene."

"Okay Irene, I'm an agent with the Internal Revenue Service. I would like to come by with my partner. We're investigating a large non-reported income. Would this afternoon, say two o'clock be convenient?"

"Yes, that would be fine. Two questions, though. Will the visit take long, and do I need to have a lawyer present?"

"The questioning should take no more than an hour," Mike answered. "About having a lawyer present, that is your call, but this is just a low-key interview to establish some facts. No formal charges are pending at this time. And lawyers are expensive."

"All right, I'll see you at two o'clock," said Irene with a slight quiver in her voice.

* * *

Mike dressed in a dark gray suit with a maroon pin stripe. Tess wore a tailored pantsuit. They stood on the wrap-around porch and rang the doorbell.

Irene Collins immediately answered the door and invited Mike and Tess into the home.

"Mrs. Collins, I'm agent Len Dravo and this is my partner Helen Jordan," a name Tess made up.

"Please come in. My sister owns this home, but she's out visiting." She led them into the parlor where a magnificent Mahal oriental rug in vivid red, blue, green and ivory covered the floor. The room was a mixture of modern and Victorian furniture. When offered a seat, both Tess and Mike opted for one of the two comfortable looking armchairs. Irene chose the Victorian sofa with a utilitarian design that discouraged coziness.

Although Mike was prepared to handle such a request, he was thankful that Irene had not asked for identification. *Today we play the role of the heartless and cruel IRS investigators*, cut into his mind.

Mike removed a recording device from his pocket and displayed it in his right hand.

"Irene, I'm going to record our conversation and you'll be supplied a copy if you so request. You'll be asked a few questions to establish your identity. Is this okay with you?"

It was not okay with Irene, but she did not want to appear guilty of some crime by being arrogant or uncooperative. "Please, go right ahead with the questioning."

Mike spoke directly into the recorder. "This is agent Len Dravo along with agent Helen Jordan. We are at the residence of Irene Day Collins on this 10th day of February 1998. Mrs. Collins agreed to this meeting from our previous phone conservation. The residence is located at 1734 L.N. Pearce Street, Alachua, Florida. Mrs. Collins has asked me to call her Irene. She ha been informed that we're investigating the possibility that she has received a large and unreported income. For authenticity, are you Irene Day Collins, whose husband is John Mark Collins?"

"That is correct."

"Have we in any way threatened you or are you intimidated by our presence?"

"Well, I am nervous as anybody would be talking to the IRS, but I'm not intimidated."

"Thank you, Irene. If you disagree with any statement made by Miss Jordan or myself, please correct us. If a question is asked that you don't understand, ask for clarification. If you do not want to answer a question, you are not required to give an answer. Do you have any initial questions for us?"

"No, you've explained the rules of engagement pretty thoroughly. You both are respectful and don't seem to want to crucify me. No pun intended." She chuckled.

"Mrs. Collins, let me outline the situation as viewed by the Internal Revenue Service, what actions the department has taken and the possible consequences if a crime has been committed," Tess said. "First, the IRS suspects you have been embezzling funds from the Sutters Hill Community Church during your fifteen years of employment from 1983 to 1998."

"But I made restitution to the church," Irene blurted.

"That was a settlement contract between the church and yourself. The church recovered a portion of their losses; therefore, you weren't prosecuted for the crime of embezzlement. *Quid pro quo*," Tess elaborated. "Second, the agency obtained a warrant for the financial records of the Sutters Hill Community Church and your banking records from the Everglades National Bank from 1983 to 1998. We believe our forensic accountants will uncover upward spiking of deposits unmatched by legitimate income sources."

For many years, Irene had had some close calls. *I'll just listen to what they have to say and not act nervous*, she thought.

Tess paused for a response. None was forthcoming, so she continued, "Third, and please listen carefully to the following: In a 1961 Supreme Court case, *Eugene C. James* vs. *the United States*, the court held that embezzled funds are includible in the gross income of the embezzler in the year in which the funds were embezzled. There is no time limit evoked because embezzlement is a fraudulent appropriation. Therefore, the Internal Revenue Service is investigating the 15-year period from 1983 to 1998."

"May I ask a question?" said Irene.

"Please let me finish," Tess said. "If the IRS takes this case to trial and you are found guilty, then the sentence will be for a period of not less than 5 years or more than 30 years."

"This is unreal," said Irene. Her face lost all color and her eyes had a watery cast. "But I'm 54 years old. Why would they want to put an old lady like me in jail? Haven't I been punished enough? Every cent we had, we gave back to the church, and now, we're being shunned by all of our life-long friends. My husband and children have been embarrassed and traumatized by this whole affair. What's the point?"

Mike took over the interview. "The point is—people perceive that you got off easy. A lot of money still hasn't been accounted for. Speculation is that your children received a great deal of this money. If we can prove that they knew the funds were the result of embezzlement, they become an accessory. Your husband is also a suspect."

"You bastards! Leave my family out of this. It was me—understand—it was all me. And holy hell, 30 years is practically a life sentence."

"Calm down, Irene, we're just pointing out possibilities, nothing has happened, yet. I'll answer the question: Why would they want to put an old lady in jail? There's a pandemic of embezzlement in the United States. People believe that the reward is worth the risk since punishment for the crime is light to nonexistent. The government has now decided it is time to change that perception. A potential embezzler will think twice if he or she believes they may face 30 years in prison and that their family may also be subjected to imprisonment. This case will bring national attention. The only way you can avoid calamity for yourself and your family is to pay the estimated taxes, develop a severe incapacity or, God forbid, expire. The IRS regrets that your options are so limited and distasteful."

Irene moaned, "The Lord has judged me for stealing from his storehouse. If God afflicts my children, my punishment is tenfold." She dropped to her knees, cupped her face in her hands, and cried uncontrollably.

The two imposters let themselves out the front door, but not before informing Irene they would be back in two days. Mike tucked the recorder into his pocket as they left. Walking to the car, Mike commented, "We did the IRS proud today."

* * *

February 10, 1998 (Tuesday)

Mike and Tess sat at a table for four in the Coral Reef Café. The Coral Reef was the less fancy, less expensive of the two restaurants in the Traveler's Inn. There, the ceiling and walls donned sundry fishnets, oars, seashells, a stuffed Marlin, a diving suit, a brass ship's clock and beautiful color prints of a coral reef.

They ordered catfish sandwiches and fried curlicue potatoes, a favorite of Mississippians. The coffee was fresh brewed, so the waitress commented, and flavored with chicory. Both Tess and Mike cut the acrid taste with one pink packet of sweetener.

Tess grinned and chided Mike, "You weren't too subtle about the choices Irene can make. She's not able to pay the taxes, she certainly isn't a stroke candidate, and so kicking the bucket is really her only escape. Suggesting jail time for the husband and her kids really dismantled her defenses."

"When I first conceived this plan," said Mike, "there was no way to predict success, but now that we have confronted the Collins woman, things are looking interesting. She is nervous and distraught with limited options. She may even confide to her husband her sense of futility. If she doesn't do herself in, we will just have to facilitate the process. She is right handed so we need to shoot her in the right temporal area with a slight upward trajectory. When they check for powder burns and get suspicious at their absence, then they'll look at the husband as the prime suspect. He'll probably have an alibi, maybe teaching class at the time, so the suspicious suicide will probably be one of those unsolved cases explored on a TV investigative program. As for us, Irene was the only one who saw us and won't be describing us. We used false identification to rent the car, so there's no lead for the cops on that account."

"You have convinced me that the emotional state is perfect, but where does she get the weapon to commit the suicide? I suppose she could sit in a tub of hot water and slash her wrists with a razorblade," said Tess.

"I brought an unregistered pistol from Jackson," Mike confessed. "One of our tool pushers confiscated a cheap .38 caliber from one of the rig hands who showed up drunk for the morning tower."

Tess knew the word "tower" as oil field jargon for "shift". "Now I've got a tough question. Where did Irene get the gun?"

"I confess I don't have the answer to that one. Maybe one of the church members gave it to her and told her to go shoot herself." Mike grinned.

Tess shook her head with derision. "You need to polish up on your sarcasm."

"She's a resourceful woman," said Mike. "Maybe she just went out and bought a hand gun."

"Let's turn in. We have a whole day tomorrow to talk about Miss Irene," said Tess.

* * *

Twenty miles to the North, another family ate their evening meal. John Mark Collins, his wife Irene, and his sister-in-law Darlene Eddiceston sat at a rectangular French country oak table. The tabletop exhibited the wear of many years, its finish worn away causing the yellow oak grain to contrast with the dark varnish. The six three-rung chairs were hand carved with curved backs. The seats were cane covered with flower patterned, tie-down pads. The wallpaper was in the same flowered pattern as the seat pads. The chandelier supported four 60-watt, bent-tip candelabra bulbs.

Irene prepared her husband's favorite foods: breadcrumb-topped squash casserole, well-baked sweet potatoes and simmered center cut pork chops. *This might be our last supper together*, she thought. *After the dessert of French lemon-almond icebox pie, I'll tell them the bad news.*

"I've got some devastating news," Irene said.

"Is one of the kids hurt?" asked John Mark.

"You know Irene wouldn't wait all day to tell you if one of the kids was hurt," chimed in Darlene. "Go on, little sis, what's the matter?"

"I had a visit from two IRS agents this afternoon, a young man and woman. I guess the woman agent was supposed to comfort me after the guy beat me over the head with a statutory blackjack. Supposedly, the IRS is auditing the church's financial records and our personal bank transactions for the last 15 years—"

John Mark interrupted, "I thought they could only go back three years."

"Can they go back that far?" asked Darlene.

"I guess the government can do anything it wants to, especially against the little guy," answered John Mark.

Irene settled the matter. "Let me finish my story. The agents told me there's enough evidence to convict me of embezzlement. The money we paid back to the church has no bearing on the case. The penalty could be up to thirty years, which in my case is tantamount to a life sentence." She sobbed as her eyes rested on her husband. "The situation gets worse. The guy, Le something or other, his name is on the card he left, threatened to prosecute you and the kids. The IRS will assert that my family accepted funds with the full knowledge it was stolen money and, therefore, have aided and abetted in this crime.

"Shit," barked John Mark. "We need to hire a lawyer first thing in the morning."

"Well, the truth is, the kids never knew where the money was coming from that we gave them. They didn't know what our salaries were or whether we made unusually wise investments. You know, just dragging them into the situation would destroy their lives. Honey, you would never have condoned what was going on, so the subject was not mentioned. I kept the records for the house, so it was easy to hide the truth from you. Then the church discovered the shortfall, and you and the kids were shocked with the truth. Oh, what a mess!"

"Sometimes I wondered how we could afford to do all the things that we did. I hoped it was your good money management. I was afraid to ask. What a coward I was," John Mark confessed.

"Water over the dam," interrupted Darlene. "The issue now is to protect the kids."

"When the church was paid what money we could scrape up, my guilt was established. There are only two choices open to me. First choice is to plea bargain. I plead guilty and the IRS does not go after you or the kids. Ordinarily this solution would be appealing, but the IRS wants to use us as an example of the penalties handed down for embezzlement. When a whole family goes down the tubes, it could be a real deterrent to a wannabe embezzler."

"I don't like that idea; what's the second choice?" asked John Mark.

"The agents said they would visit with me again on Thursday. They planned to report on today's meeting to their immediate supervisor and advise me if there is any change in attitude. My opinion is there will be a change when frogs fly." Irene inhaled deeply then let the breath forcefully flow from her lungs. "If I take my own life, that will solve the problem. I'm not going to hurt my husband and kids anymore, and I certainly will not spend 30 years wasting away in jail."

It took two hours of tears, debate and prayer for John Mark and Darlene to convince Irene of the futility in committing suicide.

* * *

February 12, 1998 (Thursday)

Agents Len Dravo and Helen Jordan were mildly surprised when a middle-aged male answered the door two days later. Mike, in a Sherlock Holmesian approach, deducted that the leather elbow patches and ill-fitting tweed sport jacket with baggy trousers marked him as a college professor. In a crowd, John Mark's plain face would not have drawn attention, but today the scowl cautioned Mike to beware.

"Come in, I'm Irene's husband and I'll be sitting in on the conversation," John Mark growled, not extending his hand to welcome the agents. He led them to the same room where the first conversation took place. Irene Day Collins sat on the Victorian sofa not rising to meet the agents. John Mark seated himself on the sofa next to his wife. *This seating is perfect for a plan that involves suicide*, thought Mike. He noticed that John Mark wore his watch on his left wrist indicating he was probably right handed. Mike motioned Tess to sit opposite Irene in one of the Sheridan armchairs; he sat down facing John Mark Collins. "Mr. and Mrs. Collins," Mike opened, "if there are no objections, our discussion will be recorded as before."

"We don't object, but we want a copy of the previous taping along with this one," John Mark said.

"No problem." Mike took the recorder from his coat pocket, pressed the record button and spoke. "This is Agent Len Dravo along with Agent Helen Jordan. We are at the residence of and speaking with Mr. John Mark Collins and Irene Day Collins, husband and wife, on this 12th day of January 1998. Would either of you like to begin the session with any comments?"

"Yeah, I would," bellowed John Mark. "You two sandbagged my wife a couple of days ago. Scared her into thinking she ought to commit suicide to save her family from ostracism. I was in Nam, wounded three times. My point is, don't push us too far."

So, he knows about guns. That's good, Mike thought. He continued, "We didn't intend to frighten your wife, Mr. Collins. A crime has been committed and as a result, the government is owed a great deal of taxes. Our conversation with your wife was brutally honest. It is regrettable that Mrs. Collins became overly depressed, but no apology will be offered."

Irene joined the conversation. "Have your superiors made any final disposition in the case after hearing the interview?"

Tess answered, "Here's the thing, Irene. Nothing's changed. You'll receive a notice in the mail outlining the taxes due, interest and penalties. At that point, you can pay the amount due or appeal to the United States Tax Court. However, as we stated earlier, the IRS is going to file criminal charges. A successful conviction would prescribe a penalty of fines and/or imprisonment. My advice to you is to seek the service of a highly qualified tax attorney."

The four people in the room sat in silence after the dire news. John Mark and Irene sat stunned with heads bowed.

Mike pulled a snub nose, S&W .38-caliber gun from a concealed ankle holster. He fired from a sitting level into the left breast of Irene Day Collins.

Irene grasped her chest. John Mark jerked his head to the left and reached for his wife. "What the hell is—" His life ended with a second shot.

Mike moved swiftly after firing the first shot, and pressed the pistol slightly upward and against the right temple of John Mark before squeezing the trigger.

"I hadn't intended to kill them both, but when he answered the door, his demise was inevitable," Mike whispered. "I'll admit, it wasn't as satisfying as pulling the trigger on Bobby Dan Cantrell. It may be that poor John Mark didn't know that his wife was stealing from the church. It's possible, but he's still guilty by association. I don't believe he could be that naïve."

"Hey, I believe they were both equally guilty, and sometimes you have the infamous collateral damage," Tess argued. "Don't be a soft-boiled egg." Tess, still the nurse, took the pulse of each victim and declared, "They're both dead as hammers. Let's tidy up and get out of here." She double-checked everything they may have touched.

Mike wiped the entire gun clean, and then placed the gun in John Mark's right hand, letting it drop naturally onto the sofa. *The local cops will certainly conclude a murder-suicide*, he thought. "Did you check for any obvious hairs, or stuff that we might have dragged in on our feet?" Mike asked.

"Couldn't find a thing," said Tess.

Mike continued, "You need to wipe down the doorknob on the way out. We can dispose of these clothes later. I've checked the street and no one seems to be investigating the gunshots. Let's get out of this death house, pronto."

* * *

The Alachua Police Department received a call from Mrs. Robert Lewis Eddiceston. She frantically informed Detective Gino DeSilva that her sister and brother-in-law had been shot while she was out of the house.

Mrs. Eddiceston told Detective DeSilva, upon his arrival at the house, that John Mark and Irene had become despondent after contact by two IRS Agents. "Irene had even thought of committing suicide, but John Mark and I talked her out of it," she told the officer. "Or so I thought."

Detective DeSilva found a neighbor who saw a strange green car parked at the house on Tuesday and Thursday, but did not know when the car arrived or left. Another neighbor heard what he thought were two backfires sometime in the late afternoon on Thursday, maybe around 4:00 o'clock.

When contacted, the IRS denied having sent agents to interview the Collinses. DeSilva did not think the IRS was telling the truth, but he was not going to take on the U.S. Government. No forensic team was called to the scene, a negligent oversight. The .38 caliber gun showed no registration, and DeSilva could not locate any area pawnshops that sold the gun. Although uneasy about their decision, the local coroner and the overworked Detective DeSilva concluded, as Mike had predicted, that the deaths were the result of a murder-suicide.

CHAPTER 14
September 17, 2004 (Tuesday)
Quantico, Virginia

The incident reports, cumulatively referred to as the Justice Lovers Case, lay aligned side-by-side on Supervisor Special Agent Clarke Gable's desk. Solving the murders, which spanned a six-year period beginning in January 1997 and ending in June 2002, had become a personal obsession. He wanted desperately to nab these particular serial killers. The resolution of this case would rebuild public respect for the FBI. Clarke wanted to author a treatise on this landmark case to fulfill his long awaited aspiration of becoming a writer. This case would earn him universal recognition amongst his colleagues and the average Joe on the street. *My boat is loaded and I'm paddling upstream. At least, now I know my destination*, he thought.

In order to simplify his problems, Clarke decided to break the case into the three components. First, he would justify his hypothesis of a new clinically undefined serial killer. Second, he would create a profile of the serial killer. Third, he would devise a protocol for the capture of the serial killers.

Clarke knew that criminologists, psychiatrists and an array of other professionals and non-professionals, from the social anthropologists to the novelist, studied, catalogued, analyzed and researched the criminal mind. The behavioral science community was now able to predict, with a degree of certainty, what type of adolescent behavior led to the creation of the psychopath. In advancing behavioral science, the description of the serial killer became synonymous with the psychopath, the sociopath and Antisocial Personality Disorder (APD). Momentum in research got sidetracked as experts argued over what terminology was applicable for what set of symptoms. Clarke believed that many in the behavioral science profession were more concerned with labeling the subject rather than understanding the mechanisms that controlled the individual. *So be it. I may just add a little more confusion to classifying abnormal behavior. Sometimes you have to be part of the problem to be part of the solution.* His thoughts triggered a flashback to an argument on psychopaths the previous week with his boss, Deputy Assistant Director G. Thomas Claiborne.

* * *

September 9, 2002 (Monday)

Deputy Assistant Director Tom Claiborne stated, “The root cause of the psychopath is in the genes. If research could isolate the psychopathic gene, alteration of that gene would restore the individual to normalcy.”

“Tom, you know that nature theory is bullshit. Are you trying to tell me that there is a gene for being a doctor, and one for being an airplane pilot and another for a bricklayer, and can you imagine a criminal on the stand saying, ‘My bad genes forced me to be a criminal?’”

Claiborne countered, “What is your answer to this hypothetical about a family with five kids? Four of them grow up to be well-adjusted. One turns out to be a serial killer. All of them had the same environment and nurturing. The bad apple had to have been predisposed to becoming a psychopath.”

Clarke said, “I’ll guarantee that the bad apple was treated differently. He was not disciplined or not disciplined forcefully in the formative years starting at age two. There is no question that lack of discipline at home and school precipitated the explosion in the number of serial killers and that goes for kids killing kids. Those teenagers were not born killers. Parents and society molded them into non-caring, irrational deviants.”

Changing the subject, DAD Clairborne said, “I agree with your basic conclusions, Clarke. Those seven people were judged, found guilty of unconscionable acts and then executed. The victims had no idea they were in jeopardy. Those poor souls were bushwhacked. The Director wants this case solved. He’s worried about a leak to the press and subsequent accusations that the FBI has stumbled around for six years. We had enough criticism for not connecting the dots on 9/11. I personally think the criticism was justified. Even after this monumental failure, I’m still proud of the Bureau. The FBI does a lot of great work and never gets any credit. And our reward for solving this complex Justice Lovers Case may only be self respect. Incidentally, can I report to Goldberg that you've made some progress?"

"Not yet, but it's my top priority, Tom, believe me," said Clarke Gable.

* * *

September 17, 2002 (Tuesday)

Clarke read the Thomas R. Shotz file; a paperboy saw two people in a car parked near the scene of the hit and run. In the Bobby Dan Cantrell case, a gas station owner observed a male and female in conversation with the victim a few days before the disappearance. Similar sightings existed in the other files. It was obvious to Clarke that a Serial Killer Team (SKT), less common than the Lone Serial Killer (LSK), was in operation. He recalled a recent SKT case in which he had correctly profiled Lee Boyd Malvo and John Allen Muhammad, the Washington D.C. area snipers. The unique factor in the Justice Lovers Case was that the present SKT was not motivated by abnormal sexual gratification, acquiescence to supernatural voices or imagined societal persecution. This SKT was pursuing an argumentatively, worthwhile goal. Clarke speculated that the two killers were ordinary citizens who became disgusted with bewildering court decisions, activist judges and people not prosecuted for wrongdoing. He theorized that the SKT believed they were committing warranted acts of excision on a society that had lost its grasp of common sense and decency. The term vigilante had no application. This SKT was not murdering to uphold the law, but murdering to change the law. Clarke thought, *Maybe I'm splitting hairs like I've accused other behaviorists of doing.*

Clarke knew it was premature to discuss his conclusions with the psychological community. However, he desired the eventual step into prestige and notoriety. With a touch of amusement and a lot of seriousness, he created the term "justitiaphilia" to identify the new sociological phenomena. "Justitia" (jus-*tish*-ee-ah) was the Roman Goddess of Justice, fitting since Clarke concluded that a woman was the dominant force in this team. "Phile" was the Greek for devotee. A Justitiaphile is a Lover of Justice or a Justice Lover. *Justice Lovers Serial Killer Team. JLSKT. Great acronym,* he thought.

He was certainly unaware that the SKT had discussed being the upholders of moral rightness and justice. In a paranormal perception, Agent

Gable conceived the term justitiaphilia, of which the Millers were the first example known to the FBI.

Clarke knew that the existence of justitiaphiles was unproved at this point. He had no type of individual to interview or from whom he could obtain test data. He prayed that other justitiaphiles did not exist. *Can we stop the spread of justitiaphilia?* Clarke wistfully wondered.

Although Clarke believed the justitiaphiles would be captured, he lamented that his project could not eliminate serial murders. It was almost like a doctor having to wait until the patient died before he could devise a treatment. Unfortunately, for many a victim, the law did not yet allow for the incarceration of an individual with the potential of developing into a serial killer, for that would be the ideal time to stop the serial killer. *It's regrettable that 10, 20 or a 100 people have to be killed before it's recognized that a serial killing spree exists*, he thought.

* * *

FEDERAL BUREAU OF INVESTIGATION
BEHAVIORAL SCIENCE UNIT
QUANTICO, VIRGINIA
JUSTICE LOVERS SERIAL KILLING TEAM (JLSKT)
PROFILER: CLARKE S.D. GABLE
SUBMISSION DATE: SEPTEMBER 17, 2002

CASE PROFILE ANALYSIS

(1) Structure:

One female and one male constitute the JLSKT. The incidents have occurred over a six-year period indicating dedication to purpose, compatibility and confidence in ability. The JLSKT are most likely united in a successful marriage.

(2) Age:

The ages of the JLSKT will range between 40 and 50 years of age. At these ages, there is sufficient maturity to activate and pursue what they consider a noble cause. The killers are still healthy and energetic and can adapt to the demands of each planned homicide.

(3) Education

Both members of the JLSKT are highly educated, possibly professionals. The patience and planning required in the JLSKT pursuit suggests trained and organized intellect.

(4) Hierarchy:
In an all-male SKT, the older male is invariably the dominant figure. In a female-male SKT, the male is normally the authority. However, in the Justice Lovers Case the female may be the stimulus. This assumption is predicated on the fact that males tend to choose female victims. Five of the seven victims in this case were males, suggesting a female selecting the victims.

(5) Background:
The JLSKT came from a strict background. They were taught to follow rules and were punished if the rules were disobeyed. Both or one member may have been nurtured in a fundamentalist religion such as Pentecostal or Baptist.

(6) Region:
Five of the murders occurred in the South and one murder in the North. The JLSKT probably lives in the South, in a large city where few people pay attention to their neighbors. The South is more conservative in its views and more severe in its attitude toward crime. One of the JLSKT may be from the North, since the team committed one murder in a northern state.

(7) Economic Status:
The JLSKT is in the $300,000-plus-income bracket. The expense to execute the crimes plus the time away from occupational income suggests wealth.

(8) Emotion:
The JLSKT will not exhibit guilt, believing their deeds are justifiable. Not considered psychopaths in the classical sense, they do exhibit some sympathy for others. To help three families reach closure, the JLSKT mailed a burial map of three murdered teenagers to a daily newspaper.

(9) Cycle:
The crimes have been committed every thirteen months. The JLSKT are not superstitious of the number thirteen, again suggesting scientific background. The reason for 13 months between crimes is yet unknown, although that may be their selected time of recharging. This 13-month cycle identified this particular SKT through computer crime analysis.

(10) Race:
The JLSKT individuals are undoubtedly Caucasian, as 85 to 90% of all serial killers are white.

(11) Family Status:
The JLSKT may not have living parents or children. This status would eliminate the dampening effect of familial consideration.

(12) Synopsis and Recommendations:
The JLSKT is a white married couple between the ages of 40 and 50. They are wealthy professional people owning a stylish home in a prominent section of a large southern city. Search for a couple without living children and parents. Both members are college graduates and respectable citizens in the community. The JLSKT is imaginative and resourceful, but probably not dangerous to law officers.

POSTSCRIPT:
This speculation is offered in the event it may trigger a response at some point in a broad investigation. The first murder was a test run for the JLSKT. It would be normal to choose a locality familiar to one member of the team. Building on this assumption, the JLSKT team may reside in Mississippi where Bobby Dan Cantrell was presumably murdered. Jackson, the capitol city; Biloxi, the tourist Mecca; Meridian with its Naval Air Station; and Hattiesburg, a college town, are the four largest cities. These cities are suspected to be the prime areas of residence for the JLSKT.

In a clinical analysis, the JLSKT is a Social Deviant (SD), but should not be overlaid with those qualities attached to psychopathic serial killers. The JLSKT does not choose similar victims, i.e., all five-foot-four blondes who weigh over 150 pounds. The JLSKT does not take souvenirs from their victims or leave taunting notes for the police (crime signature). The JLSKT is not driven by compulsion, nor is it sexually gratified by the death of the victims. Victims have been chosen for a social injustice perpetrated or commission of a crime that went unpunished. The JLSKT, using the same strategy as applied by Martin Luther King and Mahatma Ghandi, are disobeying the rules of society to rehabilitate and redeem that society. Their tactics do not reach the nobility of King and Ghandi, but their dedication to purpose is as unwavering. The profiler refers to this new psychological state as "justitiaphilia."

* * *

September 25, 2003 (Wednesday)

Clarke, experiencing *déjà vu*, traveled North on I-95 to Quantico. Deep in thought, he stayed way below the 70 mile per hour speed limit, the ethereal presence of Sherri Nelson in total control of his inner being. *Only a month ago I found the girl I want to spend the rest of my life with. Thank heavens for a car that wouldn't start. Jezzy is going to be real proud of me. Friday, August 23, 2003 was one of the best days of my life.*

* * *

August 23, 2003 (Friday)

Clarke's breakfast consisted of grits, two sunny-side up eggs and two patties of low fat, low sodium sausage. He mixed all three together to make a soupy mixture he called "glop." Jezzy, his old black maid, prayerful by nature, had just finished the blessing when the phone rang.

"No doubt a wrong number this early in the morning," Jezzy said. "Hello. This is the Gable residence."

A soft voice said, "Ma'am, this is Sherri Nelson. You don't know me, but I work at the same complex as Mr. Clarke. Is he there?"

"He sure is." Jezzy glanced at Clarke and said, "It's for you." She cupped the mouthpiece and whispered, "It's a girl and she sounds nice, Sherri something or other."

Clarke swallowed a mouthful of his mixture and grabbed the phone. "Hello?"

"Mr. Gable, this is Sherri Nelson. I'm a computer programmer with Crime Analysis. I'm on the second floor just under your section. Actually I've done some work on the Justice Lovers Case."

"I'm sorry. I can't put a face with the name. What can I do for you?"

"My car won't start. The engine turns over, but it won't start up. I would be indebted if you could pick me up at my house and give me a ride to Quantico."

"No problem. Give me your address and I'll pick you up in 30 minutes." He wrote down the address.

"You been running around behind my back?" Jezzy asked.

"At 37 you ought to trust me," Clarke said. "Her name sounds familiar, but I can't place the girl. Just giving her a ride to work. It'll be nice to have some company, especially the female kind, for a change."

Clarke left his home on Stafford Avenue and turned west on Williams Street where Sherri Nelson lived. Williams Street was also Virginia Highway 3 and intersected I-95. It was his daily route each morning. Picking up this girl caused no inconvenience.

Clarke spotted the pale blue two-story wood house and turned into the driveway. Sherri Wilson came out the front door, quickly descended the three wooden steps, hurriedly walked to the passenger side and opened the door. "Hi, I'm Sherri Nelson."

"Clarke Gable, not the movie star, and no jokes about the name. Hop in."

He was glad this lovely girl had called him. Sherri was at least five-foot-seven and in high heel shoes probably five-foot-nine. She had the slim build of a jogger or long distance runner. Her pale complexion was flawless, except for two tiny freckles below her left eye. The high cheekbones complemented the almond-shaped eyes. The pupils were a lustrous emerald green. The straight, black, silky hair fell to her shoulders. She was the perfect result of a union of Caucasian and Asian parents. Clark remembered seeing her at the office now. He had not fraternized with her.

"My boss accepts no excuses for missing work," Sherri said. "You are saving my life and my job."

"Who's your boss?" Clarke said.

"It's Mr. Perry Walters."

"Yeah, he is kind of a hard-nose. If he gives you any trouble, let me know. He owes me all kinds of favors. How did you get on board with the FBI?"

"I was a town student at Mary Washington College and started out as a music major but switched to computer science. In my senior year, the school awarded me the Ralph A. Niemann Scholarship. It was probably a stepping-stone to getting an internship at the FBI Academy. The Bureau liked my work ethic and computer literacy. Offered me a position on graduation day."

"Of course, your good looks had nothing to do with the offer," Clarke stated, with a mixture of humor and flirtation.

Sherri blushed, recovered her composure and said, "Every girl uses that weapon."

As he pulled into the parking area, Clarke could not remember making the drive to the Academy. *Am I that starved for companionship?* He thought. Aloud, "See you at five o'clock, Miss Nelson."

"Thanks for the ride, Mr. Gable."

"Hey, call me Clarke, all the other starlets do."

Sherri caught the subtle compliment and nodded in appreciation.

* * *

September 25, 2002 (Wednesday)

Clarke snapped back to the present, back in the same parking spot where his first encounter with Sherri Nelson ended. He forced himself to shift gears from the pleasant thought of Sherri to the serious thoughts of the Justice Lovers Case.

He took the elevator to the third floor, unlocked his office and let his body drop, like a well-placed putt, into his swivel chair. Again, against his will, his mind drifted back to Sherri. Oh, well, I might as well daydream for a while. He whistled a real oldie: *'I got a date with a daydream'. As I recall, she wasn't wearing a wedding band. She has a pleasant disposition, is beautiful and intelligent. I'm tall enough that she can wear high heels without embarrassing me on a date. Most of all she is biracial so we can share experiences. If I ask her out, the most she can say is 'no.' It would not be my first ever rejection.* The inner voice demanded, *Call her right now.*

* * *

The phone rang five times before a female voice answered.

"Hello?"

"Sherri?"

"No, she's away from her desk. I'll get her. Who shall I say is calling?"

"It's Clarke Gable. I gave Sherri a ride to work a month ago. I need to tell her something." He felt a pang of guilt, asking for date on company time.

"Yes, of course. Hold on, I'll get her."

"Hello, Mr. Gable. How're you this morning?" said Sherri.

"Call me Clarke. I feel ancient when someone calls me Mr. Gable. Ah . . . I have two tickets to *Les Misérables* at the Carpenter Center in Richmond for this coming Saturday. It's supposed to be a great musical. Will you join me?"

"I would be delighted Mr. Gable, uh . . . Clarke."

Suddenly, Clarke's boss, Tom Claiborne, appeared in the doorway and teased, "That doesn't sound like FBI business."

Oh shit, Clarke thought. *I break policy one time and get caught*. "Gotta go, Sherri. The boss just came by. I'll call you tonight."

"I read your initial behavioral report. Good job. Now we need to devise a plan on how to apprehend these crazies," said Claiborne.

"I know that's a catch-all phrase, Tom, but these people are far from crazy. The Track and Capture Protocol (TCP) will be on your desk by quitting time."

"Good deal. And by the way, go easy on the computer programmer on the second floor."

"Geez, I can't believe my private life is making the office rounds."

Clarke picked up the rough draft of the TCP for the Justice Lovers Case. *One last proof reading for good measure*, he thought.

* * *

FEDERAL BUREAU OF INVESTIGATION
BEHAVIORAL SCIENCE UNIT
QUANTICO, VIRGINIA
JUSTICE LOVERS SERIAL KILLING TEAM (JLSKT)
PREPARER: CLARKE S.D. GABLE
SUBMISSION DATE: SEPTEMBER 25, 2002

TRACK AND CAPTURE PROTOCOL (TCP)

(1)

Alert the Attorney General in each of the following States: Florida, Tennessee, Pennsylvania, Louisiana, Texas and Mississippi that a Serial Killing Team (SKT) may be operating in their state. Include a discussion of all six crimes in the Justice Lovers File along with the Case Profile Analysis. Request an in depth re-investigation of the crime that occurred in their state. All investigative results are to be delivered to the FBI for reprocessing.

(2)

Initiate a campaign to report the probability of a Serial Killing Team (SKT) via major newspapers and television stations in the six states where crimes have been committed. Add to the reports an abbreviated behavioral profile.

(3)

Appeal through all media to the JLSKT to begin dialogue with their local law enforcement agency or the FBI. Elimination of a death penalty sentence could be negotiated for their surrender.

(4)

Establish a reward of $ 250,000 for information leading to the arrest, capture and conviction of the JLSKT.

(5)

The JLSKT must screen major newspapers, TV stories and magazines to select their victims. Set up a group to mimic the JLSKT. The team may be able to identify a small number of potential victims. A monitoring system could then be established to give the intended victims a modicum of protection.

Clarke knew that going public had a downside. The justitiaphiles would be alerted and possibly vanish à la "Jack the Ripper". However, Clarke believed that the JLSKT would welcome the publicity. New converts could result from calling attention to the JLSKT. The justitiaphiles were a formidable challenge to behavioral analysis and apprehension.

Clarke was overjoyed to be involved in a case that would profoundly advance a greater understanding of the mind. Professional success would establish his credentials as one of the premier criminologists. *The computer boys deserve a lot of credit for discovery of the JLSKT. Don't get too excited. The protocol will be subjected to dreaded budget constraints, priorities, politics and personalities. I could even be removed from the case. Sayonara, FBI, if that happens.*

CHAPTER 15
September 28, 2002 (Saturday)
Fredericksburg, Virginia

He had the exuberance of a teenage boy on his first date. Bessie May Jacks had never made him this nervous. He forced himself to relax in the air-conditioned sanctum of his new Lexus GS300. *Hell, I'm trained to handle serious emotional stress. Get a grip!*

Clarke pulled into the driveway at 331 Williams Street, got out of the Lexus, and headed for the front door. At 6:00 p.m., it would not get dark for another two hours. The temperature cooled to only 82 degrees. Clarke dressed comfortably in a cotton, khaki-colored suit, a pale blue button-down Oxford cloth-weave shirt and a seal-blue tie with alternating large and small British tan squares. As he rang the bell, he hoped whoever answered the door could not hear his pounding heart. *Get ahold of yourself, man, you're a psychologist*, Clarke reminded himself for the second time in 15 minutes. The door opened and a thin, pale-faced man in his sixties answered the door.

"Hello, I'm Dave Nelson, Sherri's Dad. You must be Clarke Gable. Please come in."

Dave Nelson was about 6'5" tall, had graying hair with a remnant of light brown coloring. Thick lenses, resting on a pointed nose, magnified his eyes. His lips were narrow and slightly upturned at the edges, giving his face a pleasing and scholarly quality.

"My wife has made some fresh chocolate chip cookies and freshly brewed coffee," Nelson said, as he led Clarke into the den. Clarke sat down in a three-cushioned, white leather sofa that faced an entertainment center hand crafted of yew wood. To the left of the sofa were two black ergonomic chairs designed to comfort aching backs. To the right of the sofa was a small, slate fireplace that blended with the light maroon and beige ceramic tile.

A demure Oriental pixie popped into the den carrying a tray with 3-inch in diameter still-warm cookies. She was about 5'2" stretched out and looked somewhat comical standing next to her tall husband. The round face, the black hair, the saffron skin color, all testified to her Oriental ancestry. Both Nelsons wore identical drab olive scrub suits with their names printed over the left shirt pocket.

"Hello, Mr. Gable. I'm Kimiko, Sherri's Mother." She had the graceful movement and the soft melodic voice associated with geishas.

Clarke rose and said, "Hello, it's my pleasure to meet you," feeling a touch awkward in comparison to the fluid movements of Kimiko.

"Please be seated. How shall I prepare your coffee?"

"Black, no sugar. One packet of sweetener if you have any."

As Kimiko exited the den into the kitchen-breakfast area, Sherri appeared at an opposite doorway leading from a hallway. "I see my parents are taking care of you. The coffee is to keep you awake so you don't fall asleep and injure their daughter in a car wreck."

Clarke was startled at the lovely woman before him dressed in a black A-line style sheath with a V-neck. A simple strand of black pearls kept the eye from focusing on the hint of cleavage. The black leather shoes featured two-and-a-half-inch spike heels. All Clarke could think to say was, "I hope I can protect you from the two-legged wolves that are going to howl when they see you."

Everyone laughed. The foursome chatted a few minutes as they sipped coffee and then Clarke said, "We'd better get going. I always like to be there a little early. We can catch a snack at one of the concessions at the Center."

* * *

On the way to Richmond, they talked about likes and dislikes, their schools, and of course, their upbringing.

Sherri was proud of her heritage and told the story about how her parents first met. "My Dad was stationed at Camp Oji in Tokyo in 1968. He was a topographic engineer with the 549th Engineering Battalion. Thank heavens he missed the Vietnam War. One afternoon, Dad and some of his buddies were at the Meiji Coffee House in the Ginza District. A cute Japanese waitress, who spoke excellent English, waited on the American soldiers who were dressed in their civvies. Dad was smitten. He kept going back for kohi and ocha, until finally Kimiko said she would go with him to see a sci-fi film, *Planet of the Apes*. They fell in love, obtained the required special dispensation by the U.S. Army and then got married in 1969. Yours truly happened along a year later. Dad was stationed at Fort Belvoir when I was born."

"That's a neat story, Sherri. Do you ever see your grandparents?"

"Mom writes them pretty often. Mom and I visited them in Tokyo only once and they came to visit us in 1999 when I lost my baby girl." Abruptly, Sherri changed the subject: "I really am excited about seeing *Les Misérables*."

* * *

The Carpenter Center for the Performing Arts was the music hub for Richmond. Grand opera to Broadway musicals gave performances in the Center. Richmond had renovated an old Lowe's theater into a premier performance hall. The lighting was soft and restful. The sloping of the seats gave everyone a clear view of the stage. The acoustics continually astonished Clarke, giving him the sensation of surround-sound.

Les Misérables opened on Broadway, March 17, 1987. A Richmond critic considered the talent in the road show superior to the original casting. Clarke and Sherri sat in rapture as the plight of Jean Val Jean unfolded. Clarke thought that Victor Hugo would have been proud of the musical version of his classic novel.

* * *

On I-95 north, in the quiet interior of the Lexus, Clarke began to sing, "Bring him home, bring him home."

Sherri giggled and kidded, "Don't quit the FBI."

A long period of silence followed Sherri's comment about Clarke's singing. Sometimes Clarke detested his clinical self, but he knew Sherri wanted to unburden her soul. Clarke mentally shifted from date to doctor. "On the trip to Richmond, you mentioned losing a child. I noticed how down you were after that comment. Would you like to talk about that? Anything you tell me will be held in confidence. Our conversation is not FBI business."

"Oh, forgive me, Clarke." He saw tears begin to spoil Sherri's makeup. "I don't want to burden you with my past. I surely didn't go out with you to get free therapy."

"Sherri, I asked you for a date because I like you. I'm a friend who just happens to be a psychologist. It's the friend that wants to help you."

"I really identified with Eponine in the play tonight. Nothing went right for her. It really is a sad musical, even though the finale was uplifting."

Clarke remained silent, sensing Sherri would continue without prompting.

"It was my senior year at Mary Washington College. I was dating Danny Bonds—tall, dark, handsome, and the most popular student on campus. He could sing, play the piano and loved to dance. He was pampered, spoiled and immature, but I fell in love with him despite the character flaws. After our fifth date, we thoughtlessly started having sex without protection. On graduation day, I was already three months pregnant. With the blessing of both sets of parents, we got married. Danny got a job selling real estate with his dad's company. We rented a small apartment in the Fredericksburg Historical District. His parents were extremely wealthy and gladly helped out with expenses. We were really happy and looked forward to being parents."

Sherri became quiet and stared into the darkness. The moon, a giant golden disc, had a hypnotic effect on its anguished viewer. After a few minutes, Sherri continued, "The baby was born with Down's Syndrome. The pediatrician informed us that Bonnie—that's what we named her— had multiple defects, the worst of which were congenital heart disease and mental retardation. The Doctor sobbed when he told us the child would probably not live longer than two years, which he described as a blessing considering her quality of life."

Sherri grew silent. Clarke saw the tears again flood her eyes. With deep affection, he recited one of his favorite verses from Matthew's Gospel: *Come unto me all ye that labor and are heavily laden and I will give you rest. Take my yoke upon you and learn of me, for I am meek and lowly in heart: and ye shall find rest unto your souls. For my yoke is easy and my burden is light.*

Sherri drew strength from the Bible quotation and continued, "Bonnie required 24-hour attention. The trips to the doctor's office and the emergency room at the hospital were frequent and strenuous. After a year, Danny told me that he couldn't take it anymore and was leaving me and the baby. The fool thought there was a link between my being half-Oriental and the mongoloidism. I moved back with my wonderful parents. Bonnie died just short of her fourth birthday. Danny didn't even show up at the funeral or send flowers. His parents said he moved to Alexandria and was dating. They believed he still loved me and predicted he would eventually want to reunite

Finally, he filed for divorce, and I didn't contest the proceedings. After the divorce, I changed my name back to Nelson. It's been three years, and I'm just beginning to make a life for myself."

"There are many human emotions, Sherri," said Clarke, "and prolonged sadness is one that can cause severe debilitation. Remember when you were a teenager? It took months and sometimes years to get over a breakup with your heartthrob. How much more difficult to overcome the sadness when a parent loses a child? Only time can cauterize the emotional wound. Sherri, a personal question. Does the thought of suicide ever occur to you?"

Sherri answered with an emphatic, "No! Killing myself was never an option. I did feel a deep guilt that I had failed to give my baby a healthy body. But taking my own life would dishonor my parents."

Clarke stated his opinion. "After one ride to work and one date, my conclusion is that you are emotionally stable. You're not suffering from depression. What you have experienced was neurotic guilt. You believed you harmed Bonnie. You decided that some long trip you made while pregnant, some medicine you took, some vitamin you didn't take or some unknown radioactive substance was the cause of the Down's. You tormented yourself into believing there was a way to have prevented this tragedy. Finally, your willingness to discuss those feelings, as you are doing tonight, will lead you to an inevitable conclusion: Bonnie's defects were not your fault." Clarke said nothing for a few moments. A grin worthy of a Cheshire cat introduced his next remark. "By the way, there is no charge for the analysis."

Sherri burst out laughing. It was a laugh filled with relief and with appreciation for the man sitting next to her.

CHAPTER 16
January 27, 1999 (Wednesday)
Brentwood, Tennessee

Tess Miller's wealth, likeability and healthcare experience made her a good appointee to the Board of Directors for the Highland Park Medical Center (HPMC). The three-year term ran from November 1998 to November 2001. The management of the hospital was contracted to Guardian Incorporated, a company that owned 72 hospitals and managed 34 outside owned hospitals in 28 states.

Guardian knew successful hospitals were managed in conjunction with a well-trained Board of Directors. Addressing that fact, training seminars were established at the corporate headquarters in Brentwood, Tennessee. Brentwood, a suburb of Nashville, claimed the title of Nashville's business center.

The last week in January, HPMC enrolled Tess in a seminar—all expenses paid including airfare and lodging in the Brentwood Marriott Courtyard, located a few blocks north of the Guardian Headquarters. Tess decided to take Mike along, at his expense, for companionship. He could laze around or sightsee during the day, and they could eat together at night.

* * *

The radio alarm sounded at 6:00 a.m.

Mike sat upright and hollered, "Turn that dang thing off."

"Just go back to snoring while I take a shower," Tess said pleasantly. She turned off the alarm, stood up, stretched and then headed for the shower. Her routine was simple. Meet the shuttle bus out front at 7:00

a.m. and arrive at Guardian headquarters at 7:30 a.m. for a continental breakfast. Sessions began at 8:00 a.m.

After Tess showered and dressed in slacks, shirt and a pullover sweater, she opened the door and retrieved the morning paper. Bold headlines read: **GOVERNOR GOES PARDON-CRAZY**.

Tess read the article.:

In 1769, Sir William Blackstone, an English Judge, wrote these words: "It is better that ten guilty persons escape than one innocent suffer." Well, our lame duck Governor Andrew Jackson Forrest, bearing the name of two of Tennessee's most famous generals, obviously believes that utopian statement. The governor, in a sensational abuse of power, granted commutation to life without parole for all 138 prisoners on Tennessee's death row. To compound the injury to the criminal justice system, he fully pardoned eleven convicted murderers, blaming flaws in the judicial system.

The governor defended his action by stating there was a disproportionate number of blacks on death row. In addition, he believed that many inmates were defended by incompetent lawyers.

DNA testing is causing a massive review of old cases. Both death row inmates and lifers have been freed on the new scientific testing. In a Midwest state three men on death row were found to be innocent and released. "I will not have innocent men put to death on my watch," Governor Forrest voiced.

The diligent effort by district attorneys, juries, and judges was made superfluous by the governor's decision. Included in the commutations were many cases where there was no doubt of guilt and where senseless and vicious acts of murder had been committed. Relatives of the victims were infuriated. The attorney general and all of the district attorneys have condemned the action taken by the governor.

"Hey, Mike, wake up a sec and read this article on the front page about Governor Forrest. We need to talk about this jerk when I get home. If you get a chance, see if anything shows up on TV. Gotta run."

* * *

Sponsored by Guardian, the morning session and workshops starte with "Trends in Hospital Care and Individual Trustee Responsibilities." Afte lunch break, the topics changed to "Understanding Hospital Financia

Statements" and "Keep out of Lawsuits." Guardian had good instructors and good material presented in understandable terms. Tess asked several questions and volunteered her opinion during discussions. To her disgust, the article about Forrest stayed at the forefront of her thoughts, shattering her concentration. Glad when her Rolex read 5:00, she hurried back to the Marriott and the latest updates on Tennessee's political crisis.

* * *

Tess key carded the door to Room 415—neat and clean with the typical motel amenities. She stripped down to her undies to get comfortable. The black lace bra and a black bikini side-laced brief revealed her sensuality. Tess, in a playful mood, bent over and wiggled her backside at Mike.

"Man, if I had a dart, there'd be no way I could miss that big of a target," Mike spoofed.

"If you don't like it, don't be stroking it anymore," Tess quickly countered. Ignoring Mike, she lay down beside him to watch the evening news. She conjectured, *The Andrew Jackson Forrest saga will surely be picked up by the national news, and I'll catch the latest fallout.*

Mike figured he should get in the last word. "I like the outfit," he said with a sinister grin, stroking her.

"It must be attractive, a lot of people have been staring at me," Tess said with an equally sinister grin, slapping his hand away.

Mike knew when to give up, so he shifted to another subject. "Guess where I went today?"

"You went to see the Titans practice."

"Nope. Good guess, though. I took a Mid-South sightseeing bus tour, and one of the places we visited was the Governor's residence. Is that a blast or what, after this morning's news?"

"Anybody on the tour bus talk about the Governor's antics?"

"I had an interesting conversation with a woman about 35 years old. Calm yourself. I did not flirt, not one time! She wore an Oscar De La Renta red tweed, open jacket, with fluid caramel pants. Under the jacket, she wore a silk V-neck tank that revealed some serious cleavage. We're talking $2,500 before tax. I know, because the same outfit was in the Niemann Marcus catalogue you showed me. I considered buying it for you. Lucky for me I didn't. It ruined the outfit for me when I saw someone else wearing the same thing." *That comment ought to get me out of hot water*, he thought.

"Excellent recovery, Mike"

"Yeah, I thought so, too. Anyway, her hair was her best feature. She sized up as money, good looks, style and probably a University of Tennessee graduate."

Tess commented, "You sure noted a lot about her for a guy that didn't flirt once." Mike chose to ignore the barb. *At least there's no blood oozing*, he thought.

Then he told Tess about the conversation that the woman initiated.

* * *

"I guess we're seat partners for the tour," the woman said to Mike. "My name is Johnny Emory. Came up from Knoxville on business."

Mike noticed she wore a wedding ring, so he decided this pretty lady was just friendly, not making a move on him. "That's a good southern name. Mine is Mike Miller. Visiting from the Magnolia State."

The bus driver's announcement over the static of the P.A. system interrupted their conversation: "Our next stop is the home of our governor. The place was built in 1929 by a wealthy businessman and was called Far Hills. The state bought the house and ten acres in 1949 and Tennessee's governors have lived there since that time. It will take us 45 minutes to get to the mansion. As soon as I get out of this traffic, I'll give you some more facts."

After the announcement, Mike continued the conversation. "Your governor made the headlines this morning, big time. What's your take on what he did?"

"I think like a lot of other Tennessee folks. Radio station WNCC took an informal poll. In less than an hour, I don't remember the exact figures, like 500 disagreed and 50 agreed— a 10 to 1 disapproval. A.J. Forrest is having a tough time attempting to convince the public that he was acting nobly. His feeble mind must have created a false moral mandate. You know, he's being investigated for awarding lucrative state contracts to a firm owned by his son. This misuse of trust has apparently been going on for years. I think he was hoping the public would consider his clemency action as some good deeds offsetting some bad stunts. Gee, I didn't mean to get so wound up. My husband says I lecture too much."

"Don't apologize. My wife does the same thing. You've made some excellent points."

The bus driver's voice again came through the overhead speaker: "We'll be there in a few minutes. A guide will take us through the house and around the gardens. Everyone must stay together, no wandering about.

"Now for more facts about the governor's home. It's a three-story brick structure in the Early Georgian Design. There are 16 rooms and 9 baths. The first floor is used for offices, the second floor is personal living quarters, and the third floor is for recreation and relaxation. Fine art and antique furniture give the home a museum atmosphere. We will stay here 30 minutes, so every body be back at the bus by 3:30."

* * *

Mike brought his mind back to the hotel room. "We didn't get to see the governor, though. He's probably hiding out."

"I wonder if there's anything on the Five O'clock News." Tess picked up the remote and turned the huge flatscreen TV on.

The program started with a speech by State's Attorney General Lyle McAllen, whose fury was apparent in every clipped word: "Governor Forrest is to be despised for trashing the Justice System. Why should policemen, prosecutors and jurors invest enormous amounts of time, energy and mental agony in bringing a criminal to justice, if the governor strikes it all down with the stroke of a pen? Citizens feel betrayed and embarrassed for the State of Tennessee."

After the commercial, during which Tess determinedly fought off Mike's roaming hands, a reporter interviewed an elderly lady. Speaking in a halting voice tinged with unbelief, the woman related how two thugs broke into her daughter's house one night to steal everything they could lay their hands on.

Tears running down her face, she said, "My son-in-law went downstairs to investigate the noise. Olin Jacks fired three bullets into my son and left him to bleed to death on the living room rug. Jamie, my daughter, came to the top of the stairs when she heard the shots, and the other thug, Mike White, ran up the stairs, chased my daughter into her bedroom and slit her throat. My five-year-old granddaughter locked herself in the bathroom, but the bastards broke down the door and drowned her in the commode. Then they found little Andy hiding under his bed. One quick twist and his neck was broken. I wish they'd killed me, too, but they didn't see me; I hid behind the washer and dryer. My only reason to keep on living now is to see these two beasts die. I'd like to shoot the damn governor and let *him* bleed to death, the way those animals left my family."

Tess fought tears as the scene cut away to the text of a moving commentary displayed on the screen while an unseen reporter read the words:

> My Dad fought in World War II. He didn't talk much about the fighting, but he was proud to be a veteran. A lot of military people on both sides died in that war, but so did a lot of innocent civilians. Did our President Roosevelt and England's Prime Minister Churchill say, 'Stop the war?' No! We are now in a different kind war. A war against crime. If we lose, this country will be destroyed. We're not fighting Nazis and Japs this time. It's murderers, thieves and drug dealers. Yes, there'll be some innocent casualties. That's a fact of human existence. But we cannot cut and run like our irresponsible governor. Like Pearl Harbor, yesterday was a Day of Infamy.

"A few minutes ago, I was not the least bit interested in watching the news about an arrogant governor's problem," Mike confessed. "When I saw you dressed in black panties and bra, plans were formulated that did not include the head of state. My mind sent an urgent message: *Watch the T.V. for a few minutes. Then go to more personal and enjoyable business*. But Mr. Libido was blown away by Forrest's ridiculous decision to pardon so many convicts. Thinking about this tragedy left my mind numb and my you-know-what limp. Where were his brains?"

Tess, cool as ever, said in a soft soothing voice, "I've got a good idea and a bad idea. The good idea is that we had a target lined up for March, but we're going to substitute Governor Andrew Jackson Forrest."

"Well, I'll be jiggered, that's a big bite to chew. If that's the good idea, what is the bad idea?" Tess whispered something into Mike's ear and he grinned enthusiastically, "That is a bad idea! Mikey likes it."

CHAPTER 17
February 26, 1999 (Friday)
Jackson, Mississippi

Mike, dressed for comfort, had on a pair of Nantucket gray cargo pants and a black cotton Old Navy® pullover. He loved the pockets, the military insignias and the relaxed look. The fleece-lined, soft leather moccasins kept his feet warm and gave him a close sensitive feel with the BMW's responsive accelerator pedal.

Tess, not to be outdone for comfort, wore a white woven linen poncho top with taupe linen jute cropped pants. Mike dubbed the ensemble "the washerwoman outfit." Tess's feet snuggled into black suede mules with gold trim by Jacque Levine®. The couple headed North on the Natchez Trace Parkway. They loved driving the Trace. Trucks were prohibited, and mile after mile of woods on both sides of the roadbed created a scenic tunnel.

Their destination was Tupelo. The town of 45,000 boasted one of the largest under-roof flea markets in the United States. Both Tess and Mike loved patrolling the hundreds of booths that hawked wares from artwork to zit healing cream.

They drove in silence for half an hour, watching several deer ignore the speeding automobile. Mike thought about the huge cost of leasing oil and gas rights in Conecuh County, Alabama.

Suddenly Tess broke the silence. "Mike, I've been trying to figure a way that we can hit the Tennessee Governor without getting mowed down. All Governors have at least two plain-clothes guards, 24/7. When he travels there are probably, at the very least, two unmarked cars monitoring his travel, and when he speaks or appears in public, there will be security everywhere. We may have to back off this guy."

Mike was quiet for a minute, then said, "Johnny Emory, the woman who sat next to me on the tour bus, said something I forgot to mention. Her husband has a good friend who is with the Tennessee Highway Patrol. The THP is responsible for protecting the chief executive. The trooper went through the state police academy with one of the guys who followed Forrest around. This guy said Forrest is a bitch to guard. On several occasions, he broke procedure, sneaking off without the guard's knowledge. He told the two guards that he was visiting a 45-year-old divorcée, and it's none of their damn business who she is or where she lives. It's rumored his wife is going to divorce him as soon as he's out of office. This little peccadillo could help us."

"If Mrs. Forrest is intuitive, like most married women, she knows about the affair and knows the mistress. Maybe we could trick or provoke her into revealing the name of her competition," Tess suggested.

* * *

March 11, 1999 (Thursday)

In an early afternoon brainstorm, Tess went online and pulled up a web page on the office of the First Lady of Tennessee. On the off chance that she might reach Laura Lee Forrest personally, she dialed the listed number, taking the precaution of dialing *67 so that her number would not register on the caller ID system. She also taped the call.

A pleasant voice answered on the third ring, "Hello. This is the office of the First Lady of Tennessee. May I help you?"

"Yes you can. I'm an old high school classmate of Laura Lee, excuse me, I mean the First Lady. I'd like to talk with her for a second."

"You are fortunate. Mrs. Forrest is in and not in conference. May I say who is calling?"

"If you don't mind, can it just be a surprise?"

"All right, but the First Lady likes to limit her calls to five minutes. Hold the line."

The voice was husky and authoritative. "So this is an old school friend I'm thrilled you called. Who is this?"

"Mrs. Forrest, I'm sorry for the deception. This is not an old classmate but I need to talk to you, so please don't hang up."

"Well, who are you then?"

"You don't know me, but Governor Forrest has stayed at my home overnight on many occasions."

"I know who you are, Miss first name Rita, Miss last name Gallo-Jones."

Bingo, thought Tess.

"My husband," said Laura Lee, "excuse me, my stupid husband, had your phone number written on a piece of paper in his wallet. Sneaky me found it. What the hell do you want?"

Tess wasn't sure if she should hang up. She had already gotten the info she needed, but it was enjoyable to play Gallo-Jones.

"I just wanted you to know that your husband's quirky behavior is getting on my nerves. The affair is over. I thought you might be relieved."

"Listen sweetie, your affair may be over, but so is this marriage. Do me a favor; keep the old boy on the string for awhile so he has a shoulder to cry on."

Tess heard the click of the phone as the line went dead. *WOW! That is one, tough lady*, she mused. She could hardly wait for Mike to get home. She went back on the Internet, logged onto the Yahoo white pages and found the address and phone number of Rita Gallo-Jones.

* * *

As soon as Mike came in the front door, Tess told him to sit down and listen. She played the tape of the phone conversation with the First Lady of Tennessee.

Mike sat in a stupor for a few minutes. Tess knew the wheels were grinding like a gristmill, so she said nothing.

Mike finally spoke, "My bet is that the Governor's wife is going to tell him about his little tart calling while he's getting ready for bed. He won't have the time to do anything tonight, but he sure is going to want to see his sweetie pronto. Get packed, we're driving to Nashville tonight. Tomorrow we check out the Gallo-Jones place, and then we stake it out at night. If the Governor doesn't show up in a few nights, it may be that the wife didn't say anything. In that event, you call the Governor. Tell him Rita's very sick and would like to see him tonight. Let's get a move on."

"Why can't we fly?" queried Tess.

"We can drive to Nashville quicker than boarding an airplane, flying to Nashville and renting a car. It's no big deal to drive 200 miles of interstate—shouldn't take more than three and a half hours."

CHAPTER 18
March 14, 1999 (Saturday)
Nashville, Tennessee

Three days following his wife's revelation about the conversation with Mrs. Rita Gallo-Jones, Governor Forrest's thoughts were still tortured. *What the hell is Rita trying to do? If the storm over nepotism and prisoner releases doesn't end my political career, the report of this affair will bury me. I've got to call Rita and ask her why she betrayed me.*

* * *

Rita picked up the phone after the second ring. "Hello."

"Rita, this is A.J. My wife knows everything. Why did you call her?"

"A.J., are you nuts? I haven't talked to Laura Lee."

"Look, I'm coming over tonight." The governor hung up without a goodbye.

* * *

It was easy for the governor to elude his watchdogs. An old crony picked him up on South Curtiswood Lane, near the governor's mansion, and, day or night, delivered him to any destination. Andrew Jackson Forrest enjoyed his subterfuge. He never considered himself in danger.

Like many other American cities, Nashville was experiencing revival of one of its downtown areas known as Germantown. Mrs. Rita Gallo-Jones was fortunate enough to have purchased a property on Hume Street near Morgan Park before the explosion in property values. Rita was divorced from an abusive husband, for which she was thankful. She was also childless, for which she was not thankful. She supported herself by running a real estate business. A venture with several wealthy Nashville businessmen, opening two new subdivisions, proved enormously successful. From this wave of success, the Tennessee Realtors' Association elected her president. At a state convention for Realtors Rita introduced the featured speaker, newly elected Governor Forrest. An immediate mutual attraction was the foundation for the soon-to-follow *amoretti*.

* * *

Mike and Tess, in their BMW, parked across the street from the Gallo-Jones house. The one-and-one-half story house, with a full-width integral porch supported by six square posts, rested on brick piers. Latticework filled the space between the piers. The single front eight-panel door was accented with rectangular glass panes above and on the sides of the door. Shuttered windows and a chimney top were visible, and the wood siding, painted a divinity color, sported shutters and latticework painted black forest green.

"Rita's taste in houses is a lot better than her taste in men," Mike commented.

"I don't know, Mike," Tess teased. "The governor is not bad looking for 61. Still has all his hair. He must have a certain charm and appeal to've gotten elected. Also, remember, Mrs. Gallo-Jones may be using the governor to further her own career. The governor gets sex, and she gets a property re-zoned and makes a killing."

It was the third night since they had driven north from Jackson. Each night they parked in a different place to not arouse suspicion. At 6:10 p.m., the governor arrived in an unmarked car. He got out, thanked the driver, walked up the four steps to the porch and entered the front door without knocking.

Mike and Tess waited patiently in the Beemer. Eventually the porch light came on, and, at precisely 10:30 p.m., Mike rang the doorbell. After a few minutes, he rang the bell again. After a third time an angered Rita Gallo-Jones, wrapped in a full-length robe, opened the door.

"What are you doing bothering me this late at night? Hard-working, decent people are asleep at this hour. You'd better have a good story or my husband will be out here with a shotgun," she lied.

"We hate to disturb you, Ma'am, but we're assigned to protect the governor. He has broken security measures again by coming to your home without proper protection. This prisoner thing has resulted in lots of threats

Would you be so kind as to ask the governor to come to the door? We'll wait here."

Flustered and embarrassed, Rita barely whispered, "I'll go get him. You'll have to give him a few minutes so he can be presentable."

After a few minutes, the governor came to the door, barefooted and barechested, wearing an unbelted pair of woolen gabardine slacks.

"I thought I told you boys not to ever follow me when I'm visiting a lady friend. Hey, do I know you two?"

Mike thrust the ice pick forcibly upward into the governor's throat.

The Governor staggered backward.

Mike twisted the ice pick and yanked it out. Blood poured from the governor's mouth and nose.

Tess had told Mike, "This type of wound won't kill instantly. He'll exhibit the same symptoms as a stroke."

Mike held the uncomprehending Forrest upright. Mike hated to get blood on his sleeves, but he wanted to give Forrest one last message.

"You may not comprehend this, Mr. Governor, but it helps me with my anger problem. You won't give clemency or commutation to any more killers. Did you really think you could undo justice and not pay a penalty? Oh, and cheating on your wife wasn't nice either!" yelled Mike.

Mike and Tess, each holding one of the governor's arms, laid him gently on the newly varnished floor.

* * *

Rita lay uneasily under the heavy woolen blanket. She had closed the bedroom door so as not to intrude on official conversation, but she estimated 15 minutes had gone by and now, worried, she began to wonder what had happened. There was some muffled conversation, then it became eerily quiet. *How could anything be wrong with A.J. with two state agents present? I'll check anyway.*

As Rita approached the front door, she was shocked to see her lover sprawled in an ever-increasing pool of blood. She screamed, "A.J., what happened!?"

She cradled the dying governor like the infant she once dreamed of bearing. His glassy unseeing eyes stared at nothing. A gurgling sounded the death knell. Blood spurted from his nose and mouth, but Rita could not see the stab wound.

Finally, Rita, aroused from her shock, screamed and shouted, "Somebody, please help me!" Then she ran to the phone in the kitchen and dialed 911.

In an amazingly calm voice, Rita begged, "Please . . . please send an ambulance to 827 Hume Street. It's the governor. He's paralyzed and hemorrhaging. I have no idea what caused the bleeding."

With all her attention on A.J., Rita never noticed two people get into their car and slowly drive away.

CHAPTER 19
November 13, 2002 (Wednesday)
Quantico, Virginia

Clarke was apprehensive as he drove to the Academy. *I never did like dog and pony shows. That guy behind me needs to pass. He's attached like a leech.* His thoughts turned back to the upcoming meeting. *It's good the meeting is scheduled at 10:00 a.m. I'll have time to review my checklist and be ready for any surprises. The Justice Lovers Case may not be a big-ticket item for the Director, so I'll try not to be disappointed if my case is put on the back burner.*

The advanced print of the agenda listed three people in attendance: Special Agent Clarke F.D. Gable, Clarke's boss Deputy Assistant Director G. Thomas Claiborne, and Assistant Director Zachariah Goldberg from the Hoover Building in D.C. The topic of the meeting: discuss the Justice Lovers Case and prioritize recommended action. Clarke knew the biggest constraint was finding money; most of the FBI budget went toward thwarting terrorism.

As Clarke entered the conference room, he immediately spotted Assistant Director Goldberg. About six-feet-two and 160 pounds, shoulders slightly stooped and prematurely balding, Goldberg long ago had decided to shave his head. He wore out-of-style horned-rimmed glasses that contrasted strangely with the tailored $700 suit. His physical appearance led the unsuspecting to believe he was not screwed together just right. The Assistant Director had an I.Q. of 141 and a photographic memory; he could quickly analyze and solve problems. Direct to a fault, he hurt some feelings along the way as he rose to second in command of the FBI.

Goldberg sat at a solid cherry conference table with six swiveling leather chairs. One chair sat at each of the narrow ends, while two pairs sat opposite each other at the wide sides of the table. Goldberg sat in a chair at the end located to Clarke's right. Clarke's boss, Claiborne and another man sat next to each other at the opposite side of where Clarke stood. A middle-aged stenographer sat apart from the group to record the meeting and file it electronically for instant and easy retrieval. Clarke decided to take the single chair opposite Goldberg. Clarke nodded to his boss then said, "Good morning, Mr. Goldberg, sorry I'm a few minutes late."

"The time gave us a chance to get the pleasantries out of the way," said Goldberg. "The man sitting next to Deputy Assistant Director Claiborne is Special Agent Artie Majesky. I'll explain his presence later. Everyone knows Molly, probably the most knowledgeable person in the building on our activities. As usual, she'll tape our discussions for the record."

Clarke winked at Molly, and reached out his hand to Majesky, saying, "Welcome aboard. Hope you can help us on this case." *Wonder if the scowl is for my benefit or a permanent facial defect?* Clarke mused.

"Only if it's what Mr. Goldberg wants," said Majesky.

Artie Majesky stood six-foot-two and weighed a muscular 195 pounds. His crewcut emphasized his thinning blonde hair. He had hazel eyes and one long eyebrow. His beak-like nose, broken at least once, sat crooked on his face. His vacant stare made Clarke wonder if the man was on drugs. The unsmiling face announced, *I'm not Mr. Nice Guy.*

"Okay," said Goldberg. "Everybody's here that was invited. I'm pretty busy this morning, so we have 45 minutes to handle business." Goldberg shuffled some papers then continued, "I have studied Agent Gable's Profile and Protocol on the Justice Lovers Case. Catchy name, by the way, Clarke. Would've made old J. Edgar proud with this great in-depth analysis.

Goldberg scratched his temple and closed his eyes as if in deep thought. He had the rapt attention of everyone in the room. Then he spoke up. "To simply call this JLSKT a couple of vigilantes would be inaccurate and underestimate their significance. As Clarke suggests, these people are not mentally ill in the classical sense. They consider themselves the moral arbiters in determining just behavior. They have a mission, maybe even a calling, to administer punishment for wrongdoing or harm done by one individual to another. The advocates of the policy of retribution would be proud of this JLSKT, and that's a scary thought."

Clairborne said, "Zach, both Clarke and I believe we need to catch these killers immediately. They already have a six-year head start. If the FBI could crack this case, the Bureau would garner some much-needed good publicity. I believe that agent Gable would be a new star in the world of criminology, another plus for our Behavioral Science Unit. I am anxious—"

Goldberg interrupted. "It's not the function of the FBI to seek publicity, good or bad. The FBI is not, and will never be, a stepping-stone to knighthood in a psychological roundtable. This case is going to be handled quietly. It will not be the basis for some future book or movie, either. Are we clear on those points?"

Clarke assumed the remarks were directed his way. Disrespectfully he thought, *Goldberg could really use some consultation on his personality.*

"Let me give you an example of the harm that publicity can do," Goldberg continued. "In Pearl, a little town in Mississippi, a sixteen-year-old kid killed two of his classmates at the local high school. The networks put his picture on the tube, and all the reporters were hot to interview the kid. What follows? High School killings start occurring all over the United States. Some analysts believe these copycat shooters are attempting to outdo each other. You start with Luke Woodham and you end up with the massacre at Columbine. We cannot go public with the Justice Lovers Case and justitiaphilia. If we do, there'll be these justitiaphiles, as you have named them, coming out of the woodwork to serve their country."

Clarke thought that Goldberg was ignoring some strong possibilities and decided to defuse this one-sided harangue. *Mom always said I had a big mouth, so, here goes.* "Sir, permit me to interject some probabilities into this discussion. First, I don't believe that the JLSKT are the only justitiaphiles presently in the United States. This JLSKT is the first of its kind identified by a law enforcement agency. The thirteen-month cycle of homicidal episodes was the critical factor in discovery. These people may be misguided, in our opinion, but they are convinced they're morally right and have a just cause. The deterrent will be public awareness of justitiaphilia. Perhaps a public reevaluation of our laws and society would erase the just-cause element fueling our justitiaphiles. As bad as it is, the high school killings are making our citizens review policies, procedures and the emotional state of our student population. Let me quote the King James Version: *The night is far spent, the day is at hand: let us therefore cast off the works of darkness, and let us put on the armor of light.* That's Romans 13:12."

"I've always admired people who can quote the Bible and Shakespeare," retorted Goldberg. The small compliment was a gentle breeze before the hurricane. Then more sternly he said, "Here's the way the Director and I want the case handled. Clarke, your speculation that the JLSKT are husband and wife and are from a major city in Mississippi sets the groundwork for the plan we will act upon right after the first of the year. This case is not a top priority, especially if we're losing only one life a year. Some of the terror cases you're handling, Clarke, are much more important regarding potential loss of life. In January, you can get the ball rolling"

Clarke could not prevent his right hand from involuntarily slapping the table. "Sorry, Mr. Goldberg, but why the two-month delay?"

Goldberg was eerily silent. He stared at the ceiling for a moment, never acknowledging Clarke. Then he eyes focused forward and he spoke sternly, "I will repeat my last statement in the event it was not understood. In January, Clarke, you may get the ball rolling to locate the JLSKT by working with our guys in Mississippi. No state or local boys will be used at that time. In presenting the case, feel free to use any cover story plausible, but there is to be no mention of this justitiaphilia. The Bureau has some of its best agents in the Jackson Division. They've been ordered to defer present investigations and give 100 percent of their attention to this case at the appropriate time. Do I make myself clear?"

Claiborne asked, "What should we do when we determine who's the serial killing team?"

"That's not been decided, yet," answered Goldberg. "It may be necessary to violate the rights of some citizens in processing this case. The resolution of this case may be irregular in order to conceal the motivation of the JLSKT from the general public."

"Sir," Clarke interjected, "the FBI should be concerned with crime solving, not with hiding a behavioral abnormality from the public. This approach is going to result in that bad publicity you just said you didn't want. That opens the door for Congress to kick the agency in the ass. I don't think the next victim would appreciate your deferring movement on the case until next year."

"I appreciate your opinions, Agent Gable," Goldberg said sternly, "but you have your orders. You're on the edge of insubordination here. I will overlook your outbursts this one time. Now, are there any other comments?"

"No sir," everybody answered in unison.

"There is one last item," concluded Goldberg. "Artie here is part of an experimental program with a limited number of agents named the Tactical Assessment Group or TAG for short. The purpose of a TAG member is similar to that of a combat historian. He'll observe and record all elements of the case. He'll not offer advice or interfere with the agent in charge. The Bureau anticipates that this real-time look at unique cases will reveal why some agents go awry. It may simply be the innate inability of a few agents to foresee long-term consequences of each decision. The Bureau realizes that this noble experiment may yield nothing. However, we need to let our agents in the field have more control and less restraint if we are ever to be an effective organization. TAG should help us reach this goal. If there are no more questions, I've got to leave. My schedule's tight."

* * *

"Mr. Goldberg, you wanted me to stop by your office for final instructions?" said Artie.

"Yes, thank you, Artie. What I told the others about TAG this morning contains some truth. It would serve no purpose in revealing TAG's secret responsibilities. As to the Justice Lovers Case, the individual or individuals are never to come to trial. The Bureau will not allow the courtroom to be a platform for exporting their ideas for changing society. Do we have a meeting of the minds on this case, Agent Majesky?"

"Yes, sir. Don't worry about anybody ever knowing about justitiaphilia. I suppose you can control Gable from blabbing about the case to the public."

"Count on it," replied Goldberg.

CHAPTER 20
April 5, 2000 (Wednesday)
Allentown, Pennsylvania

From inside the Camry parked at the Allentown Wal-Mart parking lot, two sets of eyes followed the athletic, middle-aged man walking toward the "ENTER" sign with an almost imperceptible limp. Dressed casually in sweats, socks and sneakers, looking as though he was coming from or going to a workout session, Tommy Shotz, 37 years old, had no idea that he would never see his 38th birthday.

In the last three years, Mike and Tess Miller successfully dispatched a target for each year. Tommy Shotz had the misfortune of being their fourth objective.

The Millers, never referring to themselves as professional killers, developed a modicum of expertise in dispatching their quarry. Mike had attained the rank of Eagle Scout and still practiced the Boy Scouts of America motto: *Be prepared.* A casual observer would describe the Millers as ordinary people above suspicion of chicanery.

"The temperature is a perfect 68 degrees—perfect golf weather," Mike said playfully. "I'm wasting a great day watching this worthless jock go shopping at Wal-Mart. Worthless may be the wrong adjective. When the jury spun the insurance wheel, the pointer stopped on jackpot."

A jury had awarded Tommy $25 million for his pain and suffering and damages, the category all lawyers love. The unsuspecting defendant had not calculated that many of the jurors remembered Tommy's high school football heroics. An added bonus: The captivated jury believed insurance companies were bloodsuckers, and that it was payback time. As expected, the outlandish award was appealed and reduced to a paltry $14 million. Tommy Shotz bragged that his share was good take-home pay for a mail carrier.

Tess and Mike cataloged Tommy's movements for a week. They first became aware of him when he appeared on the afternoon television circuit and in several magazines and newspapers. They preferred targets located in the South, but Mike was familiar with the Allentown, Bethlehem, and Easton (ABE) area in Pennsylvania.

* * *

Tommy Shotz was about 5'9" tall, had wide shoulders, a thick neck and slightly bowed legs. He walked with a Charlie Chaplin waddle, but nobody dared tease him. He had wavy brown hair always neatly combed. His dark brown eyes accentuated by exophthalmia, or bulging orbs, gave his stare an aura of intimidation. A "football stare-down," Tommy called it, a great advantage against opponents of Bethlehem's Liberty High.

Tommy, vicious when provoked, still had many friends, male and female. He considered himself a ladies' man, and three marriages did nothing to inhibit his flirtatious nature. Mostly cocky and self-centered, Tommy could also be humble and humorous at times, which gave him an endearing quality.

Tommy recognized the two older people sitting in the 4-door Toyota Camry. *Nice car, nice silver gray color*, he thought. He had noticed them showing up where he did several times, but no alarms went off. Since his court case was big news, he expected reporters everywhere and did not mind—in fact, enjoyed—the attention. His wife Nancy and their two boys, Barry and Todd, complained they were bored with the endless questioning about their dad. Tommy explained to them that in a few months, the reporters would be off on another story and their lives would go back to normal. But for now, cocky Tommy Shotz enjoyed the fuss and notoriety.

As he left Wal-Mart, he was not surprised when the woman got out of her car, walked up to him and introduced herself.

"Hi, Mr. Shotz, my name is Teri Beard," Tess said. "I'm a reporter for the *Allentown Sentinel*. I tried to phone you, but your line was always busy. I know you've been interviewed by some of the large metropolitan papers, but the *Sentinel* wants a special human interest story. Your Lehigh Valley friends and fans would love a close-up special—maybe a big spread in the Sunday edition. Can I ask you a few initial questions and tape our conversation?"

"Yeah," said Tommy. "You can ask me a few questions, just as long as you don't put words in my mouth."

Used to being approached in odd places, Tommy never asked for identification. He did not consider an interview in a parking lot strange, but instead was flattered. Too embarrassed to offer her a seat in his litter-strewn car, Tommy leaned against his car as Tess removed a small tape recorder from her purse.

An expert in the art of the ogle, Tommy's mind ran in full observation mode sizing up Tess. He observed: *Definitely older than I am, maybe by ten years. Blonde hair, large brown eyes, a few wrinkles at the corner of her eyes. Nose is small. Blue slacks and a red blazer. Liberty High's colors. V-necked white blouse shows some nice tits. The first good-looking female reporter I've ever seen.*

His lawyer had told him not to speak to anyone for at least a year, just as a precaution, but his cockiness would never let him go along with that crap.

Tess began, "Mr. Shotz—"

"Call me Tommy," he interrupted.

"Okay, Tommy. Did you take the drug Noxaphene? Wasn't it an experimental drug approved for final testing by the FDA?"

"Yeah," he said, "it was an experimental drug. Me and 499 other people signed up to do the testing at no cost. Half were going to take a placebo and the other half Noxaphene. Of course, I didn't know which group I was in."

Feigning interest, Tess asked, "How often did you take the drug?"

"I took one 40-milligram tablet each morning after breakfast. We were not supposed to take the pill on an empty stomach or in the evening. It never did nauseate me like it did other people." Tommy was impressed by his answers to the reporter's questions.

"Why were you put on the Noxaphene?" Tess asked.

Tommy shuffled his feet and squinted as he waved at a passing car, and then answered, "Well, my cholesterol was pretty high, and the Noxaphene was designed to significantly lower LDL, the bad cholesterol. Well, it worked—except I developed severe pain in all my joints."

Tommy sighed and continued his narrative. "I couldn't play golf or jog. I couldn't even sit in a car for 15 minutes without hurting. Apparently, none of the other people taking the Noxaphene developed any of these symptoms. The Great Western Drug Company hoped that taking me off the drug would reverse the problem, but no such luck."

"Well, how did the lawsuit get initiated, Tommy?"

"A lawyer called me out of the blue and asked if I'd be willing to sue Great Western Drug Company. Somehow, he found out I wasn't on the placebo. He said it wouldn't cost me a cent if I won, that I could end up with a significant cash settlement, and that chronic inflammation, total disability and pain were the path to big bucks from sympathetic juries. The lawyer said that Great Western wasn't protected by the FDA due to negligence."

Tess outwardly pretended to be horrified, but inwardly, she was amused with Tommy's acting. She continued, "Did the lawyer call you before or after you became symptomatic?"

Tommy ignored that question. He knew better. Besides, he was convinced this blond bimbo reporter hung on to his every word. He decided she must be attracted to him, and that somehow excused him from answering the question. The idea of a fling with an older woman brought a stirring to his loins.

"Who's the guy with you?" he asked.

"He's my driver and protector just in case somebody gets too frisky during an interview." Tess took a deep breath, stretching her sweater, and winked at Tommy.

Assuming this was a bonafide come-on, he said, "What about *after* the interview, honey?"

In her best, sultry, Mae West imitation, Tess drawled, "If you give me the real lowdown, you can come up, pardon the pun, and see me sometime."

Tommy snickered.

"Now, let's get back to Noxaphene." Tess said, "You look pretty spry at the moment. Clue me in on the rest of the story."

"A doctor, I believe he's called a rheumatologist, examined me. He was our expert witness in court and testified that there was permanent damage to the soft tissue around my knee joints, hip joints, elbows and shoulder joints. His prognosis was that I could only walk a few steps without pain, that my strength was limited to lifting no more than five pounds, so delivering mail was out of the question. The doctor concluded by saying my sex life was extremely impaired, too. With the aid of a walker, I made my way to the witness stand.

"I testified about suffering from being impotent. I told the jury that before I used Noxaphene, we had sex twice a week. Now it was only once every three or four months. I was so inept because of pain that my wife couldn't experience any satisfaction. The lawyer called it 'lack of consortium.' So, that's about it. The amazing part is that about six months after the Appeals Court made their decision, my symptoms started to gradually disappear. It was an absolute miracle. I made a complete recovery," he said with conviction.

Tess recalled that the media reported skepticism among many doctors. The standing joke in the community was that he was up for an Oscar. No paper made any direct accusations, fearing a libel suit.

Tess stepped closer then asked, "What do you intend to do with the money, Tommy?"

"Well, I want to take the wife and kids on a two-week cruise to the Caribbean, gamble a little in Las Vegas then throw some big parties for my friends. I'm real interested in a completely restored 1948 Cadillac Series '62 convertible. That's the first year the Caddy had the tailfin. There's one for sale in Reading."

"All of that sounds so noble." The sarcasm blew over Tommy's head like a Scud missile.

Tommy lowered his voice and said, "Speaking of big parties, maybe you and I could have a little get-together? You can ditch your bodyguard and meet me somewhere. What do you say?" He tried to be smooth, covering up his eagerness.

Tess suspected that the miraculous recovery was not so miraculous. *Perhaps with a little liquor and some sweet talk, his tongue might loosen*, she thought.

"It would be a relief to mix a little pleasure with business," she lied. "There's a lounge just before you hit Route 22 at Center Street in Bethlehem called the Love Letter. The place is on the ground floor of the Sunset Motel. Meet me there at eight o'clock tonight."

Tommy Shotz blurted, "You got yourself a date, honey. I'll tell the wife I'm meeting with my buddies. She won't believe me, but that's tough."

Tess walked back to her car, opened the passenger door then slumped down into the gray leather seat.

"The little jerk is so full of cow manure his eyes are brown," Tess said before Mike could ask anything. "It's as we suspected, a put-up job. He faked his symptoms so well that even he believes they were real. I set up a rendezvous with him tonight at the Love Letter. After a few drinks, hopefully he'll spill his guts." An image of Bobby Dan Cantrell ripped apart by a shotgun appeared and disappeared. "Tommy thinks I'm his next conquest.

We discussed the possibility, so don't hate me for playing the role. You know I don't intend to do anything with that creep."

Silent, Mike started the engine and pulled out of the parking lot. They needed to confirm the worst before executing Tommy. He trusted Tess. Better yet, he loved her.

CHAPTER 21
April 5, 2000 (Wednesday)
Bethlehem, Pennsylvania

When Tess arrived at the Love Letter at 7:30 p.m., only a few regulars were there. She assumed it was permissible to choose her own booth. The rectangular room had a raised platform for Friday and Saturday night entertainment. Tonight, only the piano gave testimony to future performances. Recessed ceiling lights provided dimness in stark contrast to the glow of the Budweiser and Coors neon signs. High-back red leather booths provided comfort and privacy. A solid Philippine Mahogany Bar and an overhead TV, tuned to a girl's basketball game between U.T. and U-Conn, established the typical barroom ambience. A poster on a chrome pedestal advertised a local band named the Dead Head Trio.

Copies of original love letters, written by famous and ordinary people, covered the lounge walls. *It's obvious why the name was chosen*, Tess thought. She decided to read a few of the letters. The first letter was an endearing note to Nancy, signed Ronnie. Her eyes meandered to a letter written by a G.I. stationed in Italy in 1943. Eddie D'Argenio informed his wife that he sure could use a hot bath and a good night's rest. Eddie agonized that his best buddy was killed that day by a German sniper. He missed the kids and hoped he would get home soon. D'Argenio closed the letter by telling his wife how much he loved her and asked her to pray for his safety.

Tess could not help but wonder if Eddie got home alive. An old refrain ran through her mind: *I'll be home for Christmas, if only in my dreams.*

Tommy sat down next to her. "You look great. Let's order something to drink."

Tess did look great. Her black knit dress accentuated her small waist, unusual in an older woman. The hem, slightly below the knees, allowed her to display freshly shaved, slender and curvaceous gams. The dipping neckline drew Tommy's eyes to the ample roundness underneath. He did not complicate his life with deep thinking beyond his pet theory: a man fixated on one of three female attributes. Tommy pegged a man as an adorer of J'Lo's derriere, a drooler over a pair of shapely Betty Grable legs or a flipper-outer over Dolly Parton's breasts. He married three times, because he preferred boobs to brains.

Tommy ordered a Nuheimers, the local beer, and Tess ordered a vodka tonic. She started, "Now Tommy, I need more background on your life for the newspaper spread."

He proceeded with a typical steel-town story. "I grew up on the South Side. My dad naturally worked at Bethlehem Steel as an operator in the rolling mill. His name is Frank, middle name Xavier, a rough and tough guy, so you did what he said. Mom was just the opposite. She was a frail Irish lady, but strong enough to bear six kids, four girls and two boys. I'm the oldest, and of course, the best looking."

True, with curly auburn hair, a stocky build and the gift of gab, he owed his Irish good looks to his mother. Tommy continued, "My grades were average, but I played football like a pro. In one game against Allentown High, I scored five touchdowns and ran 242 yards. Everybody thought I would play for Penn State or Pittsburgh, but then I tore up my right knee when a ligament popped. Although the sports medicine surgeon repaired the injury, I couldn't run with the same power and agility. Not one college offered me a scholarship after the knee injury. I didn't want to work in the grime and heat at the steel company, so I went to work for the U.S. Postal Service. I lugged mail for 20 years until I got the $8.4 million break."

Tommy had several more beers while Tess nursed her first drink. She asked, "What about your relationship with women?"

Tommy smirked. "The girls always did like me. I was good-looking fast talking, and terrific in the backseat of my Mazda 626. Not a fancy car, but it and me never broke down."

Tommy craved a cigarette, but he instinctively knew this pretty woman would probably not like acrid smoke in her face. *There's no way I'm going to lose a chance for sack time with this broad.* He continued, "I met my first wife when I crashed a frat party at Lehigh. The guy she was with got looped and passed out. You can always spot a gal in distress, so I decided to help her out. We had great sex and decided to get married. When she found out later that I was continuing to see some of my old girl friends, she sued for divorce

It was a similar story with my second wife. By the time I got to my third wife, Nancy, some of my wildness abated. We have two kids, very handsome like their dad. She's aware of my occasional dalliances and insists I use protection to protect her."

Tommy Shotz liked talking but felt it was time to be paid for a good interview. "Miss Teri Beard, how about I get us a room and we continue this interview in a more comfortable way?"

"Why, Mr. Tommy Shotz, I already got us a room." Tess did not want a desk clerk recognizing them together.

They took the elevator to the third floor and walked down the narrow hallway to Room 340. Tess inserted the key card and opened the door when the green light appeared. The room was neat and clean. A nightstand separated the queen size beds. Two moderately comfortable lounge chairs sat on each side of a small, fruitwood table. The curtained window afforded a view of the patio pool. A dresser with a gold-framed mirror had a Gideon Bible lying on top. Several nondescript acrylic paintings, with splattered paint in many colors, adorned the walls.

Tess and Tommy knew what was about to happen. She dimmed the lights and both undressed in silence. Tommy pulled down the bedspread and slid beneath the clean white sheets. Tess got between the sheets and switched on a tape recorder hidden under her pillow.

Tommy snuggled close to Tess. The eight beers he consumed made him as mindless as a granite boulder, but his physical desires were unimpaired. He began his well-practiced cuddle and caress routine. Tess pretended enjoyment in an effort to quickly move this sordid tryst to an end.

Tess cautioned, "Tommy, you'd better not forget protection. Remember, Nancy made that a condition for putting up with your occasional one-night stands."

Tommy gasped. "Oh, hells bells. I didn't bring one with me. But don't worry, I don't have anything catching."

"But Tommy, I *do* worry. Three things can happen when you have intercourse without a condom and two of them are bad: pregnancy and disease. If you came unprepared, you'd better head for a cold shower."

Tommy moved away from Tess and rolled over on his back. He knew a "no" when he heard it. In an attempt to salvage the situation, he asked, "Teri, couldn't we meet some other time? I'm good and you won't regret giving me a second chance."

Tess, although overwhelmed with relief, figured she should pay Tommy a compliment. “Tommy, call me at the paper and we’ll get together again. You do have a gentle technique, which is rather surprising for a tough guy from the South Side of town.”

Tommy laughed and stuck out his chest. He liked this reporter. “Teri, you remember I told you about the miraculous recovery from being a cripple. You won’t publish this?”

Tess could honestly agree to that stipulation and quickly said, “Agreed.”

“I never had any symptoms. My lawyer had the doctor coach me on how to act and what to say. Both of them told me that the insurance companies had plenty of money, and it was time for some of the little guys to get their share.”

After Tommy left the room, Tess retrieved the tape recorder. They would send it to the Great Western Insurance Company.

* * *

April 6, 2000 (Thursday)

Mike saw Tommy Shotz step out of the elevator, walk to the front entrance and head for the parking lot. He could not help but wince at the smile of satisfaction on Shotz’s squared-jawed face. Mike was anxious to hear what Tess had inveigled out of the intended victim. A little past 1:00 a.m. adrenalin surged through his veins. He ignored the elevator and rushed up the stairs to the third floor. He keyed the door to room 348 and upon entering, he immediately heard the shower going full blast. Mike knew Tess was washing away—physically, and, hopefully, psychologically—Tommy Shotz.

“Hi, honey, I’m back. I saw Shotz leave the motel. He seemed awfully happy,” Mike half-kidded and half-admonished.

After Tess toweled off, she wrapped it around her, came into the bedroom area then dropped into one of the lounge chairs. Her hair wet and sparkling, she grinned at Mike—everything was cool.

Mike made coffee in the two-cup carafe provided by the motel and sat down in the other lounge chair. “I felt big-time upset about you being with Shotz tonight. I’m a pretty possessive guy when it concerns my wife. Of course, now there is an extra incentive for killing the bastard.”

Tess laughed, "You better feel jealous, but don't worry, after I play the tape, you'll feel much better, and you won't believe this. Tommy forgot to bring a prophylactic, so I was saved from any real intimacy."

Mike listened carefully to the excellent recording all the way to the end. He experienced a predictable disgust visualizing another man with his wife, but then he heard Tommy's confession. Their goal was to dispatch justice to the guilty, and Tommy was guilty.

"We have to get up early," Tess said. "Let's go to bed. We have a lot of work to do in the morning." The healing power of sleep washed away Mike's lingering resentment and Tess's deep-rooted shame.

* * *

Mike and Tess rose at 6:00 a.m., showered, dressed and packed up their clothes. They had checked out the night before, prepaying in cash for each night's stay. Mike had registered as Frank Beard from Pennsylvania, a name found on the Internet.

Tess put the luggage in the BMW 740 IL, which they drove from Jackson, Mississippi. She would follow Mike, who now drove a 1993 Land Cruiser purchased in Easton, ten miles east of Bethlehem. The old SUV, in good running condition, had 145,000 miles on it. Mike had used cash to purchase the Cruiser. With Mike's cash in hand, the dealer had waived bothersome legal details, including registration and taxes.

In tandem, they drove toward downtown Bethlehem on Center Street. The route led them past the somber gray sandstone Dutch Colonial buildings of the small Moravian College. Mike smiled at a sign advertising the Grover Cleveland Democratic Club. A trivia fanatic, he knew Cleveland had been both the 22nd and the 24th President of the United States.

After waiting at a traffic light, Mike turned right on Union Boulevard and drove three miles to Tenth Avenue. Their fourth and last trip to this neighborhood, Mike recalled previous episodes of surveillance . . .

* * *

March 27, 2000 (Monday)

The neighborhood was lower middle class—a mixture of well-maintained single dwellings and duplexes built in the '40s. Tommy lived at

2241 North West Street, a two story wooden structure with a projecting porch. Mike and Tess parked a few hundred feet east of the house and watched the neighborhood boys playing touch football in the street. While the Shotz boys played on the blacktop, Nancy Shotz, stocky in build but nicely proportioned, came out to sweep the front porch.

Tess and Mike, risking exposure, left the car and strolled past the Shotz home. As they passed the porch, Nancy looked up, and Tess asked, “Could you tell us where the Berger residence is?”

In a deep, almost masculine, yet appealing voice, Nancy said, “I’m pretty sure they don’t live around here.”

The woman’s eyes expressed a deep unhappiness with her role in life. Tess sensed Nancy’s despondency and futility. She wondered: *Are we doing her an immense favor, removing Tommy from her life? Maybe a fresh start will remove obvious burdens. The kids will survive; they have a way of bouncing back.*

* * *

April 6, 2000 (Thursday)

Tommy appeared in a pale-gray sweat suit and jogged west along North West, north onto Twelfth Avenue, downhill to Union Boulevard, east on Union, turned right on Tenth Avenue and then back on North West to his beginning point. The route was three quarters of a mile. Every weekday morning Tommy ran his circuit four times for a total of three miles in 30 minutes. Mike envied Tommy’s 10-minute mile with a bad knee. Tommy ran in the street, except on Union Boulevard, a heavily trafficked, major thoroughfare. He took six minutes and fifteen seconds to reach Tenth Avenue.

Mike parked the Land Cruiser on Tenth Avenue. Tense but primed, they awaited their victim. Tommy left his house at 6:25:22 a.m. At 6:31:15, Tommy made the turn from Union to Tenth.

Mike glanced up from his watch.

A young paperboy delivered the *Allentown Sentinel*.

They lowered their heads below the windshield.

The paperboy disappeared into an alley, no doubt a shortcut.

As Tommy ran by on the opposite side of the street, he glanced at the silver-gray Cruiser, paid no attention and continued his run.

They had three more opportunities to terminate the jogger.

The engine idled smoothly and quietly. Mike tapped the accelerator to be sure the car was running. They buckled their seatbelts.

Tommy appeared again on Tenth Avenue at 6:41:15.

Mike stomped on the accelerator.

The 6,500-pound mass of steel and plastic responded.

At 57 mph, Mike jerked the wheel, slewing the truck to the left side of the road.

Head lowered, unaware of the approaching car, Tommy looked up, too late. His eyes widened. His mouth gaped open—no time to scream.

Tess and Mike heard a loud pop.

Tommy cart-wheeled. The car roof crushed his pelvis. His body weight slammed him face down onto the street.

They heard a sharp crack and did not stop.

Tess left the Cruiser, walked to Eleventh Avenue, reached their parked BMW and slid into the driver's seat. She caught up with Mike on Union.

Mike, pulling onto Union Boulevard, headed for the Hill-to-Hill Bridge across the Lehigh River. He watched his speed. Tess followed two car lengths behind. He drove south on Route 378 winding up the steep side of South Mountain. After cresting the mountain, the two cars veered right taking the old narrow blacktopped Bethlehem Pike. They drove downhill until the road flattened out, and they could see twin brick smoke stacks in the distance. They turned onto a gravel road and pulled up to a rusting gate.

Mike got out of the Cruiser and looked at the crumbled brick remains of the once famous steam generating plant. Only the two tall smoke stacks resisted time and weather. He remembered as a kid that they had called this place "the Stacks" or "the Rabbit." Mike preferred the name Rabbit and imagined the relic was guarding the large oval-shaped crater. The open-pit zinc mine had gradually filled with water, making it a perfect swimming hole. He read that the ruins once housed the largest steam operated hydraulic pump in the world. Eventually, the water flow overcame the pump, and the 500-foot deep mine filled almost to the spill point. The Rabbit now offered concealment for the Cruiser.

He opened the gate and walked back toward the Cruiser, noticing the inward crush of the front bumper and grille but little other body damage. The Cruiser narrowly cleared the gate and Mike steered toward the rim of the old mine. Tess followed through the gate, stopped, closed the gate and followed him. Mike stopped about 20 yards from the rim of the mine hole and walked to the edge. Double-checking for solid footing, he peered over the edge, a sheer drop to the water 10 feet below. No jagged edges protruded on which the land cruiser could be stuck. He casually walked back to the idling vehicle, got in, opened all the windows and put the transmission in 4-wheel drive. Next, he got out of the car, stood with the door open on the driver's side and yanked the gear lever from N to D. The Land Cruiser slowly moved forward, picking up speed on the slight downward slope to the rim. The front wheels went over and the undercarriage started to catch on the rim of the crater, but the back wheels kept driving the big 6,500 pound SUV forward. Finally, with the front-end weight of the engine, the rear of the Cruiser flipped upward and the whole assembly hurtled downward. The splash reminded Mike of Fat George, a boyhood friend who did cannonballs off the diving board at the Irving Street swimming pool. For a few seconds the SUV floated, then water filled the interior and the vehicle disappeared to its final resting place.

Mike walked slowly to the Beemer, got in on the passenger side and said, "Let's get out of here." They rode in silence as Tess retraced the route, past the motel where they stayed, to the 22 West onramp.

Breaking the silence, Tess said, "Well everything went smoothly. Let's celebrate by spending a day or two in Amish Country. I read there's a great restaurant called Plain and Fancy in the village of Bird-in-Hand."

"Yeah," Mike said, "we did pretty good, but we should've killed Tommy's grubby lawyer. Not to change the subject, but we can also take an Amish buggy ride."

Rays of sunlight pierced the puffy, white cloud cover, predicting a beautiful day.

Route 22 intersected Interstate 81, which took them almost all the way back to Jackson, Mississippi, a long, 1,200-mile drive excluding the side trip through Lancaster County. In Jackson, they returned to their normal lives as good citizens.

CHAPTER 22
April 22, 2001 (Sunday)
Traxler, Alabama

A huge, newly developing oil and gas field in Conecuh County in the Southeastern part of Alabama, named Traxler after the nearby small town of 985 people, was discovered in April of 2000. The event initiated one of the "hottest plays" in the continental United States. Seismic crews, lease brokers and drilling rigs with their tool pushers, drillers and rig hands flooded the area.

Tessco, Mike's company, drilled the well that discovered the field or "discovery well." Tessco had leased the drilling rights on 3,000 acres that looked promising for trapping dynamics for oil.

Tessco now drilled a fourth development well. Mike contracted with Great Energy Drilling Company to drill to a depth of 12,000 feet on a "turnkey basis" or prearranged price. Using this method, Mike knew the exact cost of drilling the well. The drilling company would charge a premium, but would also assume all risks. On "day work," the alternative method of drilling would reduce the cost. The disadvantage, in this case, was that the operator, Mike, would be responsible for unforeseen risks. A rather common complication would be to twist off the drill pipe due to down-hole stress. The cost in recovery of a separated string of drill pipe was at least $80,000.

Mike was part owner of Great Energy, which drilled all his wildcats, the first well drilled in a previously unsearched area. If the wildcat resulted in an oil or gas producer, Great Energy would also drill the offset or field wells adjacent to the new well. Rig 7 was his favorite because the tool pusher and rig hands had been together for years. The teamwork enabled them to drill a well fast and without a lot of downtime. Mike knew the crews by their first names and occasionally played poker with them. To his chagrin, he'd discovered the rig hands were accomplished poker players, and he'd never won a big pot, which actually paid off. The crews liked that he never complained about being taken.

One day, the tool pusher and Mike sat in the pusher's trailer. The penetration rate had slowed down drastically, and they discussed changing the drill bit, although it only had 10 hours in the hole and should not have been dull.

Outside, the 7:00 a.m. to 3:00 p.m. crew was changing shift with the 3:00 p.m. to 11:00 p.m. crew. A motorman, six-foot-four, thin as a rail and nicknamed Tall Pine, who worked with the newly arriving crew, opened the tool pusher's door without knocking. He asked, "Have you heard the news about Marlene?"

"Hell, I've been here all day trying to figure out why we're drilling so slow," yelled the tool pusher over the noise of the big GM rig engines. "Come in and shut the damn door so I can hear you!"

Tall Pine closed the door, nodded to Mike and addressed his tool pusher. "Boss, you know Marlene, the gal who likes to dance and booze it up at Anny's?"

The tool pusher nodded.

"Well," continued Tall Pine, "last night she was making out with some guy, when a sheriff's deputy rushes in and tells her there's some trouble at her double-wide. When she got there, she saw her mobile home engulfed in flames. The Madisonville Fire Chief told Marlene he was awful sorry, but all four of her kids died in the fire. She just shrugged her shoulders and asked, 'Did you save any of my expensive jewelry?' Can you believe that? Can you imagine asking a question like that after your kids just got burned up?"

"The hell you say," said the stunned tool pusher.

After Tall Pine left the trailer, Mike asked, "Tell me more about this Marlene."

"Her name is Marlene Magruder. She's a peroxide blonde, can really hold her liquor, and cusses like a 200-pound truck driver. She's been married three times and had one kid with each husband. The fourth kid she has no idea who the father is. Marlene is certifiably ugly but has a great body. In the dark when you're drunk, you don't care how they look, you know."

"Was she good to the kids?" Mike quizzed.

"Marlene was not cut out to be a mother," the pusher continued. "The Department of Human Services cited her several times for child neglect, but for some reason they never took her kids. She didn't hit them or anything, but the kids were always hungry and dressed in dirty, ragged clothes. She must have used her welfare checks on herself."

"My wife and I can't have kids," said Mike, "and somebody who doesn't want any has four. It doesn't make sense."

Changing the subject, the tool pusher said, "I guess we'd better pull that bit before we lose a cone. It'll take 20 hours to round trip. No need for you to hang around here, Mike."

CHAPTER 23
April 23, 2001 (Tuesday)
Madisonville, Alabama

Mike sat in the crowded Krispy Kreme® in Madisonville, 10 miles north of Traxler. Breakfast consisted of black coffee and three lemon-filled donuts. Tess would not have approved of the breakfast, but he was tired of cereal. The *Madisonville Times* headlined an article about local District Attorney Shelby Willard. Madisonville, a town of 19,000 people, its main industry the 30-year-old paper mill, elected Willard in 1980. He was popular and ran unopposed every four years. His goal was for a law-abiding, free-of-drugs town held up by a tough prosecuting posture. Mike read the article quoting Shelby Willard.

The death of the four young children is a tragedy almost beyond comprehension. In my 21 years of law enforcement, nothing has saddened me more. Many phone calls have been received demanding prosecution and a few pleading for the county not to press charges. It is my opinion that Marlene Magruder is guilty of criminal negligence and could be charged with involuntary manslaughter. However, what would be the purpose of five years imprisonment? Marlene has suffered enough punishment in the loss of her children. In this situation, the future deterrent factor was not a viable reason to prosecute. So, with some disquietude, a decision has been made to close the matter without any arrest.

On the same page, Mike was startled to see a notice outlined in black:

Marlene Magruder is unable to afford caskets and burial grounds for her four children. A fund has been established at the Camellia Bank & Trust. Please make your donations to the Magruder Fund. The bank is making an initial donation of one thousand dollars.

Mike drove the two city blocks to the Camellia Bank to make a donation.

CHAPTER 24
April 30, 2001 (Friday)
Traxler, Alabama

The Tessco No. 1, Richland Timber & Minerals Co., Inc., drilled to a total depth of 12,226 feet. The well encountered 136 feet of Haynesville Sand, saturated with oil and gas, at a depth of 11,840 to 11,976 feet. Production casing, cemented in place, ran to 12,100 feet. Tubing ran inside the casing and was set at 11,800 feet with a Baker Packer. Schlumberger Well Service was on location and preparing to perforate the casing opposite the production sand.

There are two periods of anxiety for the well-site geologist. The most stressful time is electrically logging through the potential pay zone. This is when you find out if your ideas are right or wrong. The No. 1 Richland T & M encountered the expected pay, justifying the 2.4 million dollars spent on seismic, leases, title opinions, location costs, surface damages, drilling and electrically surveying the bore-hole. The other time of stress is perforating and testing the pay zone. High flow rates of oil or gas translate into quick payouts and good profits. Low flow rates destine the project to a long payout period and possibly a non-profit status.

The well, perforated from 11,840 to 11,860, had immediately started unloading the saltwater left standing in the tubing to prevent a blow out. Within six hours, the well was flowing to the surface at high rate. Mike, his production engineer and geophysicist were elated. On the drive back to Jackson, his two employees talked about drilling more development wells to exploit the field. Mike was quiet. He was thinking about Marlene.

* * *

Marlene Magruder, nicknamed Marly, was 5'6" and weighed about 124 pounds. Her legs were long, slender and shapely. A "leg man" would have given her a ten. Her figure was movie star quality at 36-24-36. Until her mid-twenties, she was a long-haired natural blonde. When her hair began to darken, hair coloring came to the rescue.

But Mother Nature played a couple of dirty tricks on Marly.

A teenage Marlene once overheard a high school classmate saying that the Lord made her misshapen face from a pile of rejected parts. The description may have been accurate but was excruciatingly cruel. The large, round owl-like eyes were so close together that her brother once told her, "Marly, you can look down a microscope with both eyes at the same time." The slightly upturned pug nose, permanently puckered lips and pointed chin would present a challenge to the best reconstructive plastic surgeon. Her uncomely countenance, attached to a perfectly shaped body, was the first dirty trick.

Marlene learned at age thirteen that, if she could not attract men with her face, she could lure them with her figure. She was intelligent enough to realize sex was not a substitute for love, but for a short time, she felt in control and needed. Although folks described her as loose, horny, hot to trot, wild, slutty, a whore and a Lolita, she practiced her private code of decency. Marly would not do oral sex, would not knowingly sleep with a married man, would not do drugs and would never charge for her favors. She would never bed a man who was loud-mouthed, foul smelling, unkempt or disheveled.

Anthropologists contend that sexual intercourse is a primary drive or involuntary instinct that insures the propagation of the race. This sexual instinct in females generally accompanies a motherly instinct. Marlene completely lacked this primal inner force to nurture her offspring. For reasons only known to her, she did not believe in tubule ligation, birth control pills or prophylactics. Yet she hated the unwanted pregnancies and had no interest in raising children.

Inwardly, Marlene Magruder had no remorse in losing her four children. She told those who expressed condolences that the children suffered much in their short lives and now they were at peace. Marlene, who hated children and did not have a maternal bone in her body, conceived easily. A complete lack of the maternal instinct was the second dirty trick.

Perhaps if Mike understood the mental complexities of Marlene, he might have extended some sympathy toward the shapely, heartless blonde.

CHAPTER 25
May 1, 2001 (Tuesday)
Jackson, Mississippi

Mike and Tess were reading in bed, as they did almost every night. The king size bed was a pencil post design made of solid mahogany. Tess was reading the *Love Eagle*, by Danielle Steel, the latest novel by one of her favorite writers. Mike had browsed in a used bookstore earlier that day and found a mystery novel entitled *The Big Clock*, by Kenneth Fearing, published in 1946. Mike had never heard of Fearing before and was amazed at the crisp and witty writing style. The story was spellbinding as if written today, not 55 years before.

The fan, on low, just stirred the air. Mike raised his eyes from the book and stared at the fan, hypnotized by the whirling blades.

Still staring at the fan, he uttered, “Hon, an incident happened in a town near our Alabama well. The story is almost too sad to tell. Some goofy divorcée left her four little kids alone in a mobile home. The fire marshal figured an overload caused by an electric heater started the fire. All four kids probably died of smoke inhalation before they burned beyond recognition. She claimed a babysitter was supposed to come by after she left for the bar. Nobody ever showed up to confirm her story.”

“Damn, I’d give up my right arm and your left nut to have four kids.”

“Wait till you hear the rest of the story,” Mike said. “District Attorney Shelby Willard decided not to prosecute the imbecile. Says what good would it do? I’ll tell you what it would do! It would demonstrate that you’re responsible for your own actions. She screwed up, and the kids paid the price. There is no justice in Madisonville tonight.”

"Those kids need somebody to be their intercessor," Tess suggested. "In my opinion, there's no criminal act greater than a mother allowing her children to be injured by her neglect, let alone burned to a crisp."

"Do you want to put this woman's name on our To Do list?" Tess asked, already knowing the answer.

"Yeah, her name is Marlene Magruder. They call her Marly."

"Okay then, Marly's on the list; maybe even the top of the list. Is tomorrow too soon?"

"We must be a little more careful on this job," Mike cautioned. "Some of the townspeople know me by sight and even by name. There's a nice motel in Waynesboro, Mississippi. We could stay there and make the one-hour drive east on Highway 84 to Madisonville. I suppose we can let happenstance determine when and how Marly goes down."

CHAPTER 26
May 2, 2001 (Wednesday)
Waynesboro, Mississippi

On Wednesday afternoon, the traffic was light on the highways. Mike and Tess took I-20 from Jackson to Meridian using the Ford 150. In Meridian, Mike rented a royal blue Ford Escort. In two cars, they drove southeast on I-65 to Waynesboro, a town only a few miles from the Alabama State line, which profited from the constant oil and gas activity in East Mississippi and West Alabama. They got a room at the cheap Sundown Motel.

The dark skinned, black-haired clerk, just off the boat from India, did not think it was unusual for two people in separate cars to rent one room. In America, he assumed, it was natural for husbands and wives to sneak around on their spouses. It was none of his business as long as the filthy adulterers paid their bill and no one got shot.

* * *

Around seven o'clock Wednesday evening, Mike and Tess took the Ford Escort to Anny's. The plan was to case the place, avoid anybody that knew Mike and then hopefully get a glimpse of Marlene MaGruder.

Anny's was located just outside the city limits of Madisonville where Main Street became Highway 84. The one-story building had cinder blocks showing through the cracked stucco. On each side of a singlewide door, three casement windows showed heavy signs of rust. The new facade dressed up the front and hid the flat roof. Blacktop in the front and on both sides of the structure provided parking. Across the steep part of the roof, the neon sign said: ANNY'S.

Mike told Tess, "The bar was originally owned by Danny Lisco and was called Danny's Place. The capital D and P burned out and people jokingly referred to the place as Anny's Lace. Gradually, the locals shortened it to Anny's. After remodeling, the new owner, bowing to tradition, had the new sign read ANNY'S."

Mike and Tess walked inside, surprised that the club appeared larger inside than outside. Sturdy oak booths lined all four walls, except in front of the double doors leading to the kitchen area. Single doors at the back left and back right side read Cow Belles and Cow Pokers. Mike could not help but think, *Everybody has metaphorical names for restrooms. These are cute but sappy*. Rows of pedestal tables stood adjacent to the booths. The remaining space, reserved for dancing, contained ceiling-mounted loud speakers. Five couples line-danced, Texas style, to "Achy Breaky Heart." A hostess greeted them with, "Welcome to Anny's."

The waitress led Mike and Tess to a vacant booth, where they ordered two oyster po-boys and two light beers. Mike scanned the room, *No children or teenagers, obviously a place for adults to eat, drink and fraternize. No rig hands from Rig 7, that's a relief.* Non-Smokers, Mike and Tess got headaches from the cigarette smoke hanging in the air, but in the service of justice they resolved to breathe the nasty air.

Around 8:30 p.m., a tall blonde, crammed into tight-fitting denims, came into view. Shouts rang from three or four groups of drinkers bidding Marly to join them.

"People would kill for a figure like that," said Tess. "She's wasting her time in this dump. She could make a million bucks posing for Victoria's Secret or as a centerfold in "Playboy" magazine. I can't believe she's had four kids and isn't sagging somewhere."

"I like your roundies better than her pointers," Mike interjected.

"Your loyalty is appreciated, but your bulging eyeballs say different," Tess said.

The evening passed; Marly laughed, drank and danced with half the boys, apparently looking for a good bedtime partner. Toby Keith sang, "How Do You like Me Now?" on the jukebox. Mike imagined Marly asking the guys if they liked her better now that she had no kids. He slipped the waitress forty bucks so they could just sit and listen to the music. The waitress, Tommeka, gladly took the two twenties and left them alone in the booth.

Mike and Tess sat at the booth all night staring at good-time Marly. Near 1:00 a.m. the waitresses went around telling everyone to finish their drinks. "Closing time is in ten minutes."

Tommeka thought the big tippers strange but didn't care. A forty-buck tip was unusual. *Not bad for a night's work*, she thought, *I got the money instead of Anny's*.

Mike and Tess got up, strolled across the open space and out the front door, which was held open by the owner.

"Good night, folks," the man said. "Come back again."

"You've got a nice place here," said Mike, "People can unwind a little and the place doesn't get rowdy."

"Thanks, buddy."

Mike and Tess walked to the Ford Escort, got in, and waited for Marly. She staggered out at 1:05 a.m., wove to her car, pulled out of the parking lot heading toward Madisonville, and drove half a mile before turning on her headlights.

"She might kill herself and some other poor soul before she gets home," Tess said.

"Well, we don't have to worry about her noticing somebody following," Mike said.

Marly pulled into a graveled driveway and parked her car next to a clapboard bungalow resting on concrete blocks.

Mike and Tess watched her get out of the car, flounder up two steps to the small porch that projected outward from the main structure, then stumble inside. Mike surmised she had not locked her door since she did not use a key to get in.

"What do we do now?" Tess asked. "She's obviously in for the night."

Mike ignored the question and asked, "I wonder why some guy isn't showing up? She sure was making moves like she was ready, willing and able."

Tess laughed. "The reason's simple. She's having her period. Now answer this question. Where can we get a can of gasoline this time of night?"

"Forty miles east to the intersection with I-65 there'll be some all-night places," said Mike.

Tess offered a plan. "If the attendant asks about the gas, we'll say it's for a friend who ran out of gas on 84. We'll buy a five-gallon container, fill it with gas and come back here. You know the rest. Let's go."

At a 24-hour gas and food stop, Mike purchased a 5-gallon gas can and gas, along with a couple of packs of cigarettes to downplay the purchase of a lighter.

* * *

May 3, 2001 (Thursday)

No lights were on in any of the houses on Second Avenue, no street lamps exposed them or their movements. They parked the Ford Escort two blocks from the bungalow. If anyone looked out the window, all they would see was a couple arm-in-arm on their way home. Darkness and their closeness hid the gas can.

Mike whispered, "She was extremely drunk. I don't think a bomb would wake her."

They circled around to the back of the dilapidated dwelling. There would be no effort to make the fire look accidental.

Mike poured gasoline along the rear sill of the bungalow. No need to saturate the sill, flames from the ignited gas would reach, at least five feet high. No need to ration the fuel, as the back of the house was only 45 feet wide. Mike ran a small line of gas for about six feet, then threw the gas can and the cigarettes under the house.

He bent down and flicked the flint wheel on the lighter several times. A tiny spark produced a flame which lit the gas line. A 45-foot-wide fireball flashed along the rear sill.

They ran around the house, headed for their parked car, got in, and waited and watched. Within two minutes, the entire back wall of the bungalow was on fire. Seconds later, flames covered the entire roof and belched black smoke with a pungent odor of asphalt. The entire wooden frame house was a raging inferno.

Their moment of both disquiet and triumph came. Marly Magruder did not wake in time to prevent her own cremation.

Mike and Tess sat there incredulous.

"Wow!" Mike said. "It only took a few minutes for the whole place to burn. Unbelievable!" Mike cranked up the Ford and slowly drove away. They saw no reason to watch the futile attempt by the Madisonville Fire Department to extinguish the fire.

The sky was clear and Tess wondered if any of the stars she was gazing at had orbiting planets with life on them. "It really infuriates me when kids needlessly die. A drunk killed my brother, and I often wonder what he'd be doing if he had lived. I grieve for those four kids who never had a decent life when they were on this earth. Making Marly pay for her abuse and negligence doesn't quite balance the scales."

"If it wasn't for us, that bitch would've gone unpunished," Mike replied. "I mean, in *this* world. You and everyone ought to sleep a little better tonight knowing justice has been effectuated."

* * *

Only the local television and newspaper covered the murder of Marly Magruder. One newscaster reported, ". . . found the burned body of Mrs. Marly Magruder, who recently lost her four children in a fire that destroyed her home. The police believe that this could be a vigilante crime and have peripherally brought in the FBI. Found at the scene were a melted gas can and traces of accelerant. There are no further developments in the case. Now for the weather. . ." There was no public outcry and no one spoke of an intensive investigation to identify the arsonist-murderer.

CHAPTER 27
January 12, 2003 (Sunday)
Fredericksburg, Virginia

"How long will you be in Mississippi, honey?" Sherri asked.

"Probably a day or two this trip," answered Clarke. "I'm going to do some work on my Justice Lovers Case. You may have done some computer work on the project."

"I really don't know a whole lot," she replied.

"The FBI has identified a serial killing team, or in our terminology an SKT, and believes they're operating from one of the larger Mississippi cities. I've been directed to aid the local FBI in identifying and locating the Justice Lovers SKT. Actually, I'm looking forward to visiting the Jackson office. Some of the most famous FBI Civil Rights cases occurred in Mississippi."

"It sounds a tad dangerous, sweetheart. Can't they send somebody else? I love you Clarke, and I don't want to lose you. Since meeting you, life has become wonderful again."

"Look, I'm just an advisor. Somebody else will be doing the actual apprehension and arrest. Besides, Artie Majesky is riding shotgun. He and other members of the Tactics Assessment Group are monitoring various agents. TAG has this wacky notion they can identify and isolate the qualities that make a seemingly ordinary agent into a good decision-maker under duress. No doubt, if a serious situation should develop, Artie is instructed to get involved."

Despite the anxiety of the upcoming trip, Sherri and Clarke lay around his two-story, late Georgian-style home on Stafford Avenue. Sherri was in love with Clarke—and his house. Like so many southern belles, she had an *affaire d'amour* with old houses and antiques. She loved the Flemish bond brick pattern, the gambrel, weatherworn slate roof, and the elegant chimneys, one on each sidewall of the house. The front door had six panels flanked by two ornate pilasters and capped with a half-circle fanlight. The downstairs consisted of a living room, dining room, den, breakfast room, with an elaborate entrance hall and a spiral staircase. The upstairs had three bedrooms, a bath and a study. Sherri and Clarke settled down in the den.

Clarke had finally taken Jezzy's offer to invite somebody home, and Sherri had been the honoree of an official "Jezzy dinner". Jezzy prepared fried pork chops, baked sweet potatoes and turnip greens with diced turnips. Dessert was chocolate bourbon pecan pie about which Clarke joked, "You don't want to eat too much of this pie if you're driving." They ate in the kitchen—cozier than the formal dining room. Afterward, Jezzy washed the dishes and excused herself to visit her eighty-year-old parents.

* * *

Clarke and Sherri lounged on a white leather traditional sofa in the cherry stained oak paneled den, listening to enchanting Hawaiian melodies played by Koala. The heat began to rise between them.

In a southern drawl, Sherri said, "Sweetheart, let's not waste this romantic music by talking shop, okay?" *Even 37-year-old bachelors need a nudge to get going*, she thought.

Enthusiastically, Clarke said, "Let me fix that situation, right now." He embraced Sherri tenderly pressing his lips against her slightly opened mouth. He had not pushed for a close physical relationship with Sherri before, but now, desire swept over him like a tsunami crashing onto a sandy beach. Neither one had had a meaningful sexual union for over a year. Now the two lovers filled each other with mad and wonderful pleasure. After, they continued to hold each other closely, reluctant to abandon the incredible ardor they just experienced.

Clarke broke the rapturous moment first. "Woman, we just made a triple-a baby: Asian-African-American."

"I'm afraid not," she said. "I've been on the pill ever since our night at'Les Miz.' I knew I wanted intimacy with you since that night, and you sure were slow to catch on."

Clarke passionately kissed her again.

CHAPTER 28
January 13, 2003 (Monday)
Washington, D.C.

It would take four hours to fly from Washington's Reagan International to Jackson, Mississippi, including the stopover at Hartsfield, Atlanta. Clarke liked to do two things on a flight: Read psychological thrillers, or, if it was daylight and he was seated by a window, he would stare into the vastness and meditate. On Delta flight 1037 to Atlanta, he sat in seat 34A by the porthole. His focus: The female justitiaphile he dubbed "Lady J". Clarke believed Lady J, in certain aspects, was probably a good and even moral human being. She was the type who would be eager to help an elderly person who fell, or make sure an infirm senior citizen safely got to their destination. She might sit on the board of a local bank or Chamber of Commerce. At this very moment, she might even be starring in a Little Theater production of *The Taffetas*, or directing fund raising for the American Cancer Society. Lady J may even be a respected church member, praying to God and being faithful in tithing. She certainly practiced the principle of moral exclusion. In her perception, any individual who perpetrated an injustice could not expect sympathetic treatment or take advantage of societal leniency. Perceived injustices by Lady J appeared related to her subconscious, therefore allowing her to rate the next kill, Clark decided. If a man stole a loaf of bread, as did Jean Val Jean in *Les Misérables*, there would be no punishment administered. However, if someone stole a million dollars and exacerbated the crime by causing a suicide, then they deserved a death sentence. In a murder cleverly disguised as suicide, Irene Day Collins and her husband were murdered. The enigmatic Lady J operated on logic—flawed logic, but logic just the same. As a good detective or criminologist, Clarke tried to penetrate her mind. *I wonder if she's attractive, or if I would be charmed by her beauty and sexuality? You're treading on mighty dangerous ground, Mr. FBI Psychologist*, Clarke mused. He was intellectually fascinated by Jack the Ripper and now equally fascinated with Lady J.

Clark had a skewed admiration for the woman herself, not her murderous deeds. He acknowledged her dedication for improving society in a manner she considered a higher morality. He was sure there would be no danger when meeting this "woman of intrigue." If the opportunity arose to meet Lady J, he would not carry a weapon. Carrying a firearm can have some disastrous results. Clarke remembered earlier years and earlier cases when it was good he was not packing, because somebody would have gotten whacked. Cindy Lind's brother and his two buddies were one example. The more Clarke thought about Lady J, the more he developed what C. Daniel Batson defined as "a natural empathy for her."

"Please put your trays in the upright position and fasten your seat belts. Turn off all cell phones, computers or other electronic devices. We're preparing to touch down in Atlanta in 20 minutes," announced a voice on the intercom.

Clarke stirred from his daydream and looked over at fellow agent Artie Majesky. *They told me that he was along for observation, not as a partner. He's good on that score. Hasn't said a word. No reason not to be amiable,* he thought.

"Quick and smooth flight," Clarke said to Majesky. "Nice way to start a trip."

"I noticed you were doing a lot of deep thinking, so I didn't disturb you," Artie said. "Is there anything I should mention in my report?"

"I was thinking about the female justitiaphile. I call her Lady J. It's good technique to put yourself in the shoes of your adversary. The mind and God work in mysterious ways."

CHAPTER 29
January 13, 2003 (Monday)
Jackson, Mississippi

Clarke and Artie stayed in adjoining rooms in the downtown Crowne-Plaza located in the heart of the business and government district. The McCoy Federal Building, which houses FBI offices, was only a few blocks west on Capitol Street. Clarke, being a black man and ardent Civil Rights and history buff, was particularly proud of the Jackson Division. The division was born during a 1964 crisis when 150 agents were sent to Mississippi to solve the murder of three civil rights workers. The division was housed in the McCoy Federal Building, the first government building named after a black American.

Dr. A.H. McCoy, a successful Jackson dentist and businessman, campaigned for social change and basic rights for his people before Civil Rights became a national crusade. Dr. McCoy and his family were under constant threat of violence, even to the point of gunshots fired into their home. In part, Clarke knew his rise to success became possible by the efforts of Dr. McCoy and others like him.

Tomorrow will be an interesting day, Clarke thought. *Artie and I'll need to lay out a strategy to capture Lady J and her husband.* He looked at the LCD clock on the nightstand—8:45 p.m. *Well, there's plenty of time to review the June 2002 crime by the JLSKT*, Clarke concluded. He had brought the file hoping to discover something he may have overlooked.

* * *

In his room, Artie Majesky watched the ten o'clock news. He was anxious for the apprehension of the two redneck killers so he could get back to more important work.

Clarke grabbed his black leather briefcase emblazoned with a circular emblem proclaiming "Training, Research and Consultation." These three words defined the mission of the FBI Behavior Science Unit. He removed a folder with some sadness, as he read the name Reverend J. Olivier Claxton. As far as Clarke was concerned, this man was a buffoon who became an embarrassment to the African-American community. Despite his stupidity, the reverend was dead, murdered, and no man should pay that kind of price for being stupid. Clarke kept these thoughts private, for black people, even the enlightened ones, rarely criticized other black people in public.

Clarke appreciated that the file contained a rather lengthy historical narrative. The file also included a second section describing the murder and evidence, and a third section outlining possible motives and disposition of the case. He began to read Section One.

REVEREND J. OLIVER CLAXTON

Biographical Commentary

Section One

Obadiah Baskins, a.k.a. J. Oliver Claxton, born in the small town of Corsicana, Texas, 40 miles south of Dallas, in June 14, 1953, completed his education at Navarro College, a two-year institution. He was a member of the Gospel Choir and Drama Club.

Baskins was a self-taught Biblical expert, gifted with a photographic memory and a mesmerizing baritone voice. As a teenager, he discovered he had charisma and could spellbind his listeners, even adults, with his Bible stories, some true and others fabricated in his fertile mind. So effective was his sermonizing and hymn singing that he was ordained by the congregation at the Mt. Zion Good Shepherd Baptist Church in Corsicana. Oddly, as Obadiah Baskins, he never referred to himself as Reverend. He moved—or more appropriately, fled—to Dallas at the age of twenty when a sexually mature 13-year-old black girl accused him of being the father of her newborn son.

At this point, Baskins changed his name to the more sophisticated Reverend J. Oliver Claxton. The New Africa Missionary Church, without a leader for six months, was ecstatic to hire a man who could both preach and direct a fledgling choir.

Claxton openly admitted that his goal was to supplant Jessie Jackson as the country's premier black leader. In 1980, he organized the MMP, Minority Movement for Progress. The movement initiated numerous boycotts and protest marches in Dallas. The efforts were successful, as local businesses and municipal government hired more blacks. His rising popularity led to a morning talk show airing in 1974 through 1979. The radio stint was a stepping stone to a half hour TV show, which featured Claxton interviewing, exclusively, prominent local and regional blacks, transformed him into an increasingly vitriolic spokesman for racial agitation. He loudly proclaimed that "racial harmony" was a concept advanced by "white folks," who wanted to keep "black folks" quiet.

Claxton ran for mayor of Dallas in 1988, but his blatant contempt for the majority white population lead to his defeat by a margin of 71% to 29%. Nevertheless, his popularity with the black community continued to grow, and he began to attract national attention from the news media.

Claxton styled himself as a Civil Rights leader, but the purpose of many of his exploits appeared to be for personal aggrandizement and financial gain. Claxton's role in exacerbating several major racial incidents cast a shadow on his statesmanship.

In 1994, three young black men were killed in a shootout with the Dallas Police. The three blacks, whose short lives had a long list of violations, were chased after a bank hold-up. The three robbers were able to reach an abandoned house where they decided against surrender. After one day of stand-off, a SWAT team stormed the house, and in the ensuing gun battle, the thieves were riddled with gunshots. No SWAT team members suffered wounds. Claxton organized protests, making unfounded statements that the three blacks tried to surrender and were gunned down by white executioners wearing cop uniforms. The protests resulted in riots causing 5 deaths and 42 seriously injured. Property damage estimates reached $36 million. (No penalty for Claxton.)

In 1999, the Reverend Claxton began preaching, in the pulpit, as a guest on several TV shows, and at public rallies, that the Jews were responsible for much of the despair suffered by black people. Claxton demanded that the Jewish community pay reparations to the black community. The Minority Movement for Progress would accept and administer the funds for the benefit of black people.

Robberies of Jewish businesses increased, black kids started beating up Jewish kids, black goon squads accosted customers leaving Jewish stores, and several synagogues were partially damaged by explosive devices. Claxton was arrested and charged with "acts to incite illegal conduct". Unexpectedly, the NAACP Legal Defense Fund refused to defend Claxton and his claims his First Amendment Rights had been violated. He was admonished that Freedom of Speech did not include his tactics that were the origin of felonious, mischievous and extortionary activity. In bargaining to drop the charges, Claxton agreed to publicly announce that he had made a grievous mistake and that all malicious treatment of the Jews should cease. And it did. Blacks still admired the Reverend because he had stood up for his people. (No penalty for Claxton.)

In 2001, Claxton became involved in another racial controversy, reporting that a 16-year-old member of his church confided that she was two months pregnant by an outstanding football player. Claxton persuaded the teenager to accuse Hiram Smith, a white principal, of rape. The purpose of the ruse was simple: Remove the principal of the 80% black high school and install a black principal. The pregnant and frantic girl, LaShanna Johnston, feared her parents would disown her. She eagerly accepted Reverend Claxton's way out. The public was outraged and so was the School Board. The principal was put on administrative leave pending an investigation. Claxton relished his role as champion of the innocent black girl, degraded by the heinous Mr. Smith.

Four months after the incident, a Grand Jury could find no evidence to implicate the accused rapist. A leak told a reporter that the Grand Jury determined that an evasive LaShanna Johnston was a promiscuous student. An obstinate Claxton continued to support LaShanna. An act of good fortune for LaShanna occurred in her third month with the onset of a spontaneous abortion.

Smith suffered the loss of his position, abandonment by his wife and children, and complete rejection by his associates and friends. The 43-year-old principal drove his car into the path of an oncoming 18-wheeler and was killed instantly. DNA would subsequently prove that Hiram Smith did not impregnate LaShanna Johnston. (No penalty to Claxton.)

Crime Description

Section Two

On the morning of June 14, 2002, at approximately 7:00 a.m., José Cortezzo, a 71-year-old retired clothing store clerk, raised his garage door electronically then walked down his driveway. The morning paper lay halfway between the entrance to the garage and the street. As he bent over to retrieve the paper, damp with morning dew, he noticed an SUV parked across the street. He could not see anyone inside because of the dark tinted windows. As he turned to retrace his steps, his neighbor, J. Oliver Claxton was walking down his driveway, which was parallel and 30 feet from the Cortezzo driveway.

"Hey, old-timer, how's the wife doing?" Claxton asked.

"She's a lot better. The epidural shots have the ruptured disc under control. But it looks like I'll be doing the grocery shopping for awhile," Cortezzo said.

Cortezzo stated that his eyesight is poor, but his hearing is still acute. He said he heard what sounded like a car window being lowered followed by a loud bang. Claxton had already picked up his paper and both men had their backs to the street.

"It was horrible," said Cortezzo. "I see a spray of blood and flesh come out of Mr. Claxton's chest. He staggered forward, maybe one step, and then fell flat on his face. I rushed over and turned him face up. Even I could tell from the size of the hole where his heart should have been that he was dead. The SUV must have started up and driven away while I was trying to help Claxton. I ran in my house and called 911. I told the lady that I had just witnessed a shooting and was sure the victim was dead."

Cortezzo later told the interviewer that he never did get to read that morning paper.

The Dallas police could not locate any tire tracks, the spent bullet or any useful evidence at the crime scene. Experts figured the projectile was from a .30-caliber hollow-tipped bullet. Mr. Cortezzo could not describe the make or color of the SUV. An immediate canvass of the neighborhood could not locate anyone who had seen a strange vehicle or SUV in the area.

Case Status

Section Three

The Dallas Police Force asked for assistance from the Texas State Crime Bureau and any citizen with knowledge of the crime. Black leaders made an urgent plea for calm and patience. None of the agencies investigating the crime discovered any leads. The consensus of opinion: A hate crime. Claxton had made many enemies among the white population. The case is TAAR, Temporarily Abandoned, Awaiting Resolution.

* * *

Not much from this file is going to help us, Clarke thought. *What a waste. Claxton had the natural ability to be a positive inspiration for all African-Americans, but he ended up being a hindrance to improved racial relations. That's a crime in my book*, he concluded.

He chuckled. The JLSKT may have a sense of humor, morbid as it may be. They shot J. Oliver Claxton on his birthday. Was there a clue or message there?

He looked at his watch. It was 9:45 p.m. *Hmmm, a depressing read,* he thought. *Time to take a quick shower, watch the ten o'clock news and hit the sack. Oops, I'd better call Sherri; it's already 10:45 in Fredericksburg.*

* * *

January 14, 2003 (Tuesday)

Agents Gable and Majesky walked three blocks, initially heading south on Lamar Street and then West on Capitol Street. When the McCoy building came into view, Clarke thought it looked like a gigantic pillbox, with each floor having a series of four-windowed gun ports. Maybe the architect was prophetic, expecting that every government office building in the U.S. would one day be a target for terrorists.

They entered the complex, showed their identification cards and badges, and were waved to the elevators. Clarke noticed another guard talking into his shoulder-mounted radio, probably announcing their arrival. As instructed, they stopped at the fifth floor where they were to meet with the SAC, Special Agent in Charge. As the elevator doors opened, a young female clerk greeted them. She advised them SAC Downy Westfield was waiting in a nearby conference room. The three individuals walked down a carpeted hallway until they faced a dark, fruitwood door. The conspicuous brass plate was engraved: Conference Room 5-A. The clerk opened the door and invited the two men to enter.

The man standing at the end of eight-foot conference table said in a raspy voice, "Good morning, gentlemen, I'm Downy Westfield."

Clarke moved closer and reached to shake hands, hoping the SAC's grip would not hurt. Steeled and determined not to wince, he said, "Clarke Gable, and this is Agent Artie Majesky."

"Glad you Yankee boys came down here to learn about the new south. Mrs. Lynn Stafford, who met you at the elevator, is my secretary and will record our session. You'll receive a transcript. Zachariah has warned me about confidentiality. I assure you, there won't be any leaks from this office."

Clarke believed Westfield could back up his statement. Erect like an ex-marine, the SAC stood 5'10" and looked as if he weighed 200 pounds. Clarke later described him to his boss, Claiborne, as a square head on a square body. Westfield had no visible neck or waist. His face reminded Clarke of the chiseled granite countenance of Kirk Douglas, and the crew cut screamed military service. He wore a brown leather single-breasted coat with pleated pants, cuffed to show a slight break. The coat was accented by a solid, bronze-colored handkerchief in the breast pocket. The nutmeg-colored buttoned-down shirt was combined with a silk, solid bronze tie matching the bronze pocket square. The ensemble was anchored by wing tip shoes with hand-woven vamps and heels.

"Sir, Artie is accompanying me as a member of TAG," said Clarke. "The Bureau has a new project that studies agent's responses in actual case situations. The goal is to improve the decision-making process in fast-moving or stressful situations."

"Yeah," said Westfield. "Goldberg laid that crap on me. No offense, Artie, but it's more a waste of time and money. He called me a couple of months ago and told me to give you boys my full attention. So let's get to the reason ya'll are visiting Jackson and how this district can be of assistance. Goldberg informed me that Clarke Gable would fill me in on a special case."

Clarke waited for the inevitable punch line: "'Yeah,' I said, 'and send along Gary Cooper.'"

Clarke chuckled in earnest. *Little fish should be polite to big fish,* Clarke inwardly confessed. *Besides, the comment was pretty darn original.*

"Sir, we're attempting to solve a perplexing six-year case involving an SKT." Clarke did not mention the Justice Lovers Case or justitiaphiles, remembering the admonition by Zachariah Goldberg. He continued, "The signature aspect of this case is that this team commits to one perpetration every 13 months. There've been seven victims in six incidents identified by the NCAVC, commencing in January 1997 and ending in June 2002. If the team, which we believe are husband and wife, continue to adhere to this time schedule, we can expect another murder this July. I personally would like to save that life by early apprehension of the SKT."

"I haven't seen anything in the press about a serial killing team here in the South," Westfield stated.

"The Director and the Assistant Director," said Clarke, "do not want this case made public. My objection to this position was overridden. The SKT haven't been extremely careful, because they're unaware someone's recognized their existence. We have physical descriptions, potential DNA evidence, artist's sketches and in-depth profiles on the subjects. The case could be wrapped up without public involvement."

"What's the problem with going public?" asked Westfield.

Clarke was not allowed to tell Westfield about this new type of serial killer, the justitiaphile. He had planned his response, since he knew the question would arise. "If our theory is bogus and these crimes are unrelated, a false alarm could embarrass the FBI. The public has enough on its plate with all the terror alerts. We also don't want the SKT to go underground if they suspect the FBI is aware of their activity. We're only to involve the state investigative bureau if absolutely necessary. I don't like holding info from the states, but I'm not the last word on the investigation."

"By geez," said Westfield. "If you're instructed to hold out on the states, then you're probably holding out on me. I'll let that go for now. What's the plan for the Jackson Division?"

Clarke admired Westfield for his quick insight and unabashed candor. He felt embarrassed that he could not be frank with SAC Westfield, professional to professional. "Your instructions are to identify and locate the SKT. At that time, AD Goldberg will advise on arrest and detainment procedures."

"Boys," said Westfield, "as we say here in the South, I didn't come to town on a truckload of pumpkins. The mother organization wants these people to disappear without public knowledge. We've worked hard here in Mississippi to get people to trust and work with the FBI. State and local law enforcement hated our guts in the sixties. Now they work with us. I don't want to blow that relationship for some screwed-up protocol cooked up in the Hoover Building. I'm a team player, but you're on notice. Do not, I repeat, *do not* pull another Ruby Ridge fiasco in my district."

Artie Majesky did not say a word, but thought, *Westfield just made a preemptive strike against my orders. Gotta call the AD about that later.*

Clarke reached in his briefcase, removed three reports and handed them to Westfield. "The top report is a detailed twelve-point profile with a postscript, which should be invaluable in the search for the SKT. The second report is a synopsis of the six crimes committed to-date. You can pull the complete files from your data-link with Washington. The third report is a DNA analysis. This analysis is the only hard evidence we have to tie the SKT to one of the crime scenes. A male body hair, not belonging to the victim, was found in the victim's abandoned vehicle. That's the Cantrell murder in Tipton, Mississippi."

"That's not a lot to go on, Clarke," Westfield commented. "Give me some of your ideas on moving this case forward."

"The SKT has been careful to some degree in their activity," replied Clarke. "But they didn't figure on these various crimes being tied together, probably because of the 13-month span between the murders and for the diversity of the victims. The discovery of a connection was a break for the FBI and a validation of our software. It's my opinion that the SKT may have foolishly used their own vehicle in the Tipton situation. A white, late-model Ford F-150 with a male and female occupant was seen several times in Tipton. Your agents, beginning in Jackson, need to canvas all the Ford dealers with our sketches of the SKT for any hits. The SKT is believed to be in an upward financial bracket. It's our belief that they would probably not buy a used truck. It was six years ago that the truck was probably purchased, but hopefully a salesman, service manager or some other employee will recognize them from the sketches. If no hits are made in Jackson, expand the search to the Biloxi, Meridian and Hattiesburg areas. Don't overlook small-town dealers near the large cities. If you still bat zero, make spot checks of dealers across the state lines in Alabama and Louisiana. Tennessee is too far removed from the four largest towns we're targeting. Oh, and you might also want to check with auto repair shops, large and small."

"You just laid a lot of leg work on my District, young fella," said Westfield.

"Blame that on Goldberg," said Clarke. "At least you have five months before the next predicted incident in July of 2003."

"We'll get moving on this project. If the SKT is identified and located, no arrests will be made until authorized by AD Goldberg. I got it right?"

"You got it right, sir," answered Clarke.

"Will the SKT be armed and dangerous? I need to give my men a heads-up on that."

"These people never target law enforcement or law-abiding citizens." Clarke wondered if Downy Westfield deciphered his subtly worded answer.

Artie glared at him.

Clarke shrugged his shoulders.

Westfield had a quizzical look. He stood abruptly then said, "I guess that covers everything. I know you boys're anxious to get back to Virginia. I'll keep you posted on our progress. Good luck on your flight. It's been a real trip discussing this case." Downy made no attempt to hide his sarcasm.

* * *

Back at the hotel, Clarke and Artie quickly went to their individual rooms to make important phone calls.

Clarke called Sherri to tell her that he was catching an afternoon flight and might be able to see her tonight.

Artie immediately called Zachariah Goldberg. "Mr. Goldberg, this Downy Westfield is double-one sharp. Out of the blue he implied that the FBI wants the SKT to disappear without a trace. I'm nervous about handling this matter satisfactorily. I'm also sure that Clarke is not in line with being secretive about the project."

"Don't worry, Artie. When you get back, come by the office and we'll talk this thing over," said Goldberg.

CHAPTER 30
February 13, 2003 (Thursday)
Fredericksburg, Virginia

Sherri pushed the grocery cart down aisle six at the Wal-Mart Superstore. Her mother wanted a can of hearts of palm, but none lined the shelves. She took out her cell phone to dial home. A voice said, "Hi, Sherri."

She turned around. "Oh my God! What're you doing in town, Danny? How long has it been, six or seven years?" *Well, he hasn't changed much except for maybe being a few pounds heavier. What the hell does he want?*

Danny, in stylish blue jeans, denim shirt and blue jean jacket with copper buttons, looked like an eastern version of the Marlboro Man. *How can he act like nothing's happened between us, like we're old friends? Damn. Why did he pick this time to come back? Bastard! I wonder what he wants. Well, Danny, you're going to get the old subtle brush-off. I'll give you a taste of your own medicine.* Sherri, irritated, could not get away fast enough. She tried to maintain her cool.

"I'm kind of in a hurry, Danny, it was nice seeing you. Say hello to your mom and dad for me." She abruptly walked away.

Danny followed her, pleading, "Sherri, please give me a minute. I need to tell you something. Please!"

Sherri shopped on Thursday afternoons, avoiding crowds. No one overheard private or embarrassing conversations. She spoke her mind, "For a long time, Danny, I hated your guts for abandoning Bonnie and me. With the help of a very nice person, I'm enjoying my life again. You don't need to tell me anything. Now goodbye."

"Sherri, you've always been the strong one. When the baby wasn't perfect, I just lost it. I've recently come to the realization that my love for you has grown stronger with each passing year. There've been other girls, but they didn't mean a thing. Is it possible for you to forgive me for running away from my responsibilities? Forgive me for running away from you and the baby?"

Sherri, stunned, attempted to dampen her anger. *I wonder if this is really an accidental encounter.* "Why are you in town and what are you doing in Wal-Mart?" she asked.

"I've been in town for several days and have cruised past your house hoping to run into you. That's figuratively, not literally."

The stern expression on Sherri's face unchanged, she mused, *Danny has never been big on good timing.*

He continued, "I followed you here. You didn't answer my question. It would be phenomenal if you could forgive me for being such a jerk-off."

"Look, you're forgiven, but just seeing you triggers sad and bad memories of the tremendous helplessness and desperation we experienced from your abandonment. Surely, you don't expect me to forget you just up and left me and Bonnie because she wasn't born 100 percent normal. We're divorced now. It's over. I wish you well, Danny, but you and I can never be friends. So don't follow me, don't call me and for God's sake, stay away from me," she said.

"Sherri, please don't shut me out of your life. Give it a little thought. I'm staying at my parent's house for a few weeks. I'll call you in a few days. Maybe you could come by the house and visit. My parents would love to see you. Just like old times!"

"Didn't you hear a word I just said!?" She was losing it. Her face glowed red.

He walked away to avoid a scene.

* * *

As Danny pulled out of the parking lot, his longing for Sherri overwhelmed him. He wanted her back. His parents loved Sherri and counseled him not to run away from her and his sickly baby girl. Thank heavens, they had financially supported Sherri, but she only used their money for Bonnie.

Danny's father, Harper Bonds, a major homebuilder in the Fredericksburg area, constructed two subdivisions, one for medium income buyers and the other for wealthy individuals who wanted to live in mansions. Ownership of a separate company that only did historical research and restoration put him a cut above most large contractors. Harper doted on his only child. Although he didn't approve of some of the things Danny did, he loved him without reservation. He wanted his son to eventually take over the business.

Danny remembered how unhappy his dad was when he moved to Richmond. Fredericksburg was a small community, and he dreaded bumping into Sherri and Bonnie all the time. *I'll just come back after a few years and plug into Dad's business ventures.*

Then a sweet lady named "Luck" visited Danny. Like his Father, he was a Civil War buff. How could one grow up in Virginia and not be motivated to stand on the battlefields where Americans fought Americans? Danny studied the topography near Old Church, Virginia, 15 miles northeast of Richmond. At this place, a furious engagement took place between General Matthew Butler's outnumbered Rebels and General Alfred Torbert's Union Troops on May 30, 1864. Danny discovered a 420-acre tract of undulating, partially tree covered, land for sale. Several streams, which eventually flowed into the Paunchy River, traversed the property. Instantly, Danny recognized the potential for developing a gated upper-class subdivision. Population was expanding in all directions from a revitalized Richmond.

A picture of an 18-hole, par-72 golf course, delineated by elegant homes, flashed through his mind. Danny used his cell phone and reached his father on the first ring. "Dad, I'm going to make you a rich man."

He could hear his Dad chuckle—a good sound.

"Get in your car and immediately drive to Old Church. If you okay this project, Dad, I'm back in the family business."

Hanover Estates was an immense success. The Return on Investment (ROI) ran at twelve-to-one. In the process, Danny became a millionaire and the name of the company became Bonds and Son.

Danny had his life back. He also wanted his first love back, a desire that bounced around inside his head like a ricocheting pinball. In the past seven years, he took a few women to bed, but he never reached the fulfillment he had with Sherri. He knew she had not remarried. The mantra squirreled in his brain ten times a day: "Sherri will give me a second chance. She will forgive me." Danny figured his best move was to apologize for his callous behavior. Sherri still liked his parents, so maybe they would help bring her back into the family.

CHAPTER 31
March 6, 2003 (Thursday)
Jackson, Mississippi

In the middle of March, the temperature averaged 45 degrees in the mornings and 70 degrees in the afternoons. Tess and Mike sat in two redwood rocking chairs on their patio surrounding an oval-shaped pool. The vinyl cover, still spanning the pool, had slightly filled with rainwater. Two thick ground-round hamburgers cooked on the gas grill. Tess picked up a pint of barbeque beans and made a German potato salad. The smoke from the fat drippings hitting the open flame, filled the air with the inviting smell that caused the gastric juices to rumble. The mosquitoes had not yet materialized, so they were not doused with a bug repellant to guard against the West Nile Virus.

They watched three parallel vapor trails expand from thin lines to broad, jagged, fluffy strips.

"I've been checking the papers, TV and magazines but haven't found any good candidates for our next delivery of justice," Mike sighed. "There's one of the Islamic highjackers that needs whacking, but we could never get to him."

"You know what, Mike? I'm getting a little burned out. All our victims got what they deserved, so there're no regrets. I have a strange feeling I can't shake, that someone out there, in gumshoe land, must be aware of our unusual endeavor. Maybe we should lay low for a year and recharge our batteries."

"No arguments from me. But what got you into this frame of mind?" said Mike.

"Our luck has just been phenomenal," said Tess, "but I don't think we should push the envelope. I was reading in Genesis the other day how God made the earth in six days. On the seventh day, He rested. We've been dispensing justice for six years. This seventh year, we should rest. We can start up again in another year if we're not being pursued."

"So be it. The burgers are ready. Let's eat, I'm starved."

CHAPTER 32
April 7, 2003 (Monday)
Fredericksburg, Virginia

Danny sat in his dad's Chrysler PT Cruiser across the street from Sherri's home. The elder Bonds liked the Chrysler's retro look and ease of parking. Danny did not particularly like the manual shift, but it made his dad a happy camper. Over the last two months, he had phoned Sherri a total of 22 times at home and work, followed her in her car eight times, had her house under surveillance three times, and "accidentally" bumped into her at Wal-Mart, the gas station, book store and the U.S. Post Office. He knew he was really stalking her, but the overwhelming desire to reunite with Sherri drove him to foolish behavior. To her credit, cordial but distant, she suggested he stop calling her. He was not sure she knew of the surveillance. His parents asked that he not press Sherri, that if she had feelings for him, she would contact him.

Danny felt heart-wrenching jealousy and nauseating disgust. For the first time he saw her with a black guy. Clarke touched Sherri as he helped her into the Lexus, infuriating Danny. *A black dating my ex-wife crosses a line with me.* A black should have equal rights under the law, but not the right to date a white girl. He failed to acknowledge Sherri's oriental ancestry. Her honey-colored skin was not white. Clarke was light-skinned.

The black guy closed the passenger-side door, walked around the rear of his expensive Lexus, hesitated for a moment then fixed his eyes on the PT Cruiser. He took two steps in the direction of where Danny parked. He hesitated then turned around and got into his car.

Danny felt a cold chill throughout his body. He was in pretty good physical shape, but knew he would not be able to handle the big black guy. Obviously, they were aware of him and the black guy definitely did not like it. *Screw him. I have some friends on our construction crew that hate blacks. I might just get their help to put this piece of crap in the hospital.*

* * *

Trained to be alert to his surroundings, even when off duty and relaxing, Clarke spotted the PT Cruiser parked half a block away and across the street from Sherri's home. This was the first time he saw the automobile she said was following her. He started to walk toward the car, envisioned yanking open the door and demanding some answers. But composure that accompanies maturity led him to reject that action. He reversed his direction and got back into the Lexus. *Tonight's going to be special for Sherri and me*, he fantasized. *No need to drop an A-bomb on an anthill.*

As they drove away, the PT Cruiser made a U-turn and fell in position behind them.

"Darlin', do you have any idea who's following us in the PT Cruiser? He doesn't seem to care that we know he's sticking to us like a leech."

Sherri had no need to look over her shoulder because she already knew who the leech was.

"It's Danny Bonds, my big brave ex-husband, who abandoned the baby and me. He's been successful in a real estate venture and claims the achievement changed his life. He wants to reestablish our relationship. He asked—no, begged—me to forgive him, which I did. I told him my forgiveness didn't include getting back together. I demanded he leave me alone. He's beginning to spook me. I'm getting aggravated with the persistent phone calls, the contrived accidental meetings and the shower of gifts coming to the house. Even I know this is obsessive behavior."

Concerned, Clarke asked, "How long has this stalking been going on?"

"Two months, more or less. Are you angry because I didn't tell you right away?"

"Listen, this kind of behavior should put anybody on notice for potential harm. Psychologically, you're his 'attachment figure'. The inability to involve you in his fantasy leaves him frustrated. That kind of frustration can escalate into violence. Danny might be at a cerebral fork in the road. If he takes a right, it's because he's found someone else to take your place. If he takes a left, then jealous rage destroys the love he's imagined between you. Danny won't permit anyone else to posses his attachment figure. To answer your question, yeah, I'm mad you didn't tell me sooner and worried that things have gone too far."

While Clarke explained further the danger of her situation, he made several left and right hand turns at random, but Danny continued to follow. Stopping at a red light, Danny made the mistake of pulling up behind them, probably thinking they would go through the light. Suddenly he slammed on his brakes, tires squealing. That was enough for cool and calm Clarke. He got out of the car, walked back to the Cruiser and rapped on the driver's side window.

Danny, nervous, lowered the window and asked, "Is there a problem?"

"There's a *big* problem and it's you." Clarke opened his wallet and revealed his FBI badge. "I'm agent Clarke Gable and you're about to piss me off, and believe me, you don't want to go there. Sherri's kept a log for the last two months of your harassing her. If it doesn't stop, two things are going to happen. First, Sherri files charges against you, and second, I'm going to beat your little white ass to a pulp. It's just you and me, brother. It's your word against a law enforcement officer. Is this sermon getting through to you?"

Danny was not going to let a dumb black cop intimidate him. "The light has changed, Buddy. You're holding up traffic. Oh, and about your threat, this incident ought to look good on your service record."

"Yeah, right," said Clarke. He gave Danny boy a smile of confidence.

I refuse to let that dirt-bag ruin our romantic dinner, he thought. Clarke had reserved a small room at the Hobbs House in Fredericksburg, the old landmark, a stone house erected in 1805. The original owner, a shrewd businessman named Samuel Hobbs, used the building as a halfway overnight stop on the trip from Washington to Richmond. Before the Civil War, additions were added and used through the years, as a hospital, an Old Soldiers' Home, as the town's municipal building, and then for various shops and businesses. In 1960, Harper Bonds restored the building, establishing it as an upscale restaurant. As a sturdy survivor, the name Hobbs House remained, and was later listed on the National Register.

A charming feature of the Hobbs House was the small second story rooms used for *tête-à-tête* dining. Clarke and Sherri were seated at a round solid cherry farm table, stained and varnished. The lathe-turned legs provided a rustic contrast to the French olive patina. A wrought iron chandelier with four shaded false candlesticks provided the dim romantic lighting. The only other piece of furniture was a buffet.

Clarke and Sherri finished their dinner of poached salmon with hollandaise sauce, French string beans and boiled new potatoes. As they enjoyed a cup of cappuccino, Clarke took a small white box from his coat pocket and slid it across the table.

"What's this?" asked Sherri. "It better be a ring or you're in trouble, Mr. Clarke Gable." She fumbled to get the top removed and then screamed with delight, "It's absolutely, positively beautiful!"

The ring was a three-carat, square-cut canary diamond surrounded by 24 round .15 carat white diamonds set beveled to the yellow diamond.

"I've spoken with your dad, and he gave his blessing. We've been dating seven months now, and I'd like a more permanent arrangement. Will you marry me, Miss Sherri Nelson?"

"Oh, yes, of course I will." A deep furrow appeared on Sherri's forehead. "It's just that I'm worried now that when Danny hears about our engagement, he'll go postal and do something stupid."

"Don't worry; I'll take care of Danny. I made a mistake tonight, threatening him, but I was tired of him bothering you. He had his chance and blew it. If he's got any sense, he'll get out of your life for good."

"Honey, can we go to your house tonight? I think we deserve some quiet time together to discuss our future. Oh, and by the way, I *will* marry you, or did I say that already?"

* * *

April 9, 2003 (Wednesday)

Clarke sat in the office of his immediate superior Deputy Assistant Director (DAD) G. Thomas Claiborne. When Clarke read the *Richmond Review* that morning, he knew it was not going to be a pretty day. He entertained the idea of calling in sick, but decided to bare his back and take the forty FBI lashes.

"You know the drill, Clarke. Zachariah chewed my ass out about an hour ago. Now I get to chew your ass out."

"Get it off your chest, Tom. I let my FBI badge get the better of my ego."

DAD Claiborne opened a folded newspaper and scanned the front page. Clarke's breathing was shallow as he watched his boss prepare to unleash a verbal onslaught.

"Mr. Bonds claims you got out of your car at a traffic light and threatened him because he was following too close to your car. He said you flashed your FBI badge then said you were going to beat his little white ass to a pulp. Is that true?"

"Listen, Tom, the guy's been stalking Sherri for two months. I was taking Sherri out to propose, and the guy is attached to my car like a caboose. My blood pressure must've been 150 over 90. You expect a psychologist to be self-controlled, but I'm still part of the human race. Tom, my Homo sapiens Neanderthalensis personality reared up and took over. Evolution put one of those ugly guys inside us to carry around as excess baggage."

Claiborne grinned at the lame, but original, excuse. *Damn, it's difficult to be aggravated with him*, he thought. "Clarke you're not only a psychologist, but you're one of our best FBI criminologists. Why didn't you just report the guy to the locals?"

"You know the police are handicapped in a situation like this one. Sherri's concerned that when our engagement is announced, the fool might try to harm one or both of us, and frankly, I'm not so sure he won't."

"Clarke, I see your point and you have my sympathy, but the Department believes that no response is the best approach for handling these kinds of matters. This guy's dad is Harper Bonds with lots of political and law enforcement contacts. We don't want to get into a pissing contest. You're ordered to stay away from this Danny Bonds. Just go along with me on this one."

"Tom, I'll stay away from Danny Bonds. You know this is his way of challenging me. If he shows up at my front door looking for a fight, I'll call you for advice."

"I'll take that as compliance. One other thing, this incident is going to be part of your permanent record."

"I figured as much. I can live with it."

* * *

Danny's mind rejected the electric impulses his eyes transmitted via the optic nerve. The society page of the *Fredericksburg Bugler* announced the engagement of Sherri Takahashi Nelson to Clarke F.D. Gable.

The F.D. stood for Frederick Douglass, but Clarke rarely used the initials let alone saying Frederick Douglass. He did not want to get into a discussion as to why his parents burdened him with the name of a white movie star and a black abolitionist.

Danny was elated when a reporter friend of his dad's agreed to headline the FBI agent's threat. He thought, *Maybe Sherri will come to her senses and realize what a buffoon she's dating. My parents would not approve of their ex-daughter-in-law, who they've continued to love and support after the divorce, associating with, as they would politely say, an Afro-American. Somehow I'm going to redeem our family honor.*

CHAPTER 33
May 12, 2003 (Monday)
Jackson, Mississippi

SAC Downy Westfield was frustrated and aggravated. His district spent over 300 man-hours attempting to locate the owner of the white Ford 150 pick-up truck, identified in the 1997 disappearance of Bobby Dan Cantrell. *Shit, that was six years ago,* he reminded himself. The employees who could recognize the sketches probably moved on to other dealers. It would be simple to just run the pictures of the SKT in Jackson's *Morning Chronicle.* He picked up the phone, dialed Zachariah Goldberg in Washington and immediately was put through.

"Hello, Zach, how're the FBI and the CIA boys getting along?"

"We're sharing info and breaking down the proverbial wall between the two agencies. What's on your mind, Downy?"

"The investigation of a possible Mississippi SKT has flat run out of gas. I know you've been stone-walling me on this case, and I went along with your ideas. But we haven't made any progress. As an old friend, I'm requesting two things, Zach. First, you give me all the details. Secondly, you allow me to go public with this case."

"Downy, you know we have good reasons for handling things this way. Admittedly, it's not the best approach, but it's the necessary approach in our estimation. Give me a few days to review the situation and I'll get back in touch with you."

"Thanks, Zach. We've already spent 300 man-hours on this job. We need a break."

CHAPTER 34
May 15, 2003 (Thursday)
Washington, D.C.

For three busy days after Downy called, AD Goldberg worried. He decided to let his mind brainstorm on the subject. *If the pattern recognized by Clarke holds true, the SKT will strike again in July. That's only two months away. It's looking like one more victim might be a tradeoff to expose the justitiaphiles without going public. We've only concentrated on this case for nine months because it's not been a high priority. Clarke has plenty of work to do directing several investigations that aren't as complex as the Justice Lovers Case. He's not reported the discovery of any other case involving justitiaphiles. I think I'll keep the Justice Lovers Case in the FBI domain for a few more months. I'll phone Downy and tell him his request is denied for now.*

CHAPTER 35
October 13, 2003 (Monday)
Fredericksburg, Virginia

Clarke sat at his desk watching snowflakes swirl about outside his office window. He imagined that Old Man Winter congratulated him on his smart move to marry Sherri. The date for the wedding, a small ceremony in the chapel of the First Baptist Church, was Saturday the 18th, only five days away. Sherri was doing all the planning, including organizing the rehearsal dinner. He hoped it would not snow on their wedding day, but what worried him more than bad weather was trying to figure out what Danny Bonds was up to. After the confrontation with him in April, Clarke and Sherri caught only occasional glimpses of him, and they prayed Danny had come to his senses.

On the night before the wedding, the illusion of civility shattered. Clarke received three phone calls after midnight, the caller silently staying on the line until Clarke finally hung up.

Sherri received a threatening call that night. Danny told her that she was his girl and she better not say "I do" to Gable or anyone else.

"Let me remind you, Danny," she said, "you were the one who walked out on us filing for and receiving a divorce. Why're you so upset with me after all these years?"

Tearfully, Danny said, "I never realized how powerful my love for you is. You're my first love, and I can't believe how much that's controlling my life. It took a long time to realize my big mistake. Sherri, you owe me a second chance."

"That's not going to happen, Danny. You're making a mistake. " In a firm voice, "I don't owe you anything. Now, get that through your head."

"No! You're about to make a big mistake!" The line went dead.

* * *

If the wedding and Danny Bonds were not enough to keep his mind occupied, the lack of progress on the Justice Lovers Case made for a triple whammy. Lady J and her partner, most likely her husband, did not murder a seventh victim according to his prediction. The prediction was that in July 2003, a seventh victim will be attacked. In the past three months, no reported incidents happened that met the JLSKT criteria. Clarke was in a peculiar emotional limbo. Grateful the JLSKT had not struck in July, it disturbed him that his rock-solid prognostication, presented to the Deputy Assistance Director Claiborne and the Assistant Director Goldberg, was flawed.

Clarke surmised four possibilities for the non-event. First, the JLSKT had left the country and now operated elsewhere. *Not likely*, he thought. Second, they're serving time. *Not likely*. Third, the JLSKT had met with some type of accident and were either dead or incapacitated. *Possible*. Fourth, the JLSKT had made a conscious decision to defer or to terminate their activity. *Most likely. Sherlock Holmes preached that the most logical answer was the right answer.*

Remembering the flight to Jackson with Artie Majesky when he attempted to get into the mind of Lady J, he thought, *If I'm Lady J, why would I decide not to bring a seventh victim to justice? Or eighth, if you count John Mark Collins. I've had an entire year to choose a victim, and there're several worthy of my attention. I chose a victim and they're not accessible in the month of July. I can easily select an alternate, though. Man, am I getting bored with my crusade? I cannot return justice to America by myself. I need help. Is it possible to establish a secret organization with the lofty goal of administering justice? Hmmm, 'Justice Я Us', we don't worry about technicalities and no deferments waiting fifteen years for appeals to end. Yikes, I'm scaring myself.*

Clarke closed his eyes, rested his head on both hands and thought, *What am I missing?* He decided to review the Justice Lovers profile. When he read item five, an illumination occurred. *The justitiaphiles had a deep, religious upbringing. God created heaven and earth in just six days, and He was so pleased with his creation that He rested on the seventh day. So, 2003 becomes the rest year after six years of success. Would they ever start up again? This action conclusively separates the psychopath from the justitiaphile. The former continuously kills to relieve unrelenting aberrant urges; the latter follows a twisted logic absent the compulsion factor.*

Goldberg, Claiborne and I need to review the U-turn the Justice Lovers have taken. Then Clarke concluded, *I'll demand more public involvement. If the JLSKT has stopped its activity, public involvement is our only option. There's a delicate balance. It's been foolish to withhold the sketches from the public allowing for the possibility of a seventh episode to occur. The FBI dodged a bullet for the time being. The next critical date will most likely be in August of 2004, if the JLSKT retains their 13-month cycle. That date's not a given, since the justitiaphiles have out-smarted their unknown FBI nemesis. Well, everybody needs a take-down once in awhile, just to keep the hat size from getting too large.*

* * *

October 17, 2003 (Friday)

Sherri took the afternoon off from work to attend to last minute details, meeting with the manager of Hobbs House to give final approval of the menu and to organize the seating arrangements. There were only three bridesmaids, three groomsmen, the maid of honor, the best man, the wedding consultant, the pastor and a few relatives invited to the rehearsal dinner. The rehearsal was at 6:00 p.m. and the dinner at 7:30 p.m. Clarke was to pick Sherri up at 5:30 p.m. She pulled into her driveway at 4:45 p.m. and walked toward the front door.

"Hey, Sherri, got a minute?" Danny Bonds called out.

Disgusted, she said, "Danny, I'm busy! Go away or I'll call the police!" She turned to the front door to unlock it.

"Sherri," he continued, "you're making a big mistake and I'm here to prevent that from happening."

"Danny, get the hell away from me!" She was beginning to feel frightened as she opened the door.

More forcefully, he said, "Listen to me carefully, Sherri! Some of my construction people snatched your precious FBI man and are holding him at our place at Lake Anna," Danny lied. "You come with me immediately and nothing happens to him. My men are waiting for my orders."

Sherri could not take a chance that this was a ploy. She thought, *Clarke's safety is more important than a rehearsal dinner. He's crazy enough to do this.* She closed the front door turning to Danny.

"If I go with you, will you release Clarke unhurt?"

"After the three of us work through this problem, I'll let both of you go unharmed. Believe me, Sherri, this is for your own good and you'll thank me later."

Sherri was suddenly frightened. A picture of a double murder and a suicide flashed before her eyes. "Danny, how can I be sure you aren't going to do something crazy?"

"What I do depends on what you do, babe. So, let's get going."

* * *

Clarke pulled up to the Nelson home on Williams Street and parked in the driveway. As he walked toward the house, Kimiko Nelson opened the front door and shouted, "Hurry Clarke-e-san, hurry."

Seeing a pained expression on Kimiko's face and hearing the urgency in her voice, Clarke ran to the door. Closer, he now saw the tears in her eyes.

"I'm very worried," she said with a quivering voice that immediately alarmed Clarke. "Sherri car is parked in driveway, but she never came in house. Maybe she went with someone, do you know? Why would she do that? Who she go with, do you know?"

Clarke's chest tightened and his veins felt like ice cubes flowed through them. A horrible fear struck him. At that moment, he knew. *Calm Kimiko, and come up with a plan. Calm down, I need to do things right. Time's of the essence. I hope it's not too late.*

As calmly as he could, he said, "Don't panic, Kimiko-san. I'll phone the city police and sheriff to see if any car accidents have happened. I'll also call the Mary Washington and see if Sherri was brought to the hospital. While I'm making the phone calls, you make a list of the places Sherri was going to and the people she intended to meet the best you can." Clarke did not want Kimiko to know what he knew. *Danny probably kidnapped her. Follow protocol, other areas need checking to rule them out.*

The city police and sheriff's department found no accidents reported involving Sherri Nelson. The hospital reported the same thing. Kimiko called Hobbs House, the florist, the wedding consultant, the bridesmaids and several of Sherri's close friends. No one knew where she was. The manager at Hobbs House said, "Sherri was excited and left here about four-thirty. She said she was going straight home to get ready for tonight."

Through tears, Kimiko reported her findings to Clarke.

"We need to call the Spotsylvania Sheriff's Department and Virginia State Police, to make missing person report," Kimiko suggested.

"That's a good idea," said Clarke. "But we'll have to wait until tomorrow. A person must be missing at least 24 hours before they'll act on a report." He hated to tell her that.

"Clarke-e-san, we can't sit and do nothing for 22 more hours. Please, call FBI people?"

"I'm sorry, Kimiko-san. This situation is not under Federal jurisdiction at this point."

Dave Nelson, after being silent for a while, felt frustrated and decided to voice his opinion. He picked up an extension phone. He was so upset that he suggested Clarke call in all the law enforcement people he could and "pull out all the stops". Call in favors. He said, "Hell, I can't just wait around and suck my thumb! I'm going to get in my car and drive down every street and alley in Fredericksburg until I find my daughter!"

"Now, hold on Dave, let me run an idea by you. I'm fairly certain Danny Bonds abducted Sherri. He must've waited for her to get home and then threatened her somehow if she didn't leave with him. The night of my altercation with him, he parked across the street from your house. Sherri didn't want to worry either of you, but Danny's been stalking her intermittently for the past eight months. She wouldn't file a complaint or get a Restraining Order, but several times she did get thoroughly disgusted and contemplated meeting with an attorney. Danny seemed to sense it was time to back off and would disappear for several weeks to a month. We figured that when we got married, the game would end. The only way the FBI can get involved is if Sherri is kidnapped. I did talk to my boss about Danny, though—"

Kimiko broke in, "No, no. Danny spoiled, no doubt. But he also charming and behave well. He like to party, have good time, but he never get loud. I don't believe he would take my Sherri. He like a son," Kimiko said in defense of Danny.

"That's the old Danny, Mrs. Nelson. The new Danny is letting jealousy drive him to irrationality. He's unable to put the brakes on his runaway emotions. He may be a danger to Sherri and himself," argued Clarke.

"What do you suggest we do?" Dave asked.

"All three of us need to visit with Harper Bonds this evening. We explain the situation to him and his wife. Hopefully, they'll help us find Danny and Sherri."

"He and I are still good friends," said Dave Nelson. "I'll call him. He's a reasonable man and surely doesn't want anyone to get hurt. Even after the divorce, he considered Sherri part of their family. The Bonds have always been protective of our baby and our grandbaby."

"Okay," said Clarke. "It sounds like a plan."

Dave Nelson went into the kitchen to make the call.

* * *

October 17, 2003 (Friday)

It took only 10 minutes for Sherri's parents and Clarke to drive the six miles to the Harper Bonds' residence. Dave Nelson, sitting in the passenger seat, gave directions to Clarke. "Go back from our house to Virginia Route 1, then go south on Route 1 to Mine Road, then east to Lansdowne Road, north to Artillery Ridge Road and back west."

Clarke parked in the circular drive. The octagon-shaped house loomed out of the dusk. "Harper must have plenty of cash to own this place," Clarke commented.

"Let me advise you about a quirk in Bonds' character," warned Dave Nelson. "Bonds does not hide the fact that he's extremely proud of his octagon house. It wouldn't matter if the sun rose up in the west. Before we get to the nature of our visit, you, especially as a first time visitor, are going to be subjected to what the Fredericksburg citizens call the 'House Opera'—a not so subtle play on the phrase, 'horse opera'. We need his help, so please act like you're interested."

"Got it loud and clear," answered Clarke. *The world is full of stupid people*, was his newsflash about the elder Bonds.

The three somber visitors climbed the 10 steps to a porch encircling the second floor—actually the first floor; the story below referenced as a raised cellar.

Clarke pushed the doorbell and heard the melodic chiming announcing their presence. They stared at the impressive eight-panel witch door. The lower four bottom triangular panels formed a St. Andrew's cross. The cross was to insure protection for the occupants against demons. Many visitors mistakenly thought the X-pattern was a Confederate flag symbol.

Harper Bonds opened the massive door and greeted the three callers with a hardy "Come on in, y'all."

He led the party through the foyer into the centrally located square-shaped atrium that extended vertically three stories to a massive skylight constructed with translucent tile. The group entered a short hallway and then a small five-sided room that served as Harper's study. It was informal and cozy.

Dave Nelson opened the conversation with an introduction. "Harper, please meet Clarke Gable, Sherri's fiancé."

Harper was a big man like Clarke. He had a full head of hair, combed straight back with no part. He had a pleasant round face with a few acne scars, large hazel eyes, a small nose and a slight cleft chin.

"It's good to meet you, Mr. Gable," Harper said not able to hide the amusement at his guest's name not matching the expected skin color.

"I'm pleased to finally meet you, Mr. Bonds. You're a living legend in the construction business in Central Virginia."

Clarke knew his next statement would open the door to the "Octagon Horse Opera". "This is a fantastic house, Mr. Bonds. It reminds me of Longwood in Natchez, Mississippi."

"Clarke, if I may call you by your first name, I know you obviously came here to discuss something important, but just indulge me for a few minutes while I tell you about this house. Talking about this place is an obsession, as I'm sure you have been pre-warned."

Clarke, miffed at the delay, tactfully replied, "I'd love to hear the history."

"The official name for this place is the Dr. Greenfield House. The doc, Garrett George Greenfield, III, hung out his shingle, Doctor of Medicine and Surgery, in Fredericksburg in 1859. How could he foresee that three major bloody battles would take place within one year of each other in his own backyard? Chancellorsville, Wilderness and Spotsylvania Courthouse produced 84,000 Union and Confederate casualties. Dr. Greenfield unselfishly tended to the wounded on both sides and was praised by Presidents Lincoln and Jeff Davis for outstanding service to his profession. After the war, his books and talk tours about his battlefield experiences added to his fame and fortune. During one of his tours, he met Orson Squire Fowler who, in 1850, introduced the octagonal designed home.

"Dr. Greenfield was impressed with the radical and uniquely American house style. The inventive Fowler also advocated central heating and indoor plumbing. Greenfield built this house in 1870, but unfortunately, about the same time, popularity of the octagon house faded. A century later, I bought the house in a rundown condition. My company restored it to its original splendor. Architects from all parts of the world came and marveled at the construction. That's the end of the story."

"I own an old house myself," shmoozed Clarke, "and I can relate to the pride you have in this unique building. Thank you for preserving a great American treasure."

"A most gracious comment, Mr. Gable. You've been attentive and patient. Now it's my turn to listen. What's the purpose of this visit?"

"Mr. Bonds, I have a Doctorate in Criminology and am currently attached to the FBI's Behavioral Science Unit. These facts are mentioned, not to brag, but to lend credibility to a speculation concerning your son. Both Mr. and Mrs. Nelson agree there is a measure of danger in a developing situation. I'm here at their urging and for my personal involvement."

"I assume this situation involves Sherri and my son," said Mr. Bonds. "I figured as much when you called. My wife becomes extremely distraught when Sherri and Danny are the subject matter. She decided to let me handle whatever the problem may be."

"For the last eight months," said Clarke, "Danny's been stalking Sherri. The harassment began when Sherri refused reconciliation, and then it escalated after our engagement announcement in the *Bugler*. In frustration, I mistakenly tried to handle the matter with threats, and unfortunately, the *Bugler* reported that episode. Tonight is the rehearsal dinner, so Sherri took the afternoon off to make a final check with all the parties involved. We were able to trace her activities up to five o'clock, which seems to be when she disappeared. Her car is parked in the Nelson's driveway with no sign of her. Mrs. Nelson checked with everyone she could think of, and I checked with the police and hospitals, but to no avail."

"Before you go any further, what do you consider stalking?"

"Sherri kept a log of each and every incident. Danny made three or four calls to her everyday, and when she told him she didn't want to talk to him, the silent phone calls began. He followed Sherri several times each week and contrived accidental meetings. His behavior was abnormal, and it upset Sherri. In fairness, the harassment seemed to stop for a period, but flared up again after the engagement announcement. Sherri's respect for you and Mrs. Bonds kept her from reporting Danny to the police."

"I cannot believe Danny would ever hurt Sherri. He loves her. He's a little hot-headed sometimes but has never been in trouble."

"In psychology, Mr. Bonds, Sherri is known as an "attachment figure." She's Danny's first true love, and so far, no one has replaced her in his casting of potential soul mates. It's likely Danny will not permit the final break or the marriage to another man. Also being of southern heritage, your son's most likely been socially conditioned against interracial marriages. Sherri's rejection and her relationship with a black man, an assault on one of his basic behavioral beliefs that blacks and whites don't mix, caused a mental overload."

"I have plenty of blacks in my companies," said Harper Bonds defensively. "We treat them fairly and pay them well. We even socialize on occasions. I draw the line here. Like my son, I don't accept intermarriage of the races. I'm truly sorry, Mr. Gable, if that position hurts your feelings."

"I take no offense to your position." Clarke thought, *Oh, Mr. Bonds, you should've lived in the last century, not this one.* "It's your son's mental state and Sherri's safety that are my concern."

"Then you think Danny is involved with Sherri's disappearance?" said Mr. Bonds.

"To answer your question—emphatically yes, I believe Danny kidnapped Sherri to prevent our marriage. The black and white factor is a contributor, but it's not the big issue. He'll attempt to convince Sherri to establish a reconciliation. When she turns him down again, that's the point where there could be violence. Mr. Bonds, is there a place where Danny might take her?"

"Yes," said Harper Bonds. "We have a get-away home on Lake Anna. Bought a bunch of property in 1972 right after the lake was built. We also own a home on the golf course at Hanover Estates. The Lake Anna home is secluded. If what you're saying is true, that's where Danny would take Sherri, if he really took her. We don't know that.

"It's only a 30- to 35-minute drive to Lake Anna. Harper, would you please take us there right now?" Dave Nelson begged.

"Look Dave, I don't believe Danny would hurt Sherri, if he indeed has her with him. It's only speculation. If he's trying to work something out, I'm inclined to give him that chance. My wife and I love Sherri and would like her in the family. It's also dark outside. We would scare them to death pulling in there this late at night."

"Harper-san, please at least call them. See if they are there?" asked Kimiko.

"Okay, I'll try that, but I think you're wrong." Harper dialed the Lake Anna residence. There was no answer. Then he dialed Danny's cell phone number, still no answer. "He's either not there or not answering. Meet me here at eight o'clock in the morning and we'll all drive up to Lake Anna."

Clarke was disappointed with the decision, but it was critical to have Mr. Bonds' cooperation. "Thanks for your help, sir. See you tomorrow morning," Clarke said.

CHAPTER 36
October 17, 2003 (Friday)
Lake Anna, Virginia

They rode in silence most of the way to Lake Anna. Danny attempted to draw Sherri into conversation, but she simply stared intently at the road, illuminated by the intensity of the high beams.

"I was really sad when I heard little Bonnie died," Danny offered.

Sherri turned and glared, seething. "Oh, really! As I recall you were not at the funeral."

"I wanted to come, but I was afraid it would make you more upset," he said.

"And the reason for not sending flowers or even a sympathy card?"

"That was inexcusable. I apologize for the callousness," he said.

"And how many times have you visited her grave site?"

"I abandoned you and Bonnie when you needed me the most. It almost seemed like blasphemy to kneel at her grave after running away like a coward."

"Don't say another word to me until we get to Lake Anna! I'm tired of your wimpy excuses."

The Bonds' retreat was on the shoreline of Lake Anna. The half-mile graveled access road intersected with the blacktopped Route 601. The house, a modern Cape Cod design, used tongue and groove cypress siding applied vertically. On each side, windows flanked the full height of a six-panel oak door. The deep forest-green windows, door and shutters contrasted nicely with the siding, weathered to a Spanish moss-gray. Visitors commented that the house had country elegance. The lake dwelling bordered a narrow lawn, transitioning into natural woods growth. A rectangular graveled area the length of the house provided ample parking.

Sherri was frightened when she saw no other vehicles, no sign of activity and no inside lights on. As they walked along the short path covered with cypress chips, Sherri asked, "Are you sure your goons brought Clarke to this location?"

Cocky, he said, "That was their orders."

Unlocking the front door, Danny switched on the foyer light and disarmed the security alarm. The foyer gave access to a narrow hallway, stairs led to the second floor and a doorway to the right led into the den. A switch in the foyer lit eight recessed canister lights in the den.

"Go into the den and have a seat on the sofa," he demanded.

Sherri entered through the door by a massive fireplace constructed of roughly dressed stone. A solid oak beam, eight feet long and one foot high, served as both lintel and mantle. The anthracite, gray slate hearth extended into the room. Above the mantle hung a three-foot by six-foot black and white enlargement of a photograph titled, "Their Final Charge." The picture was of nine Confederate veterans of Pickett's Charge reenacting their feat 50 years later on July 3, 1913. Sherri dropped into the royal-blue leather sofa and studied the stern expressions of the proud survivors. *I need to be a survivor like they were*, she thought.

Danny sat close to Sherri. "I lied to you, Sherri, Clarke isn't here. I lied because you never would've come."

"Have you lost what little sense you have?" She stood up and demanded, "You bastard, take me home, *immediately*!"

"Sit down, Sherri; you're not going anywhere tonight, or for that matter, anywhere tomorrow. You're going to miss your wedding day."

"You stupid bastard!" She stunned him with a roundhouse slap against his right ear.

Danny's clenched right fist caught her solidly on the left side of her jaw. That blow chipped her front teeth and cut her lip. She sprawled backward. Her head struck the slate floor. Her world went black.

Concerned, Danny immediately picked her up and laid her on the sofa. "I'm so sorry," he said. "Don't move. I'll get something to help." First, he ran to the kitchen, got a dishtowel, opened the icemaker, scooped some ice out and put it into the towel making an ice pack. He ran back to Sherri and said, "Here, hold this to your mouth." Then he ran to a medicine cabinet, got two aspirin, filled a glass with water and helped Sherri swallow the tablets.

The desperate, dispirited ex-husband and ex-wife sat facing each other without a word for what seemed like an hour—actually 20 minutes. Sherri alternated between periods of irregular breathing and deep sobbing, frightened and fearful now.

Danny attempted conversation. “I’m just so damn frustrated. A few years ago, I posted two major goals to my mental bulletin board. First, I wanted to prove myself to Dad and become wealthy in my own right. I accomplished that with the opening of Hanover Estates. After crossing that hurdle, which brought financial stability, I hoped to remarry you. I never figured you’d get involved with anybody. I was sure you’d be glad to have me back in your life.”

Trying to reason with him, she said, “Danny, don’t you see? You’re the same self-centered spoiled child you always were. Maybe you love me, but to expect me to still love you after abandoning Bonnie and me, or to still care for you, is ridiculous. Danny, please come to your senses and take me home. Don’t ruin my wedding day. Don’t make your parents ashamed of what you’re doing. I promise I won’t press charges.”

Angry, he spat, “Don’t try to use psychology on me, Sherri. I don’t care *what* my parents think of me. Without you in my life, dammit, I *have* no life.”

“Something’s wrong with this picture, Danny. You don’t contact me for seven years; you suddenly appear and confess you cannot live without me. You managed to live without me for seven years. Danny, get a hold of yourself. Find a girl without all this emotional baggage attached. My happiness is with Clarke; your happiness is with someone else.”

“How many times have you read about high school sweethearts going their separate ways? They go to college, get married and have families. After a while, their spouses die. It’s then the high school sweethearts rekindle their love and get married. Forty or fifty years later, they fall in love all over again. We’ve only been separated for seven years. It’s time to rekindle our love.”

“Danny! You aren’t listening. You aren’t thinking right.”

Not listening, Danny put his arms around Sherri, pressing his lips against her closed mouth. She dropped the ice bag and with all her strength pushed Danny away, yelling, “Don’t ever, *ever* do that again! Now take me home immediately, or suffer the consequences.”

Unmoved, he said, “You’re staying right here tonight and tomorrow. I’ll not permit you to marry that black guy. The truth is, we’re meant for each other. You must see that. No one else can ever have you.”

Sherri saw the emptiness in Danny’s eyes and sensed tragedy coming.

CHAPTER 37
October 18, 2003 (Saturday)
Fredericksburg, Virginia

At 7:30 a.m. Clarke drove to pick up Dave and Kimiko Nelson. He dialed DAD G. Thomas Claiborne on his cell phone. On the fourth ring, Claiborne answered, glancing at the caller ID, "Good morning, Clarke. You must be in trouble calling this early in the morning," he joked. "Can't find your way to the church?"

"Tom, Danny Bonds has abducted Sherri. Her parents and I believe he's holding her captive at the Bonds' vacation home on Lake Anna. We're headed up there now."

"Just in case, are you carrying a weapon?" Clairborne asked.

"Yeah, I've got my Glock .34. I may run into a complicated situation that needs handling by more than one law officer. What's the possibility of sending some of the HRT boys to the scene? I'd appreciate it."

"At this stage, Clarke, the situation cannot be considered under federal jurisdiction, but we believe in helping our own, so call me back later. I'll see what I can do"

* * *

Dave Nelson sat in front with Clarke. Kimiko Nelson and Harper and Billy Anne Bonds sat in the back. The sky was overcast—ghostly gray with a touch of mist—foreboding. Clarke thought, *A sign of things to come*?

Earlier, the morning had started off shakily. Clarke got out of his car, saying good morning to each passenger. All noticed his holstered Glock.

Billy Anne Bonds asked, "Mr. Gable is that firearm really necessary?"

The question irritated him, "Ma'am, your son has abducted my fiancé the day before our wedding. I believe Danny will harm her, himself, me or all three of us if he doesn't get what he wants. I don't intend to let that happen. I do hope, however, we can resolve this peacefully and that's why I need your help. Your influence with Danny could help immeasurably toward a good result."

Billy Anne looked horrified at what she considered over-reaction. She thought, *I'm not going to let anything happen to my son.*

Clarke thought, *In chess parlance, the black knight vanquished the white queen, for now.*

CHAPTER 38
October 18, 2003 (Saturday)
Lake Anna, Virginia

The gloomy morning mist turned into a light drizzle. The flip-flop of the windshield wipers mesmerized the five passengers. The silence was deafening.

Clarke broke through, "Mr. Bonds, would you describe the interior layout of your place? It could be important, if there's any trouble."

"Call me Harper. I don't expect trouble, but it's easy to describe the floor plan. You enter the foyer through the front door. To your immediate right is a stairway to the second floor. Before you reach the stairway, also on the right, there's a doorway into the den. Straight ahead is the kitchen-breakfast room at the rear of the house. Also off the hall, the first door to the left is the master bedroom and bath. The kitchen has a backdoor and an interior door to the laundry room. At the top of the stairs is a common area flanked on each side by a bedroom with an attached bath. A wide door at the back of the common area leads to a large storage area. The design of the home is simple and affords a comfortable getaway place."

"How about alarm systems and are firearms kept on the premises?" Clarke queried.

"Yes, to both questions. Immediately inside the front door on the right wall is the control panel for the alarm system. We secured a weapon for protection. In recent months, there have been some burglaries in the area. By some strange coincidence, it's a Glock, same type of weapon you're carrying."

"What model is it?" asked Clarke.

"It's the light-weight Model G-17. We keep one clip loaded at all times. Oh, and I forgot. We have outside cameras viewing all four sides of the house. The cameras are stationary and wide angle, and you can use any TV set in the house to monitor the outside." Harper suddenly asked Clarke to slow down. "Take the next right turn. The gravel road dead-ends at the house. Park out front."

Clarke parked the Lexus beside the PT Cruiser.

"I guess you were right, Clarke. Looks like my son *is* here."

They saw closed blinds, which was not reassuring. Harper inserted a key in the front door lock, turned it and heard the unlocking click, but the door would not open. "The deadbolt must be in place, and it can only be operated from the inside. The back door also has a deadbolt," he said. Harper pushed the doorbell and heard it chime. No one answered. He took the hinged knocker and rammed it against the brass striker plate three times. "Son!" he yelled. "We know you're in there. The Nelsons, your mother and Mr. Gable are here with me. We're getting wetter and colder by the minute.

A scream rang out.

"Danny!" yelled Harper. "Was that a scream we just heard? Dammit! Open up, Danny!"

Danny shouted, "Go home Dad, and take that FBI slob with you!"

"Is Sherri with you and is she all right? Danny, why the scream?" asked Harper.

"Yeah, she's with me. We have worked things out. She told me to tell Clarke to get lost. She just tripped going up the stairs and screamed when she fell. No big deal, Dad."

"I'd like her to tell me that herself!" demanded Clarke.

"She's upstairs right now, resting. The sex was so good last night, she plumb wore herself out," Danny said, baiting Clarke.

Billie Anne became upset with her son's behavior and pushed forward. "Danny! Open this door, *now*! This foolishness must stop this instant!"

"Mom, Dad, stay out of this! You can't do anything! Nobody'll get hurt if y'all'll just leave and go home. Oh, and I repeat. Take that useless FBI nigger with you!"

Clarke was not surprised that anger made the "N" word surface. "This useless FBI black guy ain't in trouble, but you are, Mr. Rich White Boy." Clarke immediately felt sorry for the unprofessional show of anger. He tried to calm down. "Seriously, Danny, you've crossed the line and have become a criminal. In Virginia, kidnapping is a Class-A felony. The minimum sentence is five years in prison."

"Sherri is my wife! You can't convict a man on kidnapping his own wife. Look, I'm not going to argue anymore. Leave us alone!"

Weary and wet, all five stood there silently with their heads bowed in contemplation. Each mind focused on the same question: *What can I say to make Danny come to his senses*?

After a long agonizing silence, Danny said, "Dad." His voice was calm and the word spoken expressed obvious affection. Five minds focused on the same thought: *Maybe this ordeal is over.*

"Yes, son?" replied the voice of the loving father.

"I'm armed, Dad. If anybody tries to break in, somebody's going to get hurt. I'm just warning you."

"Okay, son. Just try to calm down." The elderly Bonds were visibly devastated.

Mrs. Bonds cried as Mr. Bonds tried to comfort her.

* * *

Sherri was confined in the upstairs storage room, 10 feet by 5 feet, with shelving on three walls. The floor space accommodated the army surplus sleeping bag and the uncased pillow Danny threw into the room. A 40-watt bulb controlled by a long chain provided light. He periodically let Sherri out to use the bathroom.

On this dreary Saturday morning, Danny permitted Sherri to sit at the breakfast room table. The morning meal consisted of a bowl of cereal with milk and a glass of orange juice. As soon as she finished the skimpy breakfast, Danny took her upstairs and forced her back into the storage room prison.

Sherri guessed it was about nine o'clock in the morning. *I should be getting ready for my wedding. I hope somebody has called the church and alerted everyone involved that there probably was not going to be a Nelson-Gable wedding today. Was that a faint banging on the front door? Those are shouts, but I can't make out any of the words. Maybe if I scream, someone'll hear me.*

She screamed with all the available air in her lungs. The rescue party, standing at the front door, heard them but made no attempt at a forced entry.

* * *

Two sets of parents and a fiancé, discouraged by Danny's refusal to open the door, returned to the Lexus. They sat in silence for a few minutes, each one attempting to grip the reality of the situation.

Clarke picked up his cell phone and dialed his boss. On the fifth ring, Clairborne answered. He did not wait for the customary hello.

"Tom, we're having a problem up here. Sherri's definitely been kidnapped by Danny. He's got her holed up at the Bonds' Lake Anna house." Clarke detailed the events that transpired. "Danny Bond's mental stability is rapidly deteriorating. I'm too emotionally involved to make the wisest decisions here, Boss."

"Since you called this morning," said Clairborne, "I've been making some phone calls. Three of our guys have volunteered to go up there. You understand, their involvement is strictly off the record, and we aren't even having this phone call. Artie Majesky is backup if the crap hits the fan, Stan Chapman from HRT will do the negotiating and Al Angelo will handle the special equipment, tear gas projectiles and flash-bang grenades. He also has explosives to blow open doors for a surprise entry. We don't have a thermal imager available, sorry. And, Clarke, stay out of this."

"Thanks for the assist, Tom. I owe you big-time. Maybe Danny will respond favorably to an outside neutral party."

* * *

The troop of five waited in the Lexus, listening to the alternating sounds of soft drizzle and torrential downpours. On another day, the thump of raindrops may have been soothing, but on this day, they added to the dread.

* * *

By the time the three FBI agents arrived, the rain had ceased. The agents got out of their van and Clarke introduced them to the Bonds and the Nelsons.

Artie Majesky said, "Tom clued us in on the situation. Al and I will scout things out. Stan's going to contact the abductor by phone and begin a dialogue. We'll need a number, Mr. Bonds."

"I realize my son is acting peculiar," said Harper, "but I don't want him gunned down. Do you understand?"

"Mr. Bonds," said Artie, "the FBI's not going to initiate any risky or endangering situation." *If I get the little shit in my cross hairs, he's leaving this world. Nobody messes with one of ours. He'd better be prepared to pay the price.*

The phone rang and Danny, at an upstairs window, did not answer. The ringing stopped, but his cell phone began chirping. He decided to answer.

"Yeah . . . this is Danny Bonds. What's your problem?"

"No problem, Mr. Bonds. My name's Stan Chapman. I'm here to listen to your needs. Can I call you Danny?"

"Sure, why not?"

"Danny, do you need anything to make you and Miss Nelson comfortable?"

"No, I came prepared for the long haul. You can do me a favor, though. You and everybody else can get the hell out of here."

"Mr. and Mrs. Nelson are here, Danny. Naturally, they're worried about their daughter. Is she all right, Danny?"

"She's all right. She won't get hurt unless you guys do something stupid."

"Can Mrs. Nelson say hello to her daughter?"

"When you people go back to Fredericksburg or Washington or wherever you came from, Kimiko can call Sherri long distance. That's the deal."

"Danny, we're going to stay here until you and I work out some kind of deal. You're in real estate, right? One party sells; one party buys. They negotiate until each party is satisfied. Let's just work something out that satisfies us both."

"Stan, I'm watching two guys walking around the place and out on the wharf searching the boathouse. I have complete surveillance of the entire house. This action doesn't seem very friendly, Stan."

"I can order those guys to wait in the van, Danny, if that will make you less nervous. See, I can help you, Danny, if you help me. Could I meet with you inside where we can talk *mano a mano*?"

"Like I told my dad, I'm armed. If anybody tries to break into the house, I'll consider it a hostile act and take appropriate measures. My dad will confirm that I can hit what I aim at."

* * *

October 21, 2003 (Tuesday)

On the fourth day of the crisis, DAD Claiborne informed Clarke, "I have to recall my guys tomorrow. This matter should be turned over to the state authorities."

Clarke knew his boss ignored policy by sending the three agents. They expected a resolution in a few hours with both families involved in the negotiations. Harper Bonds even rented three travel trailers to house the families and the agents on site.

The outside temperature was 45 degrees. No wind or stormy clouds masked the penetrating warmth of sunshine that made the cold Tuesday tolerable. The Nelsons and Bonds drank coffee and discussed better days. They missed one another. The only progress in the standoff: The blinds were open. On Monday afternoon, negotiator Stan Chapman promised Danny, "There will be no forcible entries or projectiles of any sort fired through windows, if you let me talk to Sherri." Danny accepted the trade and handed his cell phone to her.

The voice was soft without any tremor, "This is Sherri Nelson."

"Miss Nelson, this is Stan Chapman. I'm with the Hostage Rescue Team and a friend of Clarke Gable. How's your physical condition?"

"I'm doing all right. The meals aren't four stars."

Stan heard the forced chuckle. "Answer these questions yes or no. Try to be nonchalant." Stan knew the information he got would be vital in a forced entry rescue.

"Has there been any physical abuse?"

"Yes, I would like you to tell my mom and dad not to worry."

"Clever answer. Do you think Danny could harm you?"

"There's a possibility, but so far we've had enough to eat."

"One last question. Are you being locked in a room? The upstairs closet appears to be the logical place."

"Sounds good to me. I hope you and Danny can come up with a solution."

Danny grabbed the phone from Sherri. "That's enough chitchat, Stan. This whole thing will be over the minute you leave and promise me that you'll not try to stop Sherri and me from traveling. I'm starting to get aggravated big-time. Apparently, you guys aren't taking me seriously. If I don't get that promise and you're not gone by five o'clock this afternoon, you'll be responsible for a murder-suicide. Is that clear enough for you, Stan!?"

Stan, about to answer, heard only silence as Danny hung up. "Oh shit," he said aloud.

* * *

Allowed out of the closet, she confronted Danny. "What do you mean, murder-suicide!?" Her face contorted with anger. "Stop feeling sorry for yourself dammit. I loved you once, but you destroyed that love by going AWOL. I've had enough of this crap! I'm leaving this second!"

She started to run, heading toward the stairs. But she had taken only two steps when Danny grabbed her from behind and pinned her arms. She screamed as loud as she could. Danny picked her up and threw her like a sack of potatoes. Sherri crashed against the shelving and fell to the floor. She heard the door lock. "You bastard! Somebody help me! Help!" she screamed out.

That was the second time the families heard Sherri scream. Obviously, things were escalating. The time for action was soon coming. Their dread deepened.

* * *

October 21, 2003 (Tuesday)

Stan Chapman, Al Angelo, Artie Majesky, Clarke Gable, Kimiko and Dave Nelson and Harper and Billie Anne Bonds crowded into one trailer.

Stan Chapman offered his ideas to the group. "Sherri advised me there was a possibility of violence. Danny gave us an ultimatum threatening violence. We all heard that last scream, probably in response to being hit, or locked up again in the upstairs closet. It's time to make our move. Danny's helped us by leaving the blinds partially open, so we can now detect some of his movements. When Danny goes downstairs again, I suggest we blow out the front door. Al has already set the charges. We toss in a couple of flash-bangs and rush for the stairs. Danny won't have enough time to react and beat us to the stairway."

"What if he doesn't come downstairs before the five o'clock deadline?" asked an impatient Artie Majesky?

Why does this guy always have to be sarcastic? Clarke wondered. *His smirk is quite irritating.*

"We have two choices, Artie. We blow the door, rush the stairs then toss the stun grenades into the common area at the top of the stairs. It should work unless Danny's reflexes are lightening fast. There's one other alternative. It would require approval from Washington. That option is a little sticky since we aren't even officially here. But anyway, if a clear range of fire is presented, we could take Danny out."

Billie Anne Bonds instantly became hysterical. "No! No! No! You're not going to kill my son! My boy is a good boy. He's not going to hurt anyone! You don't kill someone if they haven't hurt anybody—"

"Mrs. Bonds, Danny has refused to talk with you or your husband," Clarke interrupted. "I agree, we shouldn't attempt a kill shot, but Danny is no longer a good boy. You must be ready to accept the fact that he could be injured or killed during an entry operation."

"It's all your fault, Mr. Gable! Why did you have to go and get engaged to Sherri!? You blacks are always causing trouble!" shrieked Mrs. Bonds.

"Honey," Harper Bonds interjected, "you can't blame Clarke. Danny wanted the divorce. He left them for seven years. Who would've ever dreamt he was still hopelessly in love with Sherri?" He turned to face Stan Chapman. "Please, could we, at least, wait until five o'clock and see what happens? We'll do anything to help our son. We don't want him hurt. He needs help is all."

"Danny made it very clear that he intends a murder-suicide if his demands are not met," said Chapman. "We cannot let him escape and transfer this situation to another place, possibly harming even more people. We absolutely need to contain this. If our surprise entry is successful, we hope to save two lives. With respect to your request, Mr. Bonds, we'll wait to the last minute. We're trained to bring about the best possible outcome, hopefully without injury to anyone. We consider that a success. It's not our desire to hurt anyone, but we must resolve this situation. Your son, remember, has a loaded gun and a hostage. He's threatened a killing and suicide. Truthfully, how things end up is really up to your son."

All agreed on the proposed plan of action. They also thought it might be time to alert the Spotsylvania Sheriff. No one expected the situation to escalate into a life and death struggle.

* * *

The sheriff arrived at exactly 4:00 p.m. He had the forethought not to use the flashers and sirens. Sheriff Hiram Rogers was not in uniform and was unarmed except for the shotgun in the trunk of his car. Tall, thin and bespectacled, he appeared more like a bookworm than a law enforcement officer.

Clarke greeted the sheriff, described the relationship of the parties involved, the chronology of events and why the FBI was unofficially involved.

The Sheriff was satisfied to let the agents handle the situation. "For what it's worth, you're doing the right thing. You must stay in control. I'll hang around, of course. It's my district, but I do suggest we get a couple of ambulances and the fire department out here."

"We'd appreciate that."

"Consider it done."

By 4:30 p.m. Danny had made no move to come downstairs. The four agents donned body armor. Danny Bonds was no match for the FBI in firepower or skill, but the agents would not underestimate their adversary.

"Danny Bonds is no dummy," Clarke muttered. "He has to suspect we'll try to enter the house since we haven't given in to his demands. Good God, right at this moment he may be holding a gun to Sherri's head, waiting to pull the trigger if we force our way into the house. I was supposed to marry her, for God's sake."

"Take it easy, big guy," Stan said. "I know this type of coward. He thinks we'll back down and let him go. He's more worried about avoiding us after his escape than he is with a break-in. I'll grant that the last several times I've called, he hasn't answered the phone. He's sending the message he's prepared for us, so we'd better not act stupid."

"I'm going to fire the breaching charge at 4:55," Al Angelo said. "The only surprise will be that *we* pick the time. Like they say in the movies, let's synchronize our watches."

The FBI instructed the families to wait in the trailers. They objected but relented. Common sense dictated they must comply. Clarke's closeness to Sherri and lesser experience dictated he wait outside.

At 4:55 p.m. Al blew the front door. Majesky and Chapman went through the doorway and headed for the stairway. Majesky lobbed flash bangs into the common area. *Danny Boy, if you're in that room you're blind and deaf. Hope that pineapple lands at Danny's feet and kills the little bastard.*

Artie Majesky was a no-nonsense agent. His motto: If you broke the law you deserved to be punished, not mollycoddled with a slap on the wrist.

* * *

Danny and Sherri sat inside the closet, backs against opposite walls. The single bulb provided harsh lighting. Danny pointed the Glock at Sherri, forefinger resting on the trigger. Confident, in control, the weapon conferred him power and engendered her fear. *Maybe she'll finally realize she can't escape from me.*

Danny heard the muffled blast rip the front door from its frame. His heart pounded in his chest. Protected from the flash of the stun grenade, the thin closet walls offered no protection from the concussion. An already tense Danny Bonds suffered an involuntary reflex of his finger. He sat transfixed, as the Glock fired. He saw a red stain spread across the white turtleneck. Sherri slumped forward.

Majesky yanked the closet door open ignoring his training procedures then rushed inside. "God dammit! The asshole shot Sherri. Al, get the medics up here."

Danny dropped the gun. He sat eyes transfixed on Sherri. He kept shouting, "Oh my God! I didn't mean to shoot her. Oh my God! I didn't mean to shoot her." His lips moved, but he heard no words.

Stan handcuffed the babbling Danny Bonds. For an instant, he thought about putting a bullet in his head and claiming self-defense, but better judgment prevailed.

The medics covered entrance and exit wounds then moved Sherri past Clarke. Clarke behind the medics, standing helplessly as blood seeped from his beautiful Sherri's mouth, indicating a mortal wound.

As the medics put Sherri in the ambulance, Kimiko shrieked, "Is she going to be all right?"

Clarke followed the attendants. "It's serious. We have to pray for a miracle."

Sheriff Rogers contacted Life Evac, a medical transport service. The helicopter would land at a private airstrip four miles away. Rogers told Clarke, "Ride with Sherri in the ambulance to the landing strip. I'll send a patrol car to bring you back to the Bond's house." The sheriff shouted to the small group, "Listen up, everyone. I'm sending Danny Bonds to Culpeper Regional for observation. I'm placing him under arrest. As soon as he's released by the hospital, he'll be transported to the county facilities at Spotsylvania. I allowed agent Gable to ride to the helicopter pick-up site, but he'll be back shortly. The state police are sending out two of their investigators from the BCI. Nobody is to leave the premises until their statements are given. Any questions?"

"Our daughter may be dying. Can't you let us go to Richmond?" pled Dave Nelson. "We can give the damn statements any time. Please, my wife and I need to be with our daughter."

"You have a point. Let me check with the state guys," Rogers replied. After a few minutes, Rogers got out of his patrol car and walked back. "The Nelsons and Agent Gable are cleared to go to the hospital."

Clarke sat next to the collapsible gurney with the flight nurse and flight paramedic. The nurse relayed vital signs to the Medical Center. While they administered plasma and oxygen, Sherri just stared at Clarke.

"Honey, a medical helicopter is going to fly you to the Medical Center. You've got to hang on, sweetheart. We're going to have a long life together." He wanted to cry but had to be strong. "I can't fly with you in the helicopter, but I'm going to drive wide open and may be there before you."

Sherri's tears expressed a final good-bye.

The ambulance stopped near the helicopter. The mission team loaded Sherri aboard and the helicopter lifted off in dimming light. He watched its flashing lights disappear from view. *I'm drowning in an ocean of grief with no one to rescue me. Sherri, how could this happen?*

CHAPTER 39
November 21, 2003 (Friday)
Fredericksburg, Virginia

Though bitter cold outside, the real winter was in his heart. His office door closed, Clarke watched fluttering snowflakes smash and melt against his office window.

The bullet clipped Sherri's inferior vena cava—fatal internal bleeding. The Medical Center had pronounced her DOA.

At Sherri Nelson's burial, the engagement ring, worn for such a sort time, remained on her hand.

Clarke thought back to high school, dancing with Cindy Lind. He got what he referred to as "a good ass whipping" from her brother and a couple of his friends. His career began with that incident. *What a complete failure I've been. With all my training, I should've recognized Danny was dangerous and protected Sherri.*

He reflected, *It's strange how a person becomes a philosopher after a tragedy. Danny crossed the line from sanity to savagery. I'm capable of that same transformation. If Danny walked through the door right now, I'd shoot him right between the eyes without any self-condemnation. Ten to one odds, a jury would find me not guilty.* A flash of insight produced a strange bond with the justitiaphiles. *Lady J and her husband killed to balance the books. Maybe the JLSKT is not so bad. I sure can't admit that conceptualization to anybody. What a price I'd have to pay if I open my mind to such a latent emotion. At least, Danny loved Sherri enough that he didn't add rape to his crime. I'm going to solve the Justice Lovers Case for Sherri.*

Clarke realized there was only a marginal connection between the Justice Lover's Case and Sherri, but he desperately needed a reason to keep going on with living.

* * *

On November 24, 2003, the *Richmond Review* and the *Fredericksburg Bugler* reported:

The well-known real estate entrepreneur, Daniel C. Bonds, will not face first-degree murder charges in the death of Fredericksburg resident Sherri Nelson. Due to extenuating circumstances, the State of Virginia allowed Bonds to plead guilty to second-degree murder, and will probably get seven years with parole in three.

The FBI was appreciative that Sheriff Hiram Rogers praised the Hostage Rescue Team in his discussions with reporters. Good P.R. To the relief of DAD Clairborne, Rogers, on his own initiative, declared he had requested the help of the Feds. *I owe that guy big-time*, mused Clairborne. The brass never knew and no official report would ever state that three agents had volunteered to go to Lake Anna on unofficial business.

CHAPTER 40
November 24, 2003 (Monday)
Washington, DC

On the same day that the *Richmond Review* carried the article about Danny Bonds, Artie Majesky sat in the office of the Assistant Director Zachariah Goldberg. Artie had driven the short distance from Quantico to the Hoover Building in Washington, D.C.

"Artie," said Goldberg, "the Bureau may have to shift gears on the Justice Lovers Case. Downy Westfield called me back in May asking to go public with the case. I've stalled in giving the go-ahead. My dilemma hasn't changed. Protect the pubic from the killers or protect the public from copycat justitiaphiles, as agent Clarke has named the culprits. My new plan of action is to allow Downy to go public only in Mississippi with the hope that national syndicates won't headline the story. Downy will be instructed to limit the profile accompanying the sketches. He'll not be allowed to mention the words 'serial killer team or SKT.' I've reiterated that you, and also Clarke, must be part of the apprehending team if we get some concrete leads."

"Sir," said Artie, "unless these two crazies decide to shoot it out with our guys, it'll be almost impossible to take them out and make it look legit. As I told you earlier, Westfield already suspects some irregularities. He doesn't want us pissing in his rice bowl."

"I refuse to let these people use a public trial to expose their skewed administration of justice," said Goldberg. "What I'm proposing is alien to my core belief, but somebody has to use his finger to plug up the hole in the dike. I'm counting on you to find a way to fix the problem."

Artie knew Goldberg was only covering his ass. *Goldberg's not about to issue a direct order for a hit. Well, that's okay. Sometimes duty demands harsh actions.*

* * *

"Come on in, Artie, what brings you to my government cubby hole?" Clarke asked.

"I was up in Washington this morning. The AD has authorized Westfield to go public on a limited basis. If the JLSKT is from Mississippi, we should get immediate results. Stay loose! We're scheduled to head back to Mississippi on a moment's notice."

"Does Claiborne know about this change in strategy?"

"I don't think so. Zach and Downy are old buddies. Downy called Zach direct, and Zach replied direct."

"Dammit, this is my case. Without my research, no one would even know about the justitiaphiles. No offense, Artie, but why wasn't I consulted or even notified earlier?"

"I think Zach is a little pissed at you for not seeing the complexity of being involved with Sherri Nelson. It's bureau mentality, Clarke. Don't pay it any attention."

Clarke turned his back on Artie, and Artie got up and left. Clarke's scattered thoughts began to fit together like a jigsaw puzzle. *My first priority is to solve this case. Then I'm retiring. As a civilian I can publish my own report about this new psychological phenomena growing within the U.S. I've got to be careful; watch my back. Only a fool would trust Zachariah Goldberg or Artie Majesky. Maybe I can get into Artie's personnel file. No, not much of a chance. I'll just ask around about TAG.*

CHAPTER 41
November 26, 2003 (Wednesday)
Jackson, Mississippi

The front page of the *Jackson Morning Chronicle* featured the composite pictures of a female and male. The headline read, **JACKSON FBI NEEDS YOUR HELP**. Physical descriptions and a profile of the couple were included in the write-up. The FBI wanted to question the pair about several unspecified crimes. The article listed a special phone number to callers. Although they recorded the calls, the caller need not identify himself or herself because there was no reward offered.

* * *

Mike stepped out onto the front porch, comfortably dressed in cotton pajamas and fleece-lined house shoes. The waters of Ross Barnett Reservoir looked like a gold mirror reflecting the rays of the morning sun. Mike had paid $125,000 for the 2-acre lot on Cypress Point, but he considered it a cheap price. He had access to spectacular sights on the lake—east, west and north. Tall stately cypress trees framed a picturesque view of the lake. He picked up the morning paper and reentered the house. As he headed back through the house to the breakfast area, he slipped off the rubber band that held the rolled paper. Sitting down at the breakfast table, he opened to the paper to scan the headlines.

"Hey, Tess, come here, quick! I want to show you something."

"Can't it wait? I'm making up the bed."

"Nope, you need to see this, right now."

As soon as Tess appeared in the breakfast area, Mike handed her the *Jackson Morning Chronicle* and commented, "Our pictures are on the front page."

"God help me, Jesus. Those sketches look like we posed for the artist. Let me read the article."

* * *

That first day, the Jackson District received 24 calls from the Jackson area and 10 calls statewide. After seven days the calls stopped. Thirty-six calls came in from the Jackson area and 22 calls statewide. SAC Downy Westfield counted 17 calls from Jackson and 7 of the statewide calls, an amazing 41 percent identified the couple as Mike and Tess Miller. Downy picked up the phone book, jotted down their address at 100 Cypress Point Drive, and smiled with satisfaction. *I'm not calling Goldberg until we check this baby out.*

* * *

December 3, 2003

They sat in the sunroom watching sailboats tack back and forth on the reservoir.

"Well it's been eight days and nothing's happened," commented Tess.

"The FBI is checking us out. Have no doubt. They must've become aware of some common denominator that linked our executions, probably the 13 month interval between the executions. If they discovered that time frame, the process to locate us would be easy. So assume the law is going to show up at our doorstep. Got any suggestions?" Mike asked.

"It might be a blessing in disguise. We did our part, and quite successfully, I might add. A trial is a great way to inform the U.S.A. about our efforts to administer justice. We put the blame on the system. A jury might buy that and give us a free pass. Look what they did in the O.J. case," Tess replied.

"I'll bet F. Lee Bailey would love to take our case," said Mike. "It's going to be a super high profile case and would add more prestige to his persona. The book rights alone would be worth a fortune. That bait ought to reel in some kick-ass lawyer. I believe we should employ Steve Franklin. He's not only my golfing buddy, but one crackerjack lawyer. I'll talk to him after the holidays. I don't believe the FBI will make a move until after New Year's."

* * *

December 10, 2003 (Wednesday)

"Zach, this is Downy. I've got some good news for you."

"Good news is always welcome. Hit me."

"The sketches worked. A lot of calls came in, most pointing to the same couple. I believe we found your SKT. We've checked them out for an entire week to be sure."

"That's good detective work, Downy. Here's what I want you to do. Get some photographs of the Millers and e-mail them to us. I'll have pictures packaged with four other pairs and have agents approach various witnesses. As soon as we get confirmation, I'll send Clarke and Artie down there, and you boys can initiate an apprehension procedure."

CHAPTER 42
December 16, 2003 (Tuesday)
Tipton, Mississippi

Agent Chris Martein's destination was the small North Mississippi town of Tipton. Leaving from Jackson, he stopped at the Greenstown Motor Lodge. Mr. Farley Ferris still worked at the lodge, promoted from desk clerk to manager.

"Mr. Ferris, would you look at this picture lineup; see if you recognize the two people who asked about Bobby Dan Cantrell." Ferris looked and pointed to Tess and Mike Miller. "Thank you for your cooperation."

Martein continued northward to Tipton and pulled in at the Quik-Fill. The question and response were the same. Owner DeMarco remembered the two people who "conversed too damn long with Cantrell and backed up business."

* * *

December 18, 2003 (Thursday)
Alachua, Florida

Mrs. Robert Lewis Eddiceston still lived alone in her beautiful Queen Anne Victorian house on L.N. Pearce Street. She did not invite Agent Hank Thompson into the house. Darlene figured she couldn't tell a real agent from a bogus agent after her experience five years before. However, she was not reluctant to view the 10 photos. "Those are the two cold-blooded murderers who shot my sister and her husband to death. You make sure they get the chair, young man." She slammed the front door in the agent's face, but he got what he came for.

* * *

December 20, 2003 (Monday)
Nashville, Tennessee

Agent Brad Watkins was impressed with the beauty of Rita Gallo-Jones, who he met at her real estate office. *She's not a spring chicken*, he thought, *but I do enjoy being in the company of attractive women.*

Rita disliked the mental undressing and curtly said, "I'm busy, Agent Watkins. Why are you here?"

"Sorry to disturb you during the holiday season, ma'am, all's I need is for you to look at these pictures and see if you recognize who stabbed the governor?"

"Those are the two who masqueraded as members of a security detail from the Tennessee Highway Patrol."

* * *

January 5, 2004 (Monday)
Bethlehem, Pennsylvania

Nancy Shotz, whose husband was killed by a hit and run driver in April of 2000, had remarried. She now lived in a exclusive subdivision in the Saucon Valley area south of Bethlehem. Agent Lily Saunders phoned the now Nancy Banacek and made an appointment.

"Those are the two people who asked me where the Berger residence was a few days before Tommy was run over. I thought they acted peculiar."

* * *

January 5, 2004 (Monday)
Madisonville, Alabama

Agent Chance Masters felt odd being the only black man in Anny's. He felt more relaxed when a nice looking black waitress approached his table.

He asked for a particular hostess, a particular booth and a particular waitress.

"Hello. I'm Tommeka. I'll be your waitress tonight. Can I get you anything to drink?"

"Yes, I'll have an unsweetened ice tea, but first, Ms. Tommeka; I'm Agent Masters, FBI. Would you to take a look at this photo lineup, see who you recognize?"

"Yeah, those two. They paid me 40 bucks to let them sit undisturbed right at this same table. It was strange how they watched Marly Magruder all night."

By golly, Miss Molly, that takes care of business, thought Masters. *Now it's time for a little relaxation.* "May I study your menu for a few minutes?" He wondered if Tommeka would like to take a "Chance," and chuckled to himself.

* * *

January 8, 2004 (Thursday)
Dallas, Texas

Agent Stafford Louis would be the only agent to report back negatively to his headquarters. José Cortezzo could not identify anyone from the 10 pictures; he was visually impaired. He only saw the general shape of the vehicle, not the occupants.

CHAPTER 43
January 9, 2004 (Friday)
Jackson, Mississippi

"We've got to persuade Mack Franklin to take our case," Mike declared. Since their decision in December, neither Mike nor Tess exhibited any trepidation in facing the lawyer. Now doubt crept in like a thief, stealing their courage.

The couple discussed the possibility of capture, and in fact, considered eventual detection as a probability. Mike and Tess became deeply entrenched in the justification of their project. They viewed arrest and a subsequent trial not as a setback but an opportunity. The sketches in the paper made them face reality. Today they hoped Attorney Mack Franklin could devise a strategy that kept them out of prison.

When clients first met Steven Alva "Mack" Franklin, they were impressed. He was 6'5" tall and tipped the scales at 255 pounds with no sign of middle-aged pudginess.

Some clients asked how he got the nickname "Mack". Steven Alva Franklin attended the University of Mississippi from 1972 to 1976. His major was pre-law. Coach Duffy Vance needed a fullback and asked the big sophomore to try out for the team. Franklin became the most powerful fullback in South East Conference history. He flat ran over people like a Mack® truck. The team shortened his name to "Mack". Franklin led Ole Miss to the 1976 NCAA National Title and came in third place in the Heisman Trophy balloting. Teams offered huge salaries but could not lure him into pro-football. He dreamed of becoming a famous attorney in the mold of Clarence Darrow.

After getting his law degree from Yale University, he returned to Mississippi, joining the firm of Barkley, Jamison and Murray. Articulate, a master of research, pleasingly animated and commanding in stature, he became the most sought-after defense attorney in Mississippi. His exploits were the basis of two made-for-TV legal thrillers. One case involved a childcare facility director falsely accused of molesting some of the toddlers. The second case involved a cardiologist wrongly accused of terminating the lives of several patients with advanced heart failure.

Franklin's father had been a Senior Geologist with Pan American Petroleum Corporation, which eventually became AMOCO. It was natural, then, when he became a man of wealth, to invest in the oil business. When introduced to Mike Miller, Franklin invested in a number of Miller's prospects and recovered seven-fold on his investment. The two men enjoyed each other's company, both professionally and socially. Mike never beat Mack on the golf course and blamed it on their two-year age difference. Mack believed Mike just played "client golf."

Franklin's office was in a new building on Highland Colony Park Drive, Ridgeland, Mississippi. In the late '80s, some businesses and professionals left Jackson to avoid taxes and the urban blight. So began a northward migration to the towns of Ridgeland and Madison.

Tess and Mike drove to see Mack Franklin, anxious to obtain counsel.

CHAPTER 44
January 9, 2004 (Friday)
Washington, D.C.

On the same day the Millers sat in their lawyer's office, Zachariah Goldberg made a phone call to Jackson. "Downy, we have confirmed that the two suspects you identified are indeed the SKT. The agency has no doubt about our assessment. Six eyewitnesses put the pair on or near each locale at the time of the murders in five out of the six cases. Clarke Gable did one hell of a job alerting the agency to this SKT."

"I trust, when all this goes down, the Jackson District will get some kudos."

"We're still trying to determine how to keep these people under wraps," said Zack Goldberg. "We're fearful of a copycat explosion. Recognition for solving the case has to be kept within the agency and not released to the public. Either way, the Jackson boys will get their share of praise."

"Listen, Zach, I told the guys you sent down here that there's not going to be any Ruby Ridge crap in my district—shoot first and ask questions later."

Zach ignored the comment. "I sent Artie Majesky to Jackson yesterday." Then he lied, "Clarke's tied-up giving testimony on a case, but should be able to fly down before the real action begins. My guys are in a 'witness-only' mode. If you need them, okay, but they're strictly there for observation and assistance with background on the case."

CHAPTER 45
January 9, 2004 (Friday)
Jackson, Mississippi

After Mike introduced Tess to his golf partner, the justitiaphiles discussed their six projects, avoiding the word murder. They started with Bobby Dan Cantrell in 1997, Irene Day Collins and John Mark Collins in 1998, Andrew Jackson Forrest in 1999, Thomas R. Shotz in 2000, Marlene Magruder in 2001, and the Rev. J. Oliver Claxton in 2002. Tess kept copious notes on each crime and collected newspaper and magazine articles written about the victims. They talked for almost four hours, uninterrupted by Franklin, who recorded the session and wrote on a yellow legal pad from time-to-time. Mike did not read any condemnation, amazement or any other emotion from his lawyer friend. The black wavy hair with streaks of gray, the penetrating blue eyes, and the strong jaw line portrayed a look of confidence. Mike knew hc chose the right man. The question remained: Would Mack take their case?

Finally Franklin spoke. "Be back here at 8:00 a.m., Wednesday. That's the fourteenth." He rose from his leather swivel chair and added, "I'll have some questions, contracts for you to sign and an initial strategy. Forgive the appearance of being distant, but I never comment on a case without perusal. You two head straight home and do not leave the house tonight. If the FBI shows up, instruct them that you have contacted me. Get hold of me immediately, even if it's three o'clock in the morning."

"Thanks for reviewing our case, Mack. See you next week." Mike noticed that Mack did not say, "Tell the FBI that I'm your lawyer," but he expected Mack was going to jump on the case immediately.

CHAPTER 46
January 14, 2004 (Wednesday)
Washington, DC

As Yogi is purported to have said, "It's déjà vu all over again," thought Clarke. *Was it only eleven months since I took this same Delta flight 1037?* In the two-engine jet on his way to Jackson, Mississippi, he watched a shadow of the wing on the puffy white clouds below. *I was happy then because Sherri had entered my world. At that time, I also trusted the guy sitting next to me. Well both Sherri and the trust are gone. It worries me that Artie flew to Jackson on the ninth. Why would he go alone?*

The FBI electronically stores cases, financial and organizational information, agents' names and backgrounds, technical data, criminal and terrorist activities and any other areas of related significance. Certain selected agents use a special search engine named "Overlord" to access and retrieve information from this secure data bank, known as the "Realm".

Clarke called in a favor to one of his agency friends to access the Realm. The friend agreed to run TAG through the system, but refused to do any probing on Artie Majesky. The report came back to Clarke with no reference made to the Tactical Assessment Group. Clarke began asking all his fellow agents about TAG and Artie Majesky.

Only one person offered information on TAG. "Back in the '60s," the source said, "the Bureau believed Jimmy Hoffa, incarcerated in 1967, engineered the 1968 assassination of Attorney General Robert Kennedy. Hoffa hated RFK for his frenetic push to put him behind bars. Conspiracy proponents believed there was a second gunman, supposedly hired by Hoffa, aiding Sirhan-Sirhan. In 1971, Hoffa was released from prison, but the FBI wisely made no immediate move toward retribution. Then in 1975, Jimmy Hoffa disappeared. Shop talk held that TAG did the job and successfully laid the blame on the mob." The source continued, "When the FBI wanted someone removed, the shadowy TAG performed the service." Clarke wondered how a covert group within the FBI could go undetected for so many years.

He also learned little about Artie: He was not married; did not fraternize with any of the agents; was humorless and had been an Army Ranger before joining the Bureau. Clarke guessed Artie's assignment was to eliminate the justitiaphiles. Artie would probably create some type of incident during the arrest that would necessitate his shooting Lady J and her husband.

CHAPTER 47
January 14, 2004 (Wednesday)
Jackson, Mississippi

The receptionist, a perky blonde fresh out of college, ushered Tess and Mike into Franklin's personal office.

"Good morning. Can I have Mandy bring you anything to drink?"

"No thanks," both Millers chorused.

"Okay, let's get started. Before I discuss my fees and recommendations, a preamble is necessary. I realize many citizens believe our legal system is hobbled by technicality and manipulated by egotistical judges and attorneys, but despite its faults and failures, it is the bulwark against anarchy. Your method of correcting the situation is totally alien to civilized behavior and without a trace of mercy. However, as citizens of the United States, you are entitled to all the protections guaranteed by our Constitution. To that end, if you still desire to have me represent you, I promise a vigorous defense. All that being said, do you want to hire me as your attorney of record?"

Mike answered with relief and without hesitation, "You're our man. I've watched you play golf and you always play to win. I think you'll do the same for us. We realize we'll probably be convicted, maybe even get the death penalty. We want people to know that we aren't psychos, just ordinary Americans who care. With due respect to your personal thoughts, Mack, we meted out punishment to the very people who abused or ignored the law. The individuals we selected had shown no mercy or civilized behavior in the commission of their crimes."

"I'm just stating the facts of society and law," replied Franklin. He looked at Tess and thought: *How gorgeous she looks. It's difficult to associate such a beautiful face with such ugly crimes.*

Tess misinterpreted his blank look as a possible reconsideration and rejection of defending them in court.

"Mr. Franklin, are you rethinking representing us?" she questioned.

"No, no," he said, "just letting my mind wonder a little before our serious discussion. Sorry. Let's get started. When a homicide is committed in a certain state, that state will try the case, but there are some exceptions when the Feds claim jurisdiction. Crime on federal land, destruction of federal property, the killing of a federal employee and the offense of kidnapping, where the victim is transported across state lines, are a few of the incidences covered under federal purview. The choice of state: Mississippi, Florida, Tennessee, Pennsylvania, Alabama or Texas, will depend on which crime has the best chance of a successful prosecution. Another factor is which states have a good record for applying the death penalty. That would send you to Texas."

Franklin shuffled some papers as he organized his thoughts.

He continued, "I encourage you to consider requesting separate trials. This tactic will make the prosecutor's job more difficult, more expensive and more time consuming, which may open the door to deal-making."

"We have talked about jointly being tried and testifying on our own behalf," Tess piped up.

"No decision is required on these proposals at this point. Just give them some thought for now. In the future, the indictment will dictate our response," advised Franklin. "Just a couple more suggestions. I strongly encourage you surrender to the authorities. I'll call the FBI and say that the pictures in the newspaper closely resemble two of my clients. That you'll voluntarily be at their office on a certain date, certain time. The image we portray is of respectable citizens, not criminals in handcuffs waiting to be dragged from their home. Does that approach sound reasonable?"

Mike answered quickly, "We weren't planning on running, so go ahead and make the arrangements."

Franklin produced a five-page document. "This is a contract giving me exclusive rights to your story. No judge would permit your profiting from your unlawful acts. You're empowering me to stop any other party from using the material for personal gain. Don't argue or ask questions. We need to establish the lawyer-client relationship immediately. There is no time for delays in reviewing and haggling. Just sign the document." Franklin shoved the papers toward Mike and Tess. They signed without protest.

"As you probably realize, the expense of your defense will be staggering. At this point, we don't know if we're looking at a single trial or multiple trials.

An initial retainer of $100,000 will be required. At some point, monthly invoicing will be necessary. Do you have any questions?"

"No, you seem to have covered all the salient points," said Mike.

"From this point forward, you do not make any statements or sign any documents without my approval. Do not give any answers, even yes or no, to any reporters who might confront you. Just be cool."

"Tess and I get the message, Mack."

"I'll call you as soon as I get a time set up for your surrender. Stay out of sight."

Mike extended his hand to Franklin, and Tess said, "Thank you for your time and advice." No one smiled.

* * *

January 14, 2004 (Wednesday)

Careful to avoid detection by both the JLSKT and the local FBI agents, Artie Majesky tracked the Millers, monitoring their movements for six days.

Artie phoned Assistant Director Goldberg on Friday the 9th and reported that the Millers contacted an attorney named Steve Franklin.

His manner cool, Goldberg said, "The Millers obviously realize they've been identified in one or more of the killings. They may be contemplating surrendering to the authorities. That move would eliminate any chance of a planned misadventure during an attempt to arrest the Millers. I trust you have some alternative plans, Artie."

"I'm prepared to solve the problem in a satisfactory manner. When is Clarke scheduled to fly to Jackson?"

"Early evening today."

"I'll attempt to complete my assignment before he arrives. Clarke knows we're to stay together. That order, along with the possible surrender, makes for scarce liquidation opportunities. It'll be a miracle to pull this one off without Downy suspecting FBI involvement."

"That's why you get the tough jobs, Artie. Keep me posted." Goldberg hung up the phone.

Artie speculated, *Wednesday's child is full of woe. I wonder if one of the Millers was born on that day. It doesn't matter, 'cause today's going to be a big woe day for them.* He followed the Millers to the office of Steve Franklin. Since Monday, the local FBI had stopped tracking. *I don't have to worry about my fellow agents messing up my plans.*

Parking next to the Miller's BMW, he scanned the lot for witnesses. Bending next to his car as if inspecting his left front tire, he focused on the right front tire of the Miller's car. He removed the stem and replaced it with a combination valve and explosive device. Within 100 yards he could trigger the remote control. Very little air escaped changing the valve—the tire did not appear flat. Artie let out a few pounds of air of the left front tire to equalize handling.

* * *

Artie tailed the BMW along Old Agency Road, which doglegged and became Jackson Street. Artie knew the Millers would turn right off Jackson onto old 51-South, then left on Lake Harbour Drive, intersecting with Spillway Road. Spillway Road crossed the Barnett Reservoir dam. Artie intended to detonate the explosive on Spillway Road. *The directional charge will rip the right front tire apart, simulating to all but an expert a blowout. Mike Miller will lose control, jump the guardrail and roll down the embankment into the reservoir. Farewell to the justitiaphiles. What a mouthful to even pronounce.*

* * *

"The reservoir is gorgeous today," Mike said. "Maybe it's a sign that things are not as gloomy as they seem."

"Boy, are you an optimist, Mr. Miller. I guess that's why I love you, despite all the bad habits you've exhibited over the last six years."

Mike, about to answer, heard an explosion and felt the vibration in the steering wheel. The BMW veered right, smashing into the landside guardrail. The car careened off the first guardrail, and struck the opposite railing at a right angle. On impact, the car cartwheeled over the waterside railing. The battered BMW bounced and landed on the driver's side. The thin steel skin was no match for the jagged, solid boulders. The car rolled three times before splashing into the reservoir.

Artie smiled as he watched the auto float an instant, then sink in ten feet of water.

* * *

Tess remembered hearing a noise like a firecracker. She felt the car veer as Mike screamed, "Oh hell!" A sledgehammer hit her in the chest and face when the airbag inflated. Shattered windows showered safety glass in jagged, irregular pellets. Tess lost her equilibrium in the tumbling car, dazed to the point of unconsciousness. The cold water rushing through the windows shocked her alert. The BMW, oriented wheels down, gave Tess direction. The punctured airbags deflated. Tess gulped air from a small air bubble above her head. She unlatched the seat restraint and dragged her body through the missing passenger side window. She pushed off from the car roof and surfaced gasping for oxygen.

Artie stopped his car and ran to the mangled guardrail. The woman bobbed to the surface. *The man must be dead or trapped in the car*. He considered going down the rocks and drowning the woman, when a car, brakes squealing, stopped behind his car.

A teenage girl cried out, "I was a little ways back of you and saw the car go over. Have you called 911?"

"No, I haven't. Go ahead and report the accident. I'll see if I can help the two occupants." *Shit, I shouldn't have stopped to reconnoiter. My ass is going to get reamed for that stupid impulse.*

Treading water, Tess looked desperately for Mike. She saw a man standing atop the hill and yelled, "Hey! Help me save my husband. He must still be in the car."

Artie made his way down the slope, careful not to turn an ankle or twist a knee on the loose rocks.

Tess took a deep breath, jack-knifed then dove to the wreckage. Through the clear water she saw Mike held by the seatbelt. She unlatched the seat belt. Her lungs bursting, she resurfaced.

Artie took off his shoes, suit coat and weapon.

Tess surfaced, saw Artie and pleaded, "We need to get my husband to the surface, quick!"

Artie dove to the BMW. His daily exercise routine gave him strength and endurance. He grabbed the man, pulled him through the window and surfaced before his lungs demanded oxygen.

As Artie pulled the man ashore, Tess screamed. A piece of chrome protruded from Mike's sternum. Artie detected no pulse.

"Your husband's dead, lady," he called out dispassionately. *And I wish you were, too.*

Artie grabbed his coat, shoes and weapon, scaled the embankment and jumped into his rental car.

Onlookers focused on the woman, cradling the lifeless man in her lap.

* * *

The first ambulance rushed Tess Miller to the University Hospital for examination and treatment. The second ambulance containing Mike Miller headed for the Medical Center. The emergency room doctors tagged him DOA, "Dead on Arrival."

"Mr. Goldberg, this is Artie Majesky with a field report. I initiated a tire failure and one subject's dead. Tess Miller survived. She and a teenage girl, who stopped at the scene, saw me. It was an error on my part, sir."

"We cannot concern ourselves with what should have happened and if you exposed your cover unnecessarily. We have two urgent problems —how to handle the woman and how to close out this damn case. Come up with an elimination plan for the woman."

"I'm working on it, now. I've got to get my clothes changed and go pick up Clarke at the airport. I'll check back later tonight."

* * *

Although Downy Westfield, Steve Franklin and Clarke Gable were in different parts of Jackson, they were all watching the six o'clock CMTV news broadcast featuring Farley Winston and Rolanda James.

Winston announced, "Here's Rolanda with the top news story of the day."

Rolanda nodded toward Farley and then looked directly into the camera. "A tragic accident has taken the life of one of Jackson's most prominent businessmen, Michael Miller. His wife Tess Miller survived the mishap with minor injuries. The Millers were traveling southeast on the three-mile-long Spillway Road in a late model BMW, when an apparent blowout sent the car hurdling over a guard rail and into Barnett Reservoir. We now go to Reporter Kate Bower on the scene."

The camera showed a tow truck using a winch attached to a taut steel cable slowly dragging the wreckage of an auto from the lake. The TV camera scanned the damaged guardrails, the activity of a diver, several policemen doing crowd control, and the long line of traffic backed up in both directions. Kate Bower said in measured words, "I was able to talk to a teenage witness a few minutes ago. She was about half a mile behind two cars when the first car suddenly bounced from one railing to the other and then toppled into the lake. The girl said that the woman surfaced after the car submerged, but the male driver never did come up. She said a man, in a trailing car, dove into the water and rescued the man, who looked deceased. After the guy pulled the dead man from the lake, he rushed back to his car and drove off without saying a word. The witness said the man was carrying a gun. Back to you, Rolanda."

* * *

Clarke, furious, leaped from his bed, opened his door, moved directly across the hall and rapped loudly on Artie's door. As the door opened, Clarke pushed the door backward throwing Artie to the carpeted floor.

"You dirty son-of-a-bitch. I don't know how you did it, but you caused that accident. You were the guy with the gun that drove off in a hurry."

Artie slowly raised himself to a standing position. "Listen, buddy you're mistaken. Goldberg sent me down here to put the Millers under a loose surveillance. The locals terminated their coverage. I was following them when it looked like they had a tire blowout. I even tried to save the man's life. You heard it on the TV. I didn't want to blow my cover, so I left the scene. There was absolutely nothing else I could do."

"Why didn't you say anything at the airport?"

"Mr. Goldberg wanted to tell you himself tonight."

"Artie, you're not good enough to run a lie by me. I also know that TAG's not official FBI and is a little fuzzy around the edges. Here's the deal, Majesky. I don't want you anywhere around me. If anything happens to the Miller woman, I will personally accuse you of murder. Mr. Goldberg would not like that scenario."

* * *

Downy Westfield could not believe what he saw on the evening news. Steve Franklin had called him just after lunch advising him that his clients would surrender themselves at ten o'clock the next morning at the McCoy Building. The lawyer further advised that the surrender was not an admission of guilt and was in response to the similarity of the sketches shown in the newspaper. He thanked Franklin for his cooperation but wondered if Washington had something to do with the accident. His FBI heart said no, but his logical mind said yes.

* * *

Steve Franklin sat eating a TV dinner of shrimp and chicken gumbo. He and his wife often joked that they would bet no one could tell that gumbo from fresh made. As he finished eating, he saw the news flash about Mike and Tess. "Oh! My Lord! Honey, I have to go to the Medical Center to see a client."

* * *

Around 8:00 p.m. Washington time, 7:00 p.m. Jackson time, the phone rang in Clarke's room.

"Hello," he said.

"Clarke, Goldberg here. I wanted to tell you myself about Mike Miller, the male justitiaphile. Artie called and said you learned of it from the TV news. Don't be too upset with Artie, he was doing his job." Goldberg changed the subject. "You and Artie get back to Quantico tonight on a late flight. I've scheduled a meeting for ten o'clock in the morning."

CHAPTER 48
January 15, 2004 (Thursday)
Quantico, Virginia

Clarke recalled these same five people sitting in the same place in November 2002, when they first discussed the Justice Lovers Case. His eyes drifted from Assistant Director Zachariah Goldberg, to his boss DAD Tom Claiborne then finally came to rest on the visage of Agent Artie Majesky. Clarke could not resist snidely asking, "See any bad automobile accidents, lately, Artie?"

Molly, recording the meeting, sitting directly behind Clarke, felt tension permeate the room.

Still playing the tough guy, Artie said, "I have been informed that most psychologists learn about people by just listening, so listen up. One more wise-ass crack directed at me and I'm going to break my policy of not using my hands on people." He held up his huge hands.

Clarke was about to respond to the threat when AD Goldberg harshly remonstrated, "You are both out of line. I'd better not hear this kind of verbalization in my presence ever again. Is that understood?"

The two unrepentant agents nodded.

"Thank you for your attention, children," Goldberg chided. "As you're aware, there has been a tragic circumstance that must be factored into handling the Justice Lovers Case. I have instructed Downy Westfield to stand down on any movement until further orders from Washington. I'm sure each one of you has but one thought: Where do we go from this point forward on the Justice Lovers Case? This morning, I called this meeting for aid in answering that question."

Clarke thought, *Why are so many directors ostentatious? The big intro's not needed here. I'd like to knock that smug look off of Artie's ugly puss. I'd probably spend a week in the hospital patching up broken bones, but it would be worth the pain.*

"I have a critical question, Clarke. Do you think the death of her husband will preclude Tess Miller from continuing these crimes?"

Clark had already thought about how Lady J would accept the loss of her husband and partner in crime.

"As stated in my earlier reports," said Clarke, "Tess and Mike Miller, assuming they were the JLSKT, are not and were not psychopathic or sociopathic. Some authorities are using the two conditions interchangeably and others argue about the differences, but in this case, our SKT are neither, because of their conduct and divergence from standard definitions. One of the markers that identified the SKT was that they killed every 13 months for six years. This July, they did not commit a seventh murder as best as we can determine. The hiatus demonstrates that forces beyond their control did not drive the SKT. The break also leads me to conclude that they had a logical reason for cessation, evidencing a normal capacity to understand and reason. The conclusion then is that the SKT team may have decided that they had achieved their goal and terminated their crusade."

"You haven't answered my question. Will the female SK, if free, choose victims in the future now that her husband is dead?" Goldberg barked.

Clarke, with elbows on the conference table, touched the fingers of his left hand to the corresponding fingers of his right hand, lowered his head and pressed the joined thumbs to the bridge of his nose. After a short pause, he raised his head and answered Goldberg. "That long prologue was a little bit of CMA," Clarke answered wittily. "The answer to your question is speculative, but I believe my answer is correct. Besides marriage, Tess and Mike Miller bonded deeply in what they perceived as a worthwhile attempt to improve society and our administration of justice. They relied on each other as the key factor in a successful team effort. Suddenly the marriage and the team bond dematerialized. Tess Miller will not be a threat in the future unless a clone of Mike Miller appears."

"I've got two more interrelated questions for you, Clarke," Goldberg said, continuing his examination. "Do you believe this is the first and last case that will involve what you have termed justitiaphila? Do you believe going public with the case will be beneficial or harmful?"

Clarke avoided being overly dramatic and abstained from psychobabble. He spoke directly to Goldberg. "Sir, conceivably the Justice Lovers Serial Killing Team could be a one-time phenomenon. Statistics show that only 20 percent of serial killings are committed in conjunction with a partner or as a band. It's therefore more likely that crime investigators will uncover individual justitiaphiles. I subscribe to the theory that when you have a large population, there can be a multitude of individuals, independent of each other, formulating the same idea at the same time. So, the answer to your first question is no. However, let me qualify my answer."

Goldberg lowered his head and rubbed his brow with his left hand. His only expression on hearing the negative answer was, "Damn."

Clarke felt sorry for Goldberg. The AD had to make a tough decision.

Clarke added, "The JLSKT had two distinct signatures—13 months between crimes and the retribution angle. If retribution was the only signature, it would have been difficult but not impossible to link the various murders to a single serial killing team. Yes, there will be more justitiaphiles discovered, operating alone and as a team, but the FBI can handle the problem." *I'm not sure I believe what I just said, but there's no use trying to put out the fire by pouring gasoline on it!* Clarke rationalized.

"I thank you for the candid and thoughtful answers on a probable threat from other justitiaphiles," Goldberg muttered. "I hope your answer to my second question is a little more comforting."

Before Clarke continued, he wanted to clear the air about several issues. He knew he had to be careful in dealing with the AD. Surely, Artie reported their confrontation in Jackson to his controller.

"I would like to defer answering your last question, with your permission. I have one question, sir, and one comment." Clarke advised.

"You have the floor, Agent Gable."

Clarke noticed the address change from Clarke to Agent Gable. *No doubt a subtle admonition to be careful. Two can play that game.*

"Agent Artie Majesky was ordered to Jackson several days before I made the trip. You originally declared that he was to be non-involved and was to simply monitor my movements and decisions."

Artie sat straight up in his chair. The AD grinned slightly and removed his horned-rim glasses. His baldhead almost imperceptibly reddened before he answered. "Agent Gable," said Goldberg, "you're a valuable asset to the FBI. Your work's recognized as first class. The disposition of agents is not your concern, but I'll answer the question. Artie went to Jackson to monitor and grade the surveillance measures put into place by Westfield. The Jackson boys had good technique, but they prematurely stopped the surveillance. It was fortunate Artie could act as a stopgap. Now what is your comment?"

"It's absolutely imperative that I be allowed to interview Tess Miller. We have made a lot of assumptions and speculations that need verification or need discarding. I never thought I would take this type of position, but it's my viewpoint that the advancement of psychology, profiling and criminology is more important than prosecuting Tess Miller. It is essential that we study every aspect of her life and correlate those findings with the unveiling of her psyche. The primary step in recognition, cure or prevention is research. In this case, the laboratory is Tess Miller."

"The Director and I are opposed to revealing the issue of justitiaphilia to the public. I don't like the direction your comment's heading," said Goldberg.

"Mr. Goldberg, I know your concerns about a copycat explosion. To deny a complete study of this case and ultimate reporting to the medical and investigative community would be, if you'll pardon the expression, criminal." Clarke hoped this pun would soften his statement on Goldberg's second question.

"Your comments will be given serious consideration," was all Goldberg offered.

"I have one additional point of discussion," Clarke said. He turned his head and made direct eye contact with Artie before he continued. "I'll assume that it was a coincidence that Mr. Majesky was following the Millers when a sudden blowout occurred. Now, if Tess Miller was also accidentally killed, I would conjecture whether fate was aided by some human hand or TAG."

"For the second time today, you're out of line Agent Gable," shouted Goldberg. "I don't like the implication along with the disrespect to your superiors. Your career may be in serious jeopardy."

Tom Claiborne spoke for the first time. "Zach, you and I go back a long way. You moved up the ladder a little faster, but I have many influential friends in important positions in and out of the FBI structure. I happen to approve of the positions and comments of Agent Gable. You have been a little tough on one of the brightest agents we have in the BSU. So maybe both of you can back off, come up with a satisfactory plan of action and bury the implied threats."

* * *

February 3, 2004 (Tuesday)

On this blistering cold morning, received in the office of G. Thomas Claiborne, Quantico, Virginia marked F.Y.E.O., was an officially sealed envelope.

Re: AGREEMENT BETWEEN FBI AND TESS MILLER

ITEM 1: Tess Miller will be offered immunity from prosecution by the U.S. Justice Department in the wrongful deaths of:

(a)	Bobby Dan Cantrell	01/09/97 (MS)
(b)	Irene Day Collins	02/12/98 (FL)
	John Mark Collins	02/12/98 (FL)
(c)	Andrew Jackson Forrest	03/14/99 (TN)
(d)	Thomas R. Shotz	04/06/00 (PA)
(e)	Marlene Magruder	05/03/01 (AL)
(f)	Rev. J. Oliver Claxton	06/14/02 (TX)

ITEM 2: No information and evidence gathered by the Federal Bureau of Investigation will be delivered to any state or local law enforcement agency in which the above mentioned crimes were committed.

ITEM 3: Tess Miller agrees to submit to a complete psychological evaluation that will include, but not be limited to tests for behavior, intelligence (IQ) and personality disorders. Testing may also include Magnetic Resonance Imaging (MRI), the Position Emission Tomography (PET) and any other noninvasive diagnostic techniques or procedures.

ITEM 4: Tess Miller shall cooperate in and submit to unlimited interviewing and interrogation. She shall provide a written comprehensive medical, biographical, and educational history. Access to all medical and financial records shall be granted to the FBI. No financial record will be sent to any revenue service.

ITEM 5: Testing and interviewing shall be completed within a two-year period commencing with the date of this agreement.

ITEM 6: Tess Miller may not divulge any information, written, orally or electronically, or by any other means concerning the involvement of herself and her husband (deceased) in the murders listed in Item 1.

General Comments (Not to be part of Agreement):

The purpose of incarceration is to remove the criminal from society and to punish the criminal for the commission of unlawful activity. Tess Miller has suffered severe punishment, albeit mental, from the untimely death of her husband. Strong opinion holds that Tess Miller has ended her crime career. The threat of future prosecution would also be incentive for her to remain passive. The Bureau is taking this unprecedented position in anticipation of acquiring new knowledge in the science of psychology and sociology. This agreement and any material associated with the justitiaphiles will be made available to a limited number of Bureau employees. These employees are not to discuss or reveal any information on the Justice Lovers Case without expressed approval by the Director. The decision whether to go public will be revisited after studies are completed. This proposed agreement may be shown to SSA Clarke Gable for review. Please forward, under seal, any comments, changes or additions directly to Zachariah Goldberg, Assistant Director, on or before February 15, 2004.

* * *

February 6, 2004 (Friday)

Tom Claiborne downloaded and printed an interoffice memo from Clarke Gable, which read: "Tom, I have only a couple of suggestions in reference to the memo from Mr. Goldberg. Tess Miller should have a grieving period before any personal testing and interviewing, at least 60 days. I would also like to see a stipulation from the Assistant Director that I am in charge and the main participant in the proposed discovery and analysis procedure."

* * *

Washington, D.C.

"You know I follow orders without any arguments," Artie stated. "On this particular case, though, I think we're making a mistake not getting rid of Tess Miller."

"Don't worry about this one," replied Goldberg. "I've got another job for you that's more important."

CHAPTER 49
March 15, 2004 (Monday)
Jackson, Mississippi

It was exceptionally hot and muggy for March. The thermometer read 80 degrees and the humidity 95 percent. Tess recalled how Mike used to fuss about how everybody talks about the ice ages and forgets about the tropical ages in between. "Global warning is just a tropical age," he would comment. She drove to the office of Steve Franklin and neared the location where the BMW spun out of control on Spillway Road. *I'll always remember January 14, 2004 as the day my life ended. They say time heals all wounds. I wonder if I'll live that long.*

* * *

The same perky blonde, shapely legs emphasized by a hemline five inches above the knees, announced, "Mr. Franklin is ready to see you. Go right in. Down the hall, second door to the right."

The lawyer stood as Tess entered the office. "How are you holding up, Tess? I know it's been a rough couple of months since the accident."

Tess sat down and said, "It's hard to keep going when you can't see a future. I take it one day at a time."

"Let me give you some good news. The Justice Department has offered you immunity from Federal prosecution. Of course, each state in which a crime has been perpetrated could put you on trial. It would be uphill for the states, since the FBI is not going to reveal the results of their investigation. I'm going to put you in a conference room and give you enough time to thoroughly read the document. Then I'll answer your questions and get your decision. The document cannot leave this office; even your signed copy will be kept here in the security vault."

As Tess left the office, she thought: *The Ides of March is going to be a better day for me than it was for Julius Caesar.*

* * *

Downy Westfield sat in his office in the McCoy Building, chatting with Tom Claiborne in Quantico.

"Well, today is the big meeting between Tess Miller and her lawyer," Claiborne commented.

"Yeah," said Downy. "I sure was surprised at that memo I got about a month ago. You have to assume Goldberg knows what he's doing."

"His strategy," said Claiborne, "for the moment, is to keep this particular serial crime spree quiet. A decision has been made that the case file and future scientific research, if any, will not be put into the computer system. Goldberg has made me, against my wishes, the guardian of the file, so Downy, lie if you have to, but don't give out any info on this case. It's my ass if there's a leak to the press."

"Don't worry about me, Tom. I'm just grateful that the Jackson District wasn't the site for some damn shootout," said Downy. "I should hear from Steve Franklin this morning. He's a good guy. We talked this morning and he sure wants his client to take the deal. He believes acceptance will save her life. As soon as I hear from him, I'll contact you."

* * *

It was a generic conference room: rectangular, no windows and a rectangular table centered with eight chairs. A couple of yellow pads and two ballpoint pens lay on the table. Tess was making notes on the agreement when Steve Franklin came into the room and sat across from her.

He sure is good looking. But no one can replace Mike, thought Tess.

"Well, what do you think about the deal?" Steve asked politely. *Mike couldn't play golf, but he sure knew how to pick his women.*

"Mike and I figured that some day we might be arrested. We looked at a trial as a vehicle to expose our failing justice system and society. We wanted to demonstrate that individuals could stop the downward spiral. We didn't want people to abandon the law; we just didn't want the law to abandon the people. Since Mike was killed, I've lost my zeal for the whole project. No need for exposure now. I'll sign the document."

"There are plenty of things for you to do, Tess. Mike wouldn't want you to be so discouraged. Get more involved with the managing of Tessco. You're young and beautiful. Take some cruises. There may be another somebody out there that can help you through the rough spots. What you don't need is a series of trials in six different states. Incidentally, I will insist they insert a provision that any evidence discovered during their probative testing, interviewing and review of records cannot be used against you in the event of future trials, local, state or federal. You're also to be considered a patient of the specialist who evaluates you, in order to establish immunity under the doctor-patient privilege. I'll contact Downy Westfield at the local FBI office. You'll be contacted immediately when the final draft of the agreement is delivered to us for signature."

CHAPTER 50
March 1, 2004 (Monday)
Quantico, Virginia

Clarke Gable was now in full charge of the Justice Lovers Case through to final disposition. His instructions were to begin the processing as soon as they had a signed agreement. Claiborne instructed him to prepare a project procedure and submit it to Goldberg. Goldberg wanted a postulation on what the project would accomplish and how the assembled material might affect FBI routine and, if shared, the advancement of science. Goldberg also reemphasized his position that the Justice Lovers Case would not be made public, at least in the near future.

In the last month, being apart from the case, Clarke had had time to reflect on his feelings and where his future might lead. He calculated that advancement in the Bureau would be limited as a consequence of his altercation with Goldberg. He decided he would complete the Justice Lovers Case, leave the FBI and write a textbook on the justitiaphiles. He was keenly aware that publishing a book could conflict with the classified Information Nondisclosure Agreement (INA), standard form 312 that all federal employees signed. Clarke reasoned that this material was not classified— that is, not hurtful to the country, and he would not be subject to any civil court action. Clarke also figured he would need an attorney's advice on how to keep Tess Miller from being indicted on the basis of revelations in the book. As far as job opportunities, he could teach at the college level, consult as a criminologist or open his own practice.

There was also an admission that Goldberg's point of view had some basis in fact. He was grateful that despite "Black Thursday," as he referred to the meeting, Goldberg put him in charge of the final resolution of the Justice Lovers Case. *I may even call the AD and apologize for my acrimonious behavior*, Clarke reflected. As for Artie Majesky and TAG, they were best forgotten. The irony was not lost on Clarke that Majesky may be a justitiaphile. *That judgment is for another analyst,* he thought.

CHAPTER 51
April 8, 2004 (Thursday)
Jackson, Mississippi

The Jackson office provided a grey four-door sedan. Clarke drove slowly along the Spillway Road looking for the spot. Then he saw the twisted guardrails on each side of the road. Clarke thought viewing the scene would put him in a fitting mood for his first encounter with Lady J, Tess Miller.

Clarke parked in the circular drive of pebble-covered concrete. He got out of the car, took out his loose-leaf notebook, and sketched and described the house. Clarke believed that in some instances, house designs reflected the personality of the occupant. The Miller house was constructed in the modern shed style. There were five trapezoidal units, one, two and three stories high. The shed roofs pitched with different slopes. The units, joined together, produced a dramatic and appealing architectural design. The exterior walls were alternating rows of various shades of brandy-colored brick for the lower section. The upper section of the walls were white cypress cladding placed diagonally on some walls and vertically on others. Tall narrow windows emphasized the height and permitted a view of the reservoir. Clarke was impressed. This house was for the bold, the unconventional and the self-confident.

Clarke walked toward the deeply recessed entryway. He rapped the ornate brass knocker against the striker plate two times then waited.

The door opened and a gorgeous woman with a pleasant voice said, “Hi. I’m Tess Miller. You must be Agent Gable. May I see your identification please?”

Clarke answered, “Absolutely.” He showed his FBI picture identification.

“You know, I once posed as a female IRS investigator many years ago in Alachua, Florida. I’m sure you already know of that incident. You can’t be too careful nowadays. Please, come right in.”

Clarke admired the way Tess Miller so quickly established control of this first meeting. So be it, he was not there to confront, but to comprehend. He marveled at this woman's attractiveness. She possessed the three F's: face, figure and fashion.

Tess led the FBI man into her favorite room, the sunroom. She was the interviewee, but also the host. She was tastefully dressed in a taupe two-piece, tweed pantsuit with a V-neckline. The taupe square-toed pumps with inch-and-a-half heels and the gold mesh chain with a square black onyx pendant completed the elegant attire. Her blonde hair was styled in a chin-length pageboy asymmetrically parted.

"I thought we could conduct the interviews in the sun room. It was the favorite hangout for my husband and me," Tess admitted. She motioned Clarke to sit on the sofa; she took a chair to his oblique right. "The view is beautiful, and perhaps that will temper the seriousness of our conversations."

"Mrs. Miller, you'll be doing most of the talking. I will be taking notes and tape recording our sessions. By the way, this is a lovely home and this sunroom is perfect for interviewing. We are in a doctor-patient relationship. One of my goals is to assist you in a recovery process."

"Thank you for your concern. I insist you call me Tess. Mrs. Miller sounds old, and I don't feel old. Depressed a little, but not old."

"That was an unfortunate accident. We attempted to give you a grieving period before we put you under the microscope. I lost my fiancé a few months ago. She was accidentally shot by an estranged ex-husband, so I can empathize with you."

"Life can be a bitch. One can never imagine all of the twists and turns," lamented Tess.

"I've read your written medical, biographical and educational histories, but I want you tell me about those subjects orally. I may ask you to go into areas you failed to cover and to express your thoughts and emotions before, after, and during certain events. It's going to take a lot of sessions, and I apologize for that necessity."

Tess was beginning to like this black man. He was well dressed in his charcoal grey suit, white shirt and regimental tie. He spoke good English and was polite and not accusatory, even though he knew of her crimes.

"I suggest we meet Monday, Wednesday, and Friday from ten o'clock until four o'clock in the afternoon. We can have lunch here, prepared by my housekeeper. Is that a suitable arrangement?" Tess asked.

"That's an excellent arrangement. It may put less strain on us if we dress more casually," Clarke suggested.

"Blue jeans it is," joked Tess.

"Tess, I conceived a name for you, justitiaphile. It means lover of justice. From the viewpoint of a criminologist and psychologist, you and your husband are unique in the annals of behavioral science. You are and have been my case study. During our future sessions, it'll be necessary to ask probing and maybe provocative questions. Please do not be offended."

"Actually, I'm looking forward to our discussions. I want a professional opinion on what Mike and I did. Perhaps if you write about our aspirations, there may be some profound changes in society and the law. That was our goal. So, where do you want me to start?"

"Well, to use the old saw, I guess at the beginning."

EPILOGUE

On a cloudless August day in 2004, the Director of the FBI and his driver were killed when their limousine experienced a blowout. The government-owned vehicle crossed the median and crashed head-on into a tractor-trailer loaded with television sets. Zachariah Goldberg, nominated and approved as the new director of the FBI, held that position for 15 years. To the surprise of many pundits, he remolded the FBI into a no-nonsense agency. Goldberg directed the agency to track down and neutralize (legally or illegally) all terrorists in the U.S., whether foreign nationals or U.S. citizens. During his tenure, there were no bombings or terrorist incidents in the USA.

Director Goldberg no longer had the time for, or the interest in, managing the Justice Lovers Case. He delegated total responsibility to Tom Claiborne to make all decisions without review from higher authority.

* * *

Five months after the suspicious murder-suicide of Irene Day Collins and her husband John Mark Collins in 1998, the IRS completed an extensive investigation. The agency concluded that none of its agents participated in the crime. Mrs. Robert Lewis Eddiceston died in December 2003, five years after the death of her sister. Mrs. Eddiceston was 57 years old when she died of chronic renal failure, CRF, the same condition that had taken her father's life. Her deathbed wish: the murderer of her beloved sister be brought to justice.

* * *

An item for *Ripley's Believe it or Not* was the friendship that developed between Laura Lee Forrest, the widow, and Rita Gallo-Jones, the ex-mistress, of

Andrew Jackson Forrest, the Tennessee Governor murdered in 1999. Laura Lee Forrest never told anyone she was planning to ditch the "old boy" and that the timely murder eliminated a nasty divorce. Both women enjoyed their independence and remained unmarried.

* * *

In 2002, when the insurance company received the tape of Tommy Shotz admission that he duped the jury, they filed a suit for restitution. Nancy Shotz was not surprised that the $8 million windfall was about to disappear. She never did approve of the insurance scam. She was grateful Tommy's life insurance policy paid her $200,000. Nancy started oil painting covered bridges and gristmill scenes in Pennsylvania. Her artwork became popular and her paintings sold for thousands of dollars. Nancy happily remarried, and the once-bitter memories of her first husband became buried and forgotten. The two boys missed their real father, but had enough of Tommy's resilient Irish blood to insure survival.

* * *

Clarke Gable resigned from the FBI in December 2004. The Bureau released Gable from his employment agreement with the provision he would not release any information concerning IMPSP, the Identical Murder Pattern Search Program, or TAG, the Tactics Assessment Group. The FBI allowed Clarke access to the Justice Lovers Case files for a period of one year. Gable's two-volume treatise on the Justice Lovers Case was released on December 1, 2005. Volume I described the lives of Mike and Tess Miller. Volume II dealt with the justitiaphilia and the psychological implications. The volumes won acclaim in both the literary and scientific communities.

Camaraderie or an almost filial relationship developed between Clarke Gable and Tess Miller. He had to admit that he enjoyed the role as Tess Miller's analyst. He theorized he would also have liked Mike Miller. Clarke spent a great deal of time in Jackson and decided to buy a townhouse for convenience. There was never a romantic involvement between the patient and the doctor. Clarke Gable became immensely wealthy through the book, movie and television royalties. He did regret that there would probably be some copycat justitiaphiles. "Scientific advance has its cost," he would say. He still kept in touch with his mentor Tom Claiborne. He even got a congratulatory phone call about his success from a mellower Zach Goldberg. Clarke, in a spirit of magnanimity, admitted to Goldberg that he was hypercritical of the AD without a good basis.

* * *

Steve Franklin relinquished any rights he had to the Tess Miller story. He did caution Tess that one or more of the states in which the murders were committed would attempt to use the publication of the two-volume work as documentary evidence. Tess wanted her story before the American public and informed her attorney that she would accept any dire consequences.

* * *

STATES V. TESS MILLER

MISSISSIPPI:

A Long Street County Grand Jury ignored the District Attorney's presentation of the documentary evidence in the Bobby Dan Cantrell Murder and returned a No Bill. The same Grand Jury also ignored the rule against discussing evidence. The members unabashedly commented to friend and family that Cantrell was a despicable racist and murderer and deserved his fate.

The District Attorney covering Hinds County saw no legal or social benefit in prosecuting the 33-year-old mercy killing of Helene Granger or the 1985 killing of AIDS patient Ted Daws. In the Daws case, the act of spitting on the nurse, intended to cause bodily harm, was a mitigating element.

FLORIDA:

A jury in Alachua composed of nine men and three women voted to find the defendant "Not Guilty," because of insufficient evidence in what was a poorly planned strategy. The prosecuting attorney failed to breach the psychotherapist-patient privilege. The judge rejected both the dangerous exception and the lack of clinical practice arguments. It was crucial that Clarke Gable testify that the defendant admitted to him the commission of the crimes in Volume I, *The Justice Lovers Case*. Without such testimony, the book was not documentary evidence. The only witness was deceased. Defense Council offered that the tragedy had already been classified as a murder-suicide.

TENNESSEE:

The majority of the Tennessee district attorneys detested Governor Forrest for his release of eleven convicted murderers and the reduction to life sentences of another 138 death row inmates. No indictment was filed in the state as a prosecutorial requite.

ALABAMA:

District Attorney Shelby Willard did not go before a grand jury to seek an indictment. His district was comprised of four impoverished counties. He followed the Florida trial and feared a trial here would end in the same manner. In addition, the widespread hatred for Magruder would insure a pro-defendant jury. D.A. Willard was not about to waste limited funds on a probable "jury nullification case."

TEXAS:

As in Florida, a Texas grand jury brought in a True Bill. The Texas judge disallowed the therapist-patient immunity rule and declared that Clarke Gable must answer the question: Did Tess Miller personally admit to the crimes described in his treatise? Subsequently, Volume I was introduced as documentary evidence leading to a guilty verdict. The case pled before the U. S. Appellate Court.

The Appellate Court recited Jaffee vs. Redmond, a 1996 Supreme Court case. Jaffee postulated that therapist-patient privilege grew out of a greater good for the public. A promise to a patient of confidentiality is not subject to a future determination by a trial judge as to admissibility as evidence. The court stated that the Texas Rules of Evidence forced recognition of the psychotherapist-patient privilege. The appeals court was disturbed that an Evidentiary Hearing was not held by the Lower Court. The verdict of guilty was vacated, and the case was remanded for further proceedings.

PENNSYLVANIA:

The District Attorney for Northampton County was troubled with a case involving the absence of the hit and run vehicle. No forensic evidence existed that a crime was committed. Nancy Shotz's (Banacek) identification of Mike and Tess Miller, with whom she had conversation, was not significant evidence.

There was some speculation as to whether the vehicle used in the hit and run was abandoned in the old water-filled, open-pit zinc mine. Hydrologists correctly advised the mine could not be drained. The Texas case also ended any possibility of using the Justice Lovers Case, Volume I as evidentiary material. The District Attorney concluded it would serve no purpose to present it to the grand jury.

* * *

After the trials ended, Tess Miller immersed herself into managing Tessco. She gave liberally to charities. She established a free clinic to treat emotionally disturbed children. What amazed her most: A large segment of the Jackson community forgave her for her crimes. Tess prayed that if others followed her and Mike's example, they likewise would show good judgment in their selection of victims. One evening Tess remembered that when Mike and she were in Florida, they wondered who L.N. Pearce was. She discovered he was the first mayor of Alachua.

ACKNOWLEDGEMENTS

To my wife, Yvonne, who answered the same question a 1,000 times: How does this sound? To my medical doctor children, Barry and Toni, who advised on medicine and psychology. To secretaries, Shana Mitchell and Sue Hewitt, who successfully deciphered my scribble to type the first draft. To Mark and Jane Peterman of Curious Cat in Gautier, Mississippi, who advised, admonished, edited, proof read and produced the final draft. Their encouragement and friendship was my booster rocket. To petite Simone Bryan, who said, "Bob, this is a good book and it needs to be published," and then made it happen. Her talent in artwork is displayed in the unique and sophisticated jacket design. And special thanks to my sister-in-law, a splendid amateur photographer named Jane Pressgrove, who took a hundred pictures to capture the right one for the jacket.